Praise for *The Wife Before*

"Williams does give both Melanie and Samira multiple dimensions; they're flawed but also strong and determined, and the twist at the end is a surprise."
—*Kirkus Reviews*

Praise for *The Perfect Ruin*

"A delicious and decadent cocktail of jealousy, passion, and revenge. I was hooked from the very first twist. You'll love this addictive psychological thriller."
—Alessandra Torre, *New York Times* best-selling author of *Every Last Secret*

"Twisty and impossible to put down! With a cast of diverse characters, Williams brings to life a twisty thriller that'll leave you reeling long after you've read the last page. 10/10 recommend."
—Claire Contreras, *New York Times* best-selling author

"You're going to pick a side, make no mistake. And then you won't put it down until you know the truth. A shocking, sensual thriller with sharp twists."
—Tarryn Fisher, *New York Times* best-selling author of *The Wives*

"Williams is an award-winning author of romance and suspense novels; her tale of revenge will find an easy spot in fiction collections. Tailored for book clubs and for those who like to read about the sleazy side of rich elites."
—*Library Journal*

"This twisty thriller takes readers into a high-class, sinfully privileged world populated with characters who will stop at nothing for what they want. Williams stretches out the tension as readers wonder what Lola did to hurt Ivy and whether their shared past will be revealed. With diabolical turns and surprises at every corner, it's an ideal summer read for fans of May Cobb's *The Hunting Wives* (2021)."
—*Booklist*, STARRED REVIEW

"In *The Perfect Ruin*, author Shanora Williams serves up an ice-cold revenge thriller set in the glamorous and steamy hot city of Miami."
—Book Riot

"The glamour of Miami has a dark side in this twisting story where nothing is what it seems."
—WRAL-TV (NBC) North Carolina

"This is a great story of revenge and the lengths someone will go to get it, and how there are many layers to people's lives. It's a great mix of female friendship and thriller."
—*Parkersburg News and Sentinel/Marietta Times*

"This fast-paced and incredibly entertaining book is perfect for devouring by the poolside. Everyone in this book is terrible, but I mean that in the best way possible. Williams is so incredible at writing her characters that despite the horrible things they do, you still want to root for them."
—Off the Shelf

Books by Shanora Williams

The Perfect Ruin
The Wife Before
The Other Mistress

The Other Mistress

Shanora Williams

www.kensingtonbooks.com

To my siblings.
I love all eleven of you.

Dear Reader,

Before diving into this novel, I want you to be prepared for what lies ahead. While writing this book, I admit that I struggled with it—well, I've struggled with all of my books in some way, shape, or form. But *The Other Mistress* was a different writing experience for me because it took a darker turn and it triggered me, and that says a lot because I don't have many fictional triggers.

With that being said, I want you, dear reader, to be aware that there are pieces in this novel involving child abuse and sexual assault. There are moments of betrayal and moments where children are being let down by a parent/someone they trust in unimaginable ways.

Writing this really tugged at my heart, and not in a pleasant way. If anything, it ripped me wide open and I was left raw for days as I processed this story and the traumas that were created with these characters. I realize this is a work of fiction, but I would not have felt okay sending this story out to the world without a heads up or to at least encourage the reader to take note of these trigger warnings before diving in to read this book.

Reading my work is supposed to bring the reader entertainment and to (hopefully) spark conversations, but I realize everyone has their own battles and many of us are working on healing our inner child, and if reading about child abuse and sexual assault crosses the line for you, please know that I love and respect that and protecting your peace should always be your priority.

Sending love and good reading vibes,

Shanora

CHAPTER ONE

When I think of her death, I think of drowning.

She sinks with thick rope tangled around her wrists. Despite the murkiness of the water, she's looking right at me—splashing, thrashing.

She's reaching out for me, and I have the urge to jump in and save her, but I can't. I'm stuck in place, wide-eyed, as a thick blanket of fog surrounds me. My lungs feel heavier, my heart beats slower. She screams my name between gasps and blubbers. I reach for her, but a stronger hand shoves mine away.

Then the splashing ceases.

She sinks slowly, eyes wide open.

She's gone. She is no more.

CHAPTER TWO

ADIRA

Two Months Ago

No one *truly* knows their partner, do they? I mean really, *really* know them, down to the mysterious depths of their souls and the hardness of their core. You can spend years with the same person, creating memories, growing together, blossoming into one . . . but you'll never truly know what's going on inside their heads.

You'll never have access to that dark, dark corner—the space in the mind where every human keeps their wildest fantasies, their most wicked, primal thoughts, and pitch-black secrets. We all have these corners—every single one of us, even the sweetest, most kindhearted people have a sliver of darkness lurking in the crevices of their brains.

These are the things I think about when I look at my husband. He sits across from me in our kitchen, sipping his coffee as he focuses on the screen of his phone. What is he reading? An email? A *text*?

He presses his pink lips after each sip from the mug that has the words **Rugby Is Life** in a fat, bold font. It was a gift from one of the other coaches on his team.

I absorb everything about my husband, as if I'm looking at him for the first time again. There's that familiar arch of his nose, the sharp angle of his jaw. His skin appears smooth, like brown velvet, his cheekbones shaped in a godlike manner. His goatee has been trimmed neatly, courtesy of his barber, Kenneth.

The silver hair near his temples shimmers from the sunlight streaming through the arched casement windows next to us and I can't believe there was a time when I loved the gray hair on him. The maturity of it once made me feel womanly and vulnerable to him and seeing as he was five years older than I was, well, his age had always been a delicious factor. Now, I feel my belly churning at the sight of it.

Gabriel sighs and scrolls through his phone some more, his gold wedding band sparkling in the light. I study the ring and can't help but allow my mind to revert to our wedding day.

A Hawaiian breeze and a tulle ivory dress. Laughter, cheers, and applause. Twinkling fairy lights and newlywed kisses beneath milky-white moonlight. Champagne and toasts and red velvet cake with buttercream cheesecake frosting.

A sigh escapes me. What a dream that was.

"What's the matter?" Gabriel's voice fills the kitchen, a deep timbre that'd once had the power to soothe me. His voice can't be mistaken for anyone else's. I'd know his voice from across a busy room or in the thick of a crowded amusement park if he shouted my name.

"Nothing's the matter." I sip my coffee and look into his brown eyes.

"You've been quiet."

I shrug. "Just thinking."

"About what?"

"Work stuff."

He lets out a gut-deep sigh and sits against his chair, forgetting about his phone for a moment and bringing the rim of the mug up to his lips to sip. "Work stuff," he repeats after the sip.

"I'm meeting an important investor today." I flip my wrist, as if suddenly pressed for time. "I should get going. Alaina is supposed to be giving me a refresher before the pitch."

"Are we still on for dinner tonight?"

I push from the table and pick up my coffee mug and plate of half-eaten scrambled eggs and toast that he'd prepared for us. He cooks for me every now and then. He'll turn on some old-school R&B and sing while cooking what he knows how to cook, which isn't much really and is just the basics. Scrambled eggs, toast, bacon. He isn't a professional cook by any means, but it was the effort that counted. It used to mean a lot to me, having him make me breakfast. It was something special and sacred between us, but I can't shake the feeling that it's changing. A lot of things have changed between us lately.

"Of course. Tonight," I confirm.

I dump the remainder of my coffee down the drain of the farmhouse sink, scrape off the remainder of food on my plate in the trash bin, and walk around the table for my bag on the counter.

The legs of his chair scrape the floor, and I feel the heat of his body against my back.

"Try not to stand me up tonight, will you?" he murmurs in my hair. "I know you're a busy woman, but I miss spending my nights with you."

"I won't," I say without turning in his arms. I pick up my bag and move sideways. Finally facing him, I press a kiss to his cheek and murmur, "See you at dinner."

CHAPTER THREE

ADIRA

My marriage has been on shaky ground lately, and I get the sense that my husband hasn't been telling me the whole truth about what he does with his time when he's not at home.

Of course, it's not healthy to spy on your spouse—I know that—and in most cases, you're bound to find out something you don't want to know . . . but how can I *not*? He's been coming home later, texting more often, and going out of town more too. Things are changing, and there's a deep feeling in my gut that burns and sizzles and yearns for answers, so instead of driving straight to work, I drive down the block and park.

I wait exactly fifteen minutes before spotting my husband's Range Rover pass by. Putting my car in Drive, I follow him, making sure to stay a car apart so he won't recognize my Audi. The stadium for rugby is only thirty minutes away from our mansion in Noir Hills, and he has to take Interstate 275 to get there. So why isn't he taking the interstate?

He makes a right turn to drive through the city. I don't feel good about it at all, but I tell myself perhaps he's going for a coffee or needs to make a stop for gas. But we pass by his favorite coffee shop, and there are many gas stations he could've stopped at by now. He continues driving until he's turning his signal on to make a left into the parking lot of the mall.

I follow him into the lot before the light can change signals, but instead of continuing after him as he finds a parking spot, I keep driving. I keep a careful eye on his car, the clean silver gleaming beneath the Florida sun, and watch until he parks. When he does, I find a place to park where I can see him but where he won't see me, and that's when I watch him climb out of the car and walk toward one of the mall entrances with his phone pressed to his ear.

He stops and stands next to the entrance, lowers the phone, and then raises his chin. His eyes are pointed in my direction, and I lower into the leather seat, hoping he can't see me. His eyes light up with recognition, a smile sweeps across his lips, and I begin to panic, thinking he's caught me. He's onto me and now he'll know I don't trust him.

But then I realize that he's not looking at me at all, but at a woman who is rushing toward him. She meets up with him, dressed in a pink floral dress and wedged brown heels, and as soon as she does, he opens his arms and hugs her. This isn't a friendly hug, or the kind of hug you'd give to someone for a meeting or for business. This is a familiar hug—one he's given me time and time again.

And if I think that was all, I'm sadly mistaken because right there—right in front of the mall, with many bystanders and even *myself* to witness it—my husband kisses another woman.

CHAPTER FOUR

JOCELYN

If there's one thing I know, it's that life is what you make it. In life, I've learned that I have to roll with the punches, stick the landings, and if the lemons are rotten, grow my own damn lemons with the seeds and try again later to make some damn lemonade.

Failure is not an option for me and, yes, I can be headstrong and rebellious, but if I weren't, who would I be? Where would I be?

Another issue I have is constantly proving I'm a woman of value. However, a real woman wouldn't be doing what I'm doing. She wouldn't be shopping for lingerie, then going to get her hair done, all to rush to a snazzy hotel for a *man*. And yet here I am, plucking out a black lingerie set from the rack. The push-up bra will do nicely.

I take it to check out and lay it on the counter, where the cashier smiles at me. "Would you like to apply for our store credit card and save ten percent today?" she asks, continuing a bright smile.

I think about it. I have a feeling I'll need lingerie much more often now, and it's not like I can't afford to have another credit card. "You know what?" I say, smiling. "Why don't I make both of our days? Sign me up."

After I do, I collect my bag and my papers for the new credit card I've applied for and leave the store with a smile bigger than the cashier's. After my hair appointment and a quick pedicure, I'm on my way to the Ritz-Carlton downtown, Musiq Soulchild pouring from the speakers, getting my mind prepared for the night.

Pulling up to the valet, I hand them my keys, trot into the lobby of the hotel to check in, and stroll to my room on floor fourteen. I shower, freshen up, then order a light meal and a bottle of wine, which arrives just in time for me to eat before he arrives.

A spritz of Love by Kilian on the wrists and neck, a light brush of my teeth, and I'm ready. I sit on the bench at the bottom of the bed with a glass of wine, and it only takes two minutes for the hotel door to click and for Gabriel to walk into the room.

He smiles wide at me, and I giggle and place my wineglass down as he rapidly strips out of his clothes and kicks off his shoes. Rushing toward me, he scoops me up in his arms and I cross my legs around his waist, kissing him hard, deep, fiercely.

"I've been looking forward to this all day," he rasps on my lips, laying me on the bed. "I love meeting you here. Being with you. Seeing you like this."

I smile as he kisses my neck, savoring his kisses, his love.

"You really missed me that much?" I sigh.

"Trust me," he says, sitting up between my legs to unbuckle his belt. "I most definitely did."

Then he's on top of me again, easing me out of the new lingerie and making me his. It's awful, really, because he's married, and I'm sure it would kill his wife to know he's sneaking to hotels with another woman and having his way with her. After all, if it were me, I'd be devastated. But there's also something *empowering* about doing this—knowing that he's running to me, and only me, when he could literally have anyone else in this world. It makes me feel desired and sexy, like a goddess. I feel on top of the world, and there's a spring in my step and a flare in my confidence that hadn't thrived before.

Would I want it to happen to me? Hell no, and it never will because I don't plan on tying myself down and getting married. Plus, what Gabriel and I are doing won't last forever. One day he'll get bored, things will become stale, and we'll go back to what we were before, colleagues, friends. For all I know, his wife will never find out.

So yes, I'll take this. I'll take it all if it means I get to feel *something* for once in my life.

CHAPTER FIVE

ADIRA

When my eyes flutter open, I taste blood. I sit up, wiping the corner of my mouth, only to notice a streak of red on the back of my hand. My tongue stings a familiar sting and I sigh. Of course, I bit my tongue while asleep.

"Damn nightmare," I grumble, turning over in the king-size bed. My eyes wander to the window, at the sheer beige curtains hanging from golden rods. This morning is darker than the previous morning. Through the slit of the curtains, I spot gray skies and thick clouds that are ready to create a downpour. Tampa weather is always a hit or miss.

I stretch my arms. Sigh again. Then I prepare myself mentally when I turn my head and find that my husband isn't in bed with me. It's been three weeks of this—of him not showing up at night. Most times he's traveling for work. But during the other times? Oh, those other times make me sick to my fucking *stomach*.

Still, I climb out of bed and follow my daily routine. After all, I have to get to work. I'm the one who keeps the roof over our heads and pays the bills. I'm the one who put the down payment on our house and provided him his own entertainment space, where he can drink his beer, scratch his balls, and watch all the televised sporting events he wants to.

You'd think he'd show his appreciation by showing up— be a little more grateful. I scoff at the idea as I start my morning skin-care routine. I apply the cleanser, toner, serum, rub in some SPF, and then saunter to the walk-in closet built for three, taking down the outfit I planned out last night—a black pantsuit with a silky, silver blouse.

After taking the bonnet off my hair to unleash my twist out, giving my curls a refresher with water and my favorite hair cream, I top the morning off with final touches of make-up, perfume, and silver jewelry in front of my vanity.

I hear my phone vibrate aggressively on my nightstand as I check my appearance in the mirror. Everything is in place. My clothes are crisp and ironed, my hair is as neat as I can make it, but with rain on the way, I can't count myself lucky enough for a full-length good hair day. The humidity is often brutal.

Blowing a breath, I leave the bathroom and grab my phone— and what do you know? A text message has arrived from my loving husband, Gabriel.

G: Good morning, babe. So sorry I couldn't make it home last night. Got caught up with Tray at the bar and you know how he gets when he's had one too many. Crashed at his place to make sure he was good but I'll see you soon!

Home. Such an ironic word for him to call it. Certainly, he can't consider this his home. A home is where one feels safe and comfortable. Home is where you build trust with your loved ones, not stab them in the back repeatedly.

My jaw ticks. The urge to call and shout my head off at

him is strong, but I resist and instead send a quick message back. **Don't worry about it. Hope Tray is ok!**

Then I leave our bedroom and head to the kitchen to take my medication. After gulping the pills down, I grab my purse, work folders, keys, and leave the house, giving the door a slam behind me.

CHAPTER SIX

ADIRA

I park my car in the parking lot of Velvet's Café and kill the engine. Sitting for a moment, I realize that I've been coming here much too often. Soon, the employees will recognize me as a regular, and that's the last thing I need because if they notice, so will others. However, this is important, and I must admit I'm a little addicted to the habit I've created now.

Picking up my Saint Laurent bag from the passenger seat and climbing out of my car, I lock it behind me and walk toward the café in nude Louboutins.

I'm swallowed whole by the scent of brewed coffee beans and freshly baked pastries. Silver globes with gold lights hang from the ceiling, attached to thick black wires. The floor is black and white, reminding me of a vintage kitchen, as well as the wooden antique furniture.

At the counter, I order my usual iced caramel coffee with an extra shot of espresso. I thank the barista when she hands me my drink and then make my way outside, taking up one of the two-top tables beneath the black awning that faces the street. Placing my coffee down on the square wooden table, I flip my wrist to check my watch for the time. Only a few more minutes to go.

As I wait, I sip my drink and scroll through my phone, acting casual, but nothing about what I'm doing is casual. If the people around me knew what I was doing, they'd consider me unhinged. Frankly, I don't care. No one at Velvet's knows who I am—at least not that I'm aware of. And it isn't like I stay for very long. Other than my usual coffee, I only come here for one thing—well, one *person*, rather.

I hear a car door slam shut and swing my gaze up to the ridiculous bubblegum-pink Mercedes-Benz parked at the curb. A young Latina woman walks away from it, dressed in pink sneakers, high-waisted pink leggings, and a gray tank top. Her hair is in a messy topknot, a few loose strands hanging around her heart-shaped face, which is clear of makeup, minus her glossed lips.

She smiles as a man holds the door open for her. I clutch my coffee cup, feeling the heat of the liquid seeping through the sleeve. I bet men hold doors open for her all the time.

When she's inside, I watch through the window while she orders what I'm positive is her go-to now: an avocado, banana, and mango smoothie with vegan protein powder—I've overheard her order this several times—and after she pays, she waits for it at the counter.

I sip my coffee casually, phone still in hand, but I'm unable to pull my eyes away from her. She's fit and her physique could make a mediocre woman jealous, but not me. I'm not mediocre and I'm also very fit.

I go to the gym three days a week, I take part in a dance class, and on weekends I perform Ashtanga yoga in my home studio. Meditation is essential to me, but I haven't been able to meditate in weeks. My mind has been so crowded and busy lately—too occupied with betrayals for it to dwell in silence.

This woman has a little more curve to her hips than I do, but my breasts are bigger. She also has back dimples, which I don't have, but other than that, she doesn't have much else I don't.

When her order is ready, she takes it with a smile and a wave, then saunters out of the café to get back to her obnoxious car.

I've watched her come to this café and leave it for the past three weeks, and when she leaves, I'm always tempted to follow her, just to see what else she does with her time.

I know exactly who she is . . . and I hate her. I hate her with every fiber of my being. Her name is Julianna Garcia. She's a makeup artist well known by influencers in Tampa, and especially Miami. She owns a water-view apartment and visits Velvet Café for her vegan smoothies every Tuesday morning after her barre class, which is only two blocks away from here. On Thursdays, she goes swimming at a private golf club with her best friend, Victoria.

She has a golden Labrador retriever named Goldie, which I find beyond cliché, and her favorite color is rose gold. All of this I know after scouring her social media. She's the most basic human being I have ever come across . . . and she's *fucking my husband*.

CHAPTER SEVEN

ADIRA

When I first saw Julianna, I wanted to run into her and tell her exactly who I was and how much of a homewrecker she is, but then I quickly realized she had no idea who I was at all.

I sat at this very table the first time I waited to confront her woman-to-woman, and she looked right at me and didn't bat an eyelash. Just smiled at me like I was some sad stranger who needed a friendly smile. When that happened, I assumed she had no clue who I was.

The people of Tampa know my name, as well those in Miami. Though I keep my head down and mostly focus on work, I attend events when necessary and network with some of the finest people around. Whether people see me or not, most of the reputable people in this city know of me. However, I'm a private individual, and I like it that way. You only know my husband is mine if you've met us together in person. I don't post him. I don't share my life all over social media like she does.

Prior to finding out about his affair, I didn't even have social media for myself, only my company, and I don't run that account, an agency my assistant hired does. Are you kidding?

I see what social media does to people. It brings out the most vain, toxic, jealous parts of a human, and for my mind to stay healthy, I tried avoiding it at all costs . . . until I found out about *her*.

To the world, it seems I'm not married at all unless you see the ring on my finger, and it's like that for Gabriel too. He has an Instagram account but hardly posts, and never has he posted about me. I don't mind it. We like it that way. Our privacy, our marriage only being ours. What was the use in sharing something so sacred in a space so distracting and damaging?

But I realize that being as private as we are hasn't been a completely beneficial thing for us after all. He could have his affair with her and never talk about his marriage—or even mention if he was married at all, for that matter—and then come home to me, pretending he's a saint.

When I first found out about this Julianna girl, I wanted to scream at him, divorce him on the spot. But then I became curious about *why* he was doing it, and no matter how much I thought about it, nothing made sense.

I'm a good wife. Am I perfect? No, but I am good. I cook for him when I have time and when I don't have time, I'll order dinner or have someone cook and leave a meal for us. I clean when I'm home or hire a maid. I take his clothes to the dry cleaner and schedule for his new clothes to get tailored. I give him my body as often as I can when I'm not working, but lately that hasn't been a lot. Yes, we've had our rough patches, but what marriage hasn't?

Still, I can't figure out why he's having an affair—and with *her*? A girl who claims her favorite color wasn't even a *real* color ten years ago. A girl who's half his damn age.

Why would he cheat when he has *me*? A woman who has built her empire from the ground up. A woman who has accumulated millions of dollars during our marriage that not only ended up providing for us, but also invested in the launch of his national rugby team. A woman who'd been with him through thick and thin. A woman who'd given him *everything*.

I need to know why my husband is doing this to me, no matter how angry it makes me or how heartbroken I become in the end.

CHAPTER EIGHT

ADIRA

My hope is that no one is on the elevator when I ride it up to my floor, but as of late, my hope runs thin.

I press the shiny round Up arrow button belonging to the elevator, and when the silver doors spread apart, my secretary, Alaina, is there. She comes in through the main lobby because she likes to make sure she gets her steps in with her Apple Watch. Apparently, she has a competition going with one of her friends to see who can get the most steps by the end of the day.

"Alaina," I greet her, entering the elevator. "How are you today?"

"I'm great, Adira. Oh my gosh, I have to tell you about my date last night." And that's why I like to ride the elevator alone. Don't get me wrong, I adore Alaina. She's quirky and positive and she's so well organized that it puts even my OCD to shame. I wouldn't work with someone who annoys me, and she doesn't always. But ever since she and her boyfriend of four years broke up, all she can talk about is having a "glow up" and making her ex-boyfriend eat her dust. Not to mention I think Alaina is a very sexual human, so she has these random one-night stands now that are awkward to hear about, but they give her confidence and empowerment, so, like a good boss and friend, I listen.

I study her a moment, while she's deep in talk about some man named Larry who "*is a little older but really packin'*." She's wearing a gray pencil skirt and a teal blouse today. Her hair is neatly brushed up into a curly dark puff, the edges sleek with gel, and her makeup is simple—mascara, eyeliner, and lipstick. It's all she needs, really, because her golden-brown skin is flawless. She's always presentable. I like that about her. She's crazy about organization and appearances, which makes me feel not-so-crazy about how much I love organization.

I launched Lovely Silk ten years ago. This was three years before I met my husband. I was only twenty-one at the time, and a girl who had a dream and decided to invest in it. I didn't know much of anything at twenty-one, but what I know now is that I *love* my job and I love my twenty-one-year-old self for paving this lane for me. I'm passionate about it and it keeps my mind busy when what I really want to do is find a blow-torch and burn everything to ash.

Work is my escape. When I work, the chaos in my brain is minimal. I suppose because there is structure and routine here. It's normally the same schedule every week, minus out-of-town business trips, and I prepare for those months in advance.

I love walking onto my floor after stepping out of the elevator and going into an office that gives me a stunning view of Tampa through the wall of windows. Yes, it's a muggy day today, but the view still stuns me.

I enjoy sitting at my desk in the mornings, leaning back in my ivory-cushioned rolling chair and absorbing the scenery. It's breathtaking and I'm fortunate to be where I am. Of course, all the calls, meetings, and emails drive me a little crazy, but it's the price one must pay to run their own company.

There's never a dull moment at Lovely Silk. And why should there be? I built this company from scratch. All of the original designs are mine. To start, I found a wonderful vendor who produced good-quality, affordable silk, and hired someone to make pieces for me to start selling. The items range from robes to gowns to lingerie. I'd started on Etsy in 2011 and sold so much that I'd decided to hire employees, a design team, and launch my own real company within a year. It'd been a goldmine for me ever since, my products now in popular department stores, malls, and boutiques. Even the famous are wearing my items, giving proper credit.

Despite how exhausted I am some days, and how it pulls me away from my personal life, I can never let this company go. Other than Gabriel, this is all I can really claim as mine. But I suppose Gabriel *isn't* really mine anymore, is he? He's hers too, and the thought of that makes me queasy.

I place my pen down, needing a break from staring at the gold and taupe design on my computer screen. I rub my temples and sigh, then send a text to Alaina, requesting a chamomile tea. I need to calm my mind and body, practice some breathing techniques. Damn it, I really need to meditate.

Alaina brings in my tea moments later with a smile and places it on my desk. She has her headset on and is clearly on a call with someone because she's speaking indirectly.

"Anything else I can get you?" she whispers while covering the mouthpiece of her headset.

"No, I'm good. Thank you, Alaina."

"Anytime." When she leaves, I pick up the tea, blow at it, and then take a tiny sip. I settle into my chair and close my eyes. A nap would be nice. I haven't been sleeping well lately—all those damn nightmares. My tongue hurts just thinking about it.

I eye the love seat against the wall, my body yearning to walk over and curl into the fetal position and sleep for the rest of the afternoon, but I can't. I have to confirm designs for Vito before our meeting tomorrow, and even if I wanted to, I wouldn't be able to rest. I've been restless for weeks. *Thanks, Gabriel.*

A buzzing starts up on the desk and I lower my gaze, reading the name on the screen.

Dina.

I should've known she was going to call. I swear, Dina has a sixth sense when it comes to me.

"Yes, Dina?" I answer with a sigh.

"Did you have to answer the phone with that much attitude?" Dina laughs. "You okay?"

"Yeah, sorry. I'm just a little tired. I had a nightmare last night and didn't sleep well."

"Aww, I'm sorry to hear that. What was it about?"

"The same one," I murmur.

"Ah. That one only pops up when you're stressed, beloved."

"I know. I am a little stressed."

"With work . . . or something else?"

"Yes, work," I lie.

"You've been like this for a couple weeks now. You sure you're okay?" I can hear the concern cloaking her question.

"I'm fine, Dina," I tell her, but that's a lie. I'm not fine and things are not okay. My husband is cheating on me with some ditzy girl, I haven't confronted him yet, and I've been watching her every week for the past three weeks like it's normal. What I'm doing is far from normality and, sadly, I can't stop. Not to mention all this stress isn't good for trying to conceive a baby. I'll have to deal with this affair soon if I want that to happen.

"How are you and Gabriel?" asks Dina.

I chew the inside of my cheek. I haven't told her about my discovery of Gabriel's affair, nor have I told her about us trying for a child. If I tell her, I'm going to have to tell the whole truth, and she'll worry about me. Dina always worries about me. She's always been like a mother, so I suppose she has the right to, but I don't like telling her everything I go through . . . at least not right away because she tends to over-react.

"We're doing really good," I lie again. "He's going out of town for work again this weekend. His rugby team is doing really well."

"Oh, okay. That's great. Well, listen, I'll be coming your way soon, so make sure the guest room is ready for me."

"Dina, please don't tell me this is another one of your 'wellness' visits. I told you, I'm okay! Seriously, you have nothing to worry about."

"Well, what do you expect, Adira? You're overworking yourself, so I have to make sure you're taking time for you and taking care of your mental health! Besides, I want us to spend some quality time together. Maybe get our nails done or have facials with Tamika and Mazie. You need breaks from work, you know? Humans weren't built to be at such de-mand. And I know you say you're okay, but I like to *see* you are for myself. You know how I am, beloved."

Yep. I know exactly how she is. Dina doesn't believe hu-mans are supposed to work themselves to the bone. She'd grown up with two parents who loved and provided for her. Her mother was lucky enough to stay home with her while her father worked as a private-practice lawyer. She'd seen her father come home bone-tired and weary with not even enough energy to chat with her, and when he did have the energy, he'd use it to do more overtime at work.

Dina's mother always told her he worked hard for them, but Dina grew up resenting her father's job, and from there on, began to resent any job that took too much of anyone's energy or time. And this is why Dina is now a traveling heal-ing therapist. I'd never heard of such a thing until I was in her care. When I was younger, she'd always tell me she was going to travel and help people in their homes. During that time, though, she was bouncing from job to job, sometimes work-ing retail, sometimes working restaurants, but she was always happy and never took any of the jobs too seriously. She did just enough to get by and provide for me—and to finish the courses required so she could become said travel therapist.

Dina is great and I don't deserve her, but she loves me and I love her and I can never deny her visits.

"Okay," I say, smiling. "I'll have the guest room ready for you. We can hang out and have quality time and then you'll see everything on my end is perfectly fine."

CHAPTER NINE

Claudette always said demons live inside every single one of us. No matter how hard a person prays, no matter how much they beg, their demons still linger.

But there's no way one could have been inside Panda. She was the happiest person I'd ever come across and her smile lit up every room she stood in. Her face was soft and kind and she loved to give people hugs—even strangers.

There were no demons inside her. She was an angel.

If anything, I'm pretty sure the demons are inside of me.

CHAPTER TEN

ADIRA

After a long and mentally draining workday, I pick up Thai from my favorite restaurant on the way home. The spicy aroma swims around the confines of my car and my belly growls ferociously as I drive toward Davis Islands. I didn't eat much today. I coasted along on coffee, tea, and a nibble of a banana muffin that Alaina picked up from the bakery down the block.

I'm eager to get home, change into silk pajamas, and curl up with my food and a glass of wine on the brand-new ivory leather love seat I ordered while reviewing the designs again. It sounds like a promising night—that is until I pull into the custom-paved driveway. I can't help sighing when I spot Gabriel's Range Rover parked in front of our house, near one of our three oversize garages.

"Oh, sure. Be home *now* when I actually want to be alone for once," I grumble, snatching up the to-go bag, along with my purse and laptop bag.

I trot to the house in my heels, expecting to find the door unlocked as it usually is when he's home, but it's not.

With a frown, I step back and dig into my purse, rooting around until I feel the cool metal of my house keys. I unlock the door and enter, stepping into the foyer. Air from the AC cloaks me, and I hear music playing faintly from the kitchen. Candles are lit on the tables of the foyer and the elegant light fixtures in the ceiling are dimly set. My eyes wander to the stairs that wind up to the second floor and the cathedral ceiling above that gives the house an airiness that soothes me.

The music continues and I place my things down by the door, minus the Thai, step out of my heels, and walk barefoot along the shiny wooden floors. I pass by two French doors that lead to my office and notice the door is cracked open and the chandelier is on, as if Gabriel was in there recently. The start of the marble kitchen floor appears, and the music grows louder. My eyes wander over to the six-top dining table that's set with three candles in gold votives and two white ceramic bowls, no food. I check the stove and there is a pot with a lid on top, steaming lightly.

"Gabriel?" I call, walking deeper into the kitchen. No answer. I step around the counter and flip on the light switch to the refrigerated wine cellar and pull down the bottle of Chardonnay I've had my taste buds set on the whole drive. Taking the bottle to the counter, I pull out the electric wine opener, pop the bottle open with ease, then retrieve a glass from one of the half-glass, half-wooden cabinets.

"Gabriel?" I call again.

"Coming, babe!" he shouts, and I sigh, leaving the kitchen to get to the dining room. I stand in front of one of the elongated windows, my usual spot after a long day, and sip my wine while staring out past the heated pool and the bay.

The stairs creak and I turn back and return to the kitchen as Gabriel rushes down.

"I was hoping to get the food plated before you arrived." He walks toward me in black jeans and a crisp white button-down shirt, a smile gracing his lips. He's shaved since I last saw him two days ago. As always, my husband is handsome. Six feet and three inches of delicious melanin that I love. His smile is dazzling—white and straight and perfect. I have the urge to run my fingers along his naked jaw like I always do, greet him with a kiss, but I don't. Not after knowing what I know.

"Hey, baby," he murmurs, planting a kiss on my cheek.

"What is this, Gabriel?" I ask as he walks past me to get to the stove. He takes the lid off the pot, grabs a spoon, and walks to the dining table.

"I had this made for us. It's one of your favorites." I watch as he carries one of the bowls over and dumps penne alla vodka on the plates.

"That's nice of you, but I already ordered food for myself," I tell him, lifting my to-go bag in the air.

"You can save that for tomorrow. Come on. Sit," he says, taking my wineglass from me and placing it down on the table. "Have dinner with me." He wears a soothing smile as he looks over his shoulder at me. Now would be the perfect time to throw the hot pasta in his face and demand answers as to why he's cheating. Instead, I sigh and place my to-go bag down on the quartz island counter and take the seat on the opposite side of the table from him.

He grabs a beer from the wine fridge, removes the lid, and pours some into his glass.

"Are we celebrating?" I ask.

"Yes, we are."

"And what are we celebrating exactly?"

"I'm gonna get to that." He chuckles. He finally sits and spreads a cloth over his lap. Such a courteous man. But courteous men don't betray the women they love. I try not to frown at the thought.

"Gabriel, come on. You know I hate surprises."

"Okay, okay." He smirks. "Well, thanks to you, the team is finally able to add a bigger locker room to the stadium."

"Oh." I press my lips. I want to be happy for him.

"Oh? Is that all you have to say? This is great news, Adira! *Huge* news! The team is growing and we need more space for new players, so it's in the works! And not only that, but we've been getting a lot of new donors. People are starting to believe in the team and in what we can create with rugby in Tampa."

"I—I know! You're right. I'm just surprised, is all." I force a smile and pick up my glass of wine.

"It wouldn't have happened without you, you know? The team is so thankful—that's why we went out last night. Me and Tray. We wanted to celebrate. I wanted to tell you properly. With a good dinner and drinks. You know, wine and dine you?"

I fight to smile. "Well, that's nice of you."

"They'll be starting the process in September. I get to oversee a lot of the architectural details with Tray. We're really excited about this." Gabriel shakes his head and grins, as if he can't believe it's happening. "I owe you so much, babe. So damn much." He pushes out of his chair and walks around the table. Dropping to his knees, he grabs one of my hands and smiles up at me. "You're incredible, Adira."

"I'm happy to help, Gabriel." Well, I was. Four months ago, before I found out he was sleeping with another woman.

He kisses the back of my hand and stands again. "Okay. Well, anyway. Enough with the mushy stuff. Let's dig in before the food gets cold."

Gabriel falls asleep with me tonight, his arm wrapped around my middle, his warm breath running over my cheek. He spoons me from behind and I want to take comfort in this. I almost do until I remember that he probably holds *her* like this too.

What does she have that I don't? What makes him run to her instead of spending every night with me? I would drop everything for Gabriel—give him the world and more—and yet it appears he's not satisfied with that. He needs more, *more, more*. He's a greedy man, and I loved that about him once, but a greedy man is insatiable and even I, a woman who has it all, am not enough.

"Gabriel?" I call.

"Hmm," he murmurs.

"Do you really love me?"

"Of course I do. What kind of question is that? I love you so much." He kisses the curve of my neck. "Like I said, you're my everything."

And I suppose that's enough for me to hear for now.

CHAPTER ELEVEN

ADIRA

The moonlight swathes me in its milky-white light. I can't help staring at it as it shines through the thin slit of the curtains of the double doors. Just outside the doors is a stunning water view—one that my husband and I used to spend many of our nights enjoying. But not tonight.

Tonight, we're in bed and my husband lightly snores next to me, but there's no way I can sleep. I tried, I swear I did, but my mind has been racing nonstop since I laid my head on the pillow.

I peel his arm from me and plant the bottoms of my feet on the floor. I walk to his side of the bed and stop at his nightstand, picking up his phone.

I glance at him as he rustles around in his sleep. He won't wake up. Once Gabriel is asleep, he's dead to the world. I unlock his phone with the passcode and go to his messages.

Of course there's nothing there but messages from other coaches, Tray, his barber, and some automatic messages for doctor appointments and meal pickups. He most likely deleted them before I arrived. It's probably why he was upstairs when I came home. He was cleaning up his shit.

I place the phone back down and leave the bedroom quietly, taking the stairs down, the cool marble shooting through the soles of my feet. When I make it to my office, I close the doors, settle into the leather of the chair behind the desk, and open my laptop.

Gabriel may have his messages deleted, but I'm sure he didn't get to his emails. It's a reach, yes, but perhaps he knows I'm onto him. He could be taking precautions now. I log into his account, glad the password remains the same. When I'm in, I scroll through his inbox. Nothing but work and promotions from companies appear on the first page. But when I click to the second page, I see the subject line: *Can't wait to see you again.* Beneath it is the name Jocelyn Vann.

Hold on. *WHAT?!*

Who in the hell is Jocelyn Vann?

CHAPTER TWELVE

ADIRA

My brows draw together and I click the email immediately.

From: Jocelyn Vann
To: Gabriel Smith

I had so much fun with you the other night. The Chardonnay was incredible! I can't wait to see you again. Let me know when you're free.

My heart sinks, but I proceed to read Gabriel's reply.

From: Gabriel Smith

It was really fun. I didn't know you could get so wild. Still turned on by it. We'll definitely see each other again, I'm sure.

I grip the mouse, my eyes stinging. I read the email exchange several times before exiting out of it and dropping my face into my palms.

There's another woman. Of course there is! He's not happy with me, he's not satisfied with fucking Julianna, so now he's entertaining *another* woman.

I refresh the screen and copy the woman's email address, pasting it into my notes. I then log back into an old email account with a username of mine that I mostly use to give to stores or for online purchases: coolgurl_269. I paste her email address into the sender's box and then type up my email rapidly.

From Coolgurl_269@cmail.com
Stop fucking my husband!

They're the only words I send. No names, no numbers—nothing to trace back to me.

Satisfied for now, I push out of my chair and leave the office, charging back up the stairs, ready to shake Gabriel out of his sleep and settle this shit with him once and for all. But when I walk into our room, I notice my phone screen has lit up.

I walk over to it, giving a quick glance at Gabriel before picking it up.

It's an email to my old account . . . from Jocelyn Vann. I open it quickly.

From: Jocelyn Vann
Nice way to hide behind a screen.

"What?" I hiss. *That bitch.*

"Babe?"

I gasp and look back at Gabriel. He peers up at me, squinty-eyed and confused. "What's going on? Why are you up?"

"Nothing—it's nothing. Go back to sleep. I—I have to

pee." I walk to the bathroom, shutting and locking the door behind me.

I drop the toilet seat and sit on top of it, then quickly reply to Jocelyn.

From: Coolgurl_269@cmail.com
I'm not hiding anywhere. I just found out about you and have no idea who tf you are, but I know you're sleeping with him.

She responds within minutes.

From: Jocelyn Vann
You don't know me, but you can get to know me. Let's meet up. I'll gladly tell you everything you want to know about your husband.

I stare at her message, stunned. I've never heard of a woman wanting to face the wife of a man she's sleeping with. She's bold . . . and that shocks me to my core.

Instead of responding, I close out the email app and flush the toilet to distract myself. I then walk to the counter, gripping the edge of it and staring at my reflection in the mirror. It's early in the morning, but I look like I've seen a ghost. My bottom lip is trembling, my heart racing. I open the medicine cabinet and reach inside it, taking down one of the pill bottles. I open it and dump one into my hand, tempted to take it.

But I don't. I drop it back into the bottle and shove it back into the medicine cabinet.

I don't need it. And besides, I can't fight the ideas crossing my mind with medication—the main one being that, no matter what happens, I *need* to meet this other woman.

CHAPTER THIRTEEN

ADIRA

I pretend to be asleep when Gabriel wakes up. He goes through his usual routine of showering, getting dressed, putting on cologne, and leaving. He kisses my forehead, whispers, "I love you," and takes off.

When I hear the door close and his steps drift down the staircase, I climb out of bed and rush to the window to look out of it. I watch as he walks out of the house and brings his phone to his ear before climbing into his vehicle. He's probably calling one of his *other* women. He starts the car and leaves, and when he's out of the driveway, I go back to bed and sit with my phone in hand.

If I email this Jocelyn woman again, there's no turning back. For all I know, she's taunting me and when it comes to their emails, they're talking about seeing each other for something else, like business or another matter.

Shit. Who am I kidding? It's not business. Every woman knows not to respond to an email like the one I angrily sent last night unless they're guilty of it.

I lift the phone and open her message to reply.

Be honest with me. Are you sleeping with him?

It takes a minute for her to respond.

Jocelyn Vann: Yes. I was.

Cool Gurl: Was? When???

Jocelyn Vann: I'd prefer to have this conversation in person.

Cool Gurl: There's no way I'm meeting up with you. How do I know you aren't lying?

Jocelyn Vann: I don't have time for games. You contacted me and accused me of sleeping with your husband and I said I did. If you want to have a discussion, meet me at Jessa's Lounge downtown at eight. I'll be wearing orange.

CHAPTER FOURTEEN

JOCELYN

The last thing I have time for is a desperate housewife trying to blame me for her failing marriage.

When I first read the message, I couldn't help the chuckle that slipped out of me. I had a feeling this would happen. There is never a circumstance within an affair where the wife doesn't find out, and yet I slept with Gabriel anyway. Why? Because I'm an idiot, that's why.

I needed to put this to rest and jump on it before he could try to throw me under the bus. Because that's what men do, right? They gaslight and lie to get their way out of deceit. Gabriel may be charming, but he's no different.

I laugh as I browse my closet for something to wear. It's hard to decide what to go with when the closet is the size of two damn bedrooms, but a sliver of orange smacked between nudes catches my eye. The orange midi dress from Nordstrom. I'll wear that. After all, I'll be meeting the wife in less than an hour. She'll be surprised to see me as it is. I can't go without looking *somewhat* worthy of her husband's affair.

I send my final email to the wife to let her know where to find me and what I'll be wearing, then I pluck the dress on the velvet hanger off the rack and lay it gingerly on the back of the nearest chair.

Tonight should be interesting.

CHAPTER FIFTEEN

ADIRA

Jessa's Lounge is a swanky lounge in downtown Tampa. According to Yelp and other online reviews, it's a place with a soothing atmosphere, perfect for grabbing a drink and catching up with a friend, or somewhere to unwind with a lover. I researched and studied every detail of the location Jocelyn Vann had suggested online to make sure I wasn't walking into some sort of trap.

I also read the About page, but there was no owner's name listed, just a short explanation of where the name Jessa came from and how it had won several awards for outstanding customer service and bartending.

I know this is outrageous. It would be much easier to just confront Gabriel and demand answers from him, end it once and for all, but I'm intrigued by this Jocelyn woman—despite how much it terrified me and how calm she was in her responses.

How did she know I was his wife? What if I was some random psychopath who wanted to lie and manipulate her? Whatever the case may be, it's too late to turn back now.

I walk up the steps that lead to the main entrance of Jessa's and grip the shiny gold handles of the glass door to swing it open.

The first thing I notice is how dimly lit the lounge is. I suppose that's to be expected. But it's not lit in a way where a person can't see the details of each section. No, it's lit up all over, but the lighting is soft and soothing. There's a hum to the lounge as people speak that immediately comforts my soul.

Pillar candles in lanterns flicker from the center of the tables. A black railing connected to floating thick wood treads leads up to a second floor, and at the top of it is a dangly, gold chandelier. It's classy, chic, serene, and the most interesting part about the lounge is that every chair at every table is different. The chairs range from wooden to painted to velvet and even suede. A private section at the far end of the lounge is set up with deep purple-velvet sofas and directly across is a bar busy with patrons.

"Hi there. Welcome to Jessa's!" a woman greets me in a singsong voice. "Can I get you settled in?"

I turn my head, coming face-to-face with a round-faced Caucasian woman. She's wearing a purple button-down suit that combats her red hair. She's behind the hostess stand with a pen in her hand and a wide, welcoming smile on her lips. *Ah, the delightful customer service.*

"Uh . . . no. That's okay. I'm actually meeting someone."

"Oh, okay! Well, let me know if you need anything." She continues a smile and I thank her before turning away.

I scan the lounge with a careful eye as I walk deeper inside. I hope to find a woman in orange—most likely beautiful, if she's involved with Gabriel.

My eyes lift to the staircase, and I catch a glimpse of orange. Standing at the top is a woman in a sleeveless, mid-length dress and strappy black heels. Her hair is pulled up in a curly black bun, and she wears gold bangles and hoops. A clear drink in a cute bubble glass topped with a lime is in her hand and she sips from it with her eyes on mine, and then she smiles, as if she knows exactly who I am. That alone should be enough for me to bolt, but I don't.

With a simple flick of her fingers, she orders that I come up before walking away from the staircase. I glance around before following her lead.

The second floor is much quieter than the first. There's another bar, but only one bartender and two people seated there, a couple, talking over drinks. Through my periphery, I spot the sliver of orange again and turn my head.

The woman in orange is making her way past the bar toward a door with the words PRIVATE ROOM in bold letters on it. She pushes it open and disappears inside, and I hurry in my spiked heels to catch up to her.

Gripping the door handle, I swing the door open and enter a room with a poker table in the center. Four chairs are set up around the table and burgundy curtains are high on the wall across from me.

The woman in orange stands in front of a wet bar with a smile on her lips. "So, you're the wife," she says without so much as a glance my way. It's not a question but a blanket statement.

I remain standing by the door, giving her a suspicious once-over. "And you must be Jocelyn."

"Well, that depends on who you ask." She turns with the same glass in hand and smirks. "Drink?"

"No, thank you."

"Suit yourself." She saunters across the room and there's an elegance to her that, for some odd reason, intimidates the hell out of me. I watch her pull out one of the chairs from the poker table and sit in it. "You play poker?"

I don't answer.

"Probably not. Your face reveals too much."

I step deeper into the room, gazing around. What if there are cameras? What if she's bullshitting me?

"Adira," she says, and I whip my head to find her eyes.

"How do you know my name?"

"He's said it before," Jocelyn murmurs. "Sit, will you?"

I work hard to swallow, staring at her a moment longer before moving forward anyway. Taking the chair opposite hers, I place my bag on my lap and aim to settle my nerves. She places her drink on a coaster and plucks out a poker chip from a tray on the tabletop.

"I'm sure you're full of questions." She sighs.

"Can we please not beat around the bush?"

"Fine."

"Why were you so ready to meet me? The last thing a woman involved in an affair would do is meet up with his *wife*."

"Yeah, well, what can I say? I'm a different kind of woman." She shrugs, flipping the chip between her fingers. Up close, she's striking. I can see why Gabriel is attracted to her. Her almond-shaped eyes, the way her baby hairs are so sleek and swooped into a long ponytail. Her light brown face is clear of blemishes—that or she has some damn good makeup—and her lips are full. Natural, I'm sure—the color of raspberries beneath a clear coat of gloss.

"Are you trying to blackmail me? You know who I am. You had to have done research on me. Do you want money, is that it?" I ask.

The woman tosses her head back to laugh. "Trust me, I don't have time for blackmailing. And I have plenty of money, so why would I need yours?" She lifts her hands, gesturing to the room around her. "I own this place."

"Your name's Jessa?"

"God, no," she scoffs. "That's my sister's name."

"Okay," I say evenly. "How did you meet Gabriel?"

"Oh, we go way back. We were friends for a really long time."

"He never mentioned you to me."

She shrugs. "I guess he liked to keep our friendship . . . quiet."

"And now you're *sleeping* with him?"

"I suppose so," she murmurs, and I frown, anger sizzling in my veins. "When you emailed me, I knew it was you. It's not like me to sleep with married men but, like I said, Gabriel and I are good friends, and I guess things escalated. We drank too much one night, feelings got involved—you know how that goes. He talked about you a lot to me. I looked into you some time ago and I have to say, I admire your hustle. A seven-figure Black woman, killing it in the game. I have mad respect for that. And as much as I adore Gabriel, I believe you deserve better than to deal with his bullshit. Now that you know he has a mistress, you should probably leave his ass."

I narrow my eyes at her. "Why? So you can have him all to yourself?"

"Girl, I do *not* want him—well, not in the way you're thinking. Besides, after all this, I think he and I might be done." She rolls her eyes and takes a long sip of her drink. "I'm just trying to help you move the hell on from all this, so you aren't emailing other women in the future the way you did me. It makes you look desperate."

"Wow. Well, that's nice," I snap, slinging my purse over my shoulder. "But I don't need your goddamn help. And I don't understand what you're so smug about. You realize you aren't the only one he's been fucking behind my back, right?"

Her smug smile drips away and I *almost* find satisfaction in that. Almost. It is true that misery loves company, but it sucks to linger in this despicable feeling. Still, who is she to think she can get under my skin and gloat, like she's some higher-up princess? I have to shut her down.

"What are you talking about?" she asks in a calm manner, but her expression is anything but. Her jaw is ticking, her nostrils flaring at the edges. Her grip has tightened around her glass too, making her knuckles more pronounced beneath the gold light.

"There's another woman. I found out about her first. You're not the original mistress. You're just his *other* mistress."

Her chin tips and she clicks her tongue. "I see."

I stand up. "Great. And now that you know, I'll be going."

I push my chair in and head to the door, but before I can get away, I hear her say, "If what you're saying is true, I have a feeling this won't be your last time seeing me, boss lady."

I peer over my shoulder. She's smiling, her chin raised again, like she's so sure of herself. She rises out of her chair gracefully and walks to me in her heels. Extending an arm, she offers something to me. I take the object from her hand—a black business card with gold cursive font printed on it. "Give me a shout when you need me. Even if it is like last time, at three in the morning."

I have no idea why she thinks I'll ever see her again and I damn sure don't want to talk to her after this, so I stuff the card in my pocket, pull the door open, and leave the private room without looking back.

CHAPTER SIXTEEN

ADIRA

When I get home, I hurry to the den, where the minibar is set up.

I pour two fingers of whiskey into a glass tumbler and guzzle it down. Then I pour another and gulp it. I normally prefer my whiskey on ice, but tonight doesn't call for that. I need to feel the burn, let it simmer in my veins, which is awful, considering my urge to conceive.

I'm not pregnant. I've checked twice this week. The reminder of it lingers in my bathroom, wrapped in a wad of toilet paper, the box torn to shreds out of rage several days ago.

With a slow exhale, I leave the den and enter the kitchen. I place the glass down on the gleaming white counter and sag my body onto one of the upholstered barstools.

My eyes wander to the pill bottles lined up neatly on the rack next to the coffee and teas. A couple of Oxy would knock me out cold, I know it, but I resist because that isn't the pill I should have at the forefront of my mind. I start to wonder why I even have the concoction of fertility treatments there. Why have a baby with a man who doesn't give a shit? Hell, does he even want a baby? Is that why he's doing this? Seeing other women behind my back? Lying to my face? Because a family isn't what he wants? We've discussed it and he knows it'll make me happy . . . but maybe it won't make him happy.

I shift my gaze to the paper next to the bottles on the counter. Pushing off the stool, I walk toward the paper—the first page of an article my friend Kellan sent to me via email. Some man was stabbed to death in a prison only a few miles away from me. Kellan thought I'd find it interesting and, oddly enough, I did. I found it so interesting that I printed it off just so I could read it again and again and again. It's not like the man didn't deserve it. He'd murdered a mother and her daughter. He was a criminal.

Kell does that often. Anytime I express interest in a topic, he'll take it upon himself to find the biggest cases and email them to me. Prison was the last thing we talked about, and that's only because I told him I might end up in prison for "slappin' a hoe" (the hoe being Julianna, but he doesn't know that). I read the note Kell typed above the article: *Think about how you might get shanked in prison before you go around slappin' a hoe.*

I read the article a few more times, then I fold the paper, slide it across the counter away from me, and leave the kitchen, dragging myself through the halls with my drink and my purse.

How can Gabriel do this to me? I thought we were happy, but all this time he's been sleeping with other women. And they're both *beautiful* women—women who could have any man they want, but they want mine. I don't get it.

The thought of it makes my belly churn and my head throb. I drop my purse on the nightstand and climb into my king-size bed, burying the side of my face into the silk pillows. I normally hate lying down with makeup on, but I don't have the energy to wipe it off right now.

My phone buzzes in my purse. I open it and pull the phone out, and it's a text from Dina. She's sent a video, something spiritual, I'm sure. I'm not in the mood to watch it. Hell, I'm not in the mood for anything right now.

I sit up and drop my face into my hands. My head shakes repeatedly and my throat thickens. I so badly want to cry, but I don't. Gabriel clearly doesn't love me anymore and I don't understand why.

We were so happy once upon a time. I can still remember it.

He was just a man, sitting by the food court in the mall. I hate malls with all their busy-ness, chaos, and greasy food, but I had to go for a meeting with a retail store. I was ordering a smoothie when I felt him staring at me. I didn't have to look to realize that someone was looking my way. I could feel a heaviness on the back of my neck, a prickling running up my spine.

I glanced over my shoulder as casually as possible and took a sweep of the area. Not a single person was looking my way.

"Ma'am? Can I help you?" the cashier behind the register asked. I hurried to her and ordered a citrus smoothie. But as I waited, I could still feel eyes on me, so I turned to look again, and that's when I saw him.

He hadn't been seated in the food court area where the tables were. He was sitting on a bench next to the exit of a bookstore nearby. A hardback novel was in his hand, but I couldn't make out the title. A frown took hold of me as he looked me up and down. What the hell was he looking at?

I turned away, relieved when my smoothie was slid across the counter to me. Collecting a straw, I left quickly and walked toward the exit of the mall, but before I could make it, someone called after me.

"Excuse me?" The voice was deep and sultry. I'd never heard a voice like it, but it stood out among all the other voices—all the chattering and humming and laughter.

I glanced back slowly, smoothie in one hand and my purse in the other. There he stood—the man who'd been staring at me. He was much taller than I expected. He stood about only four steps away, but I could smell him and his expensive cologne. His hair was cut and lined up neatly, and I finally saw the title of the book he had in his hand: Devil in a Blue Dress.

Noticing where my gaze had fallen, Gabriel looked down at the book and lifted it. "A Mosley fan?" he asked.

"I've read a few." I stood taller. "Is there a reason you stopped me?"

"Oh, yes. Well, you see, I was tempted to come and buy your smoothie for you, but then I figured you're a woman who knows exactly what she's doing and what she wants."

I narrowed my eyes at him. Really? *I wanted to ask.* Is that all you've got?

"I, um . . . well, it's just that it's not every day I see someone like . . . you around here. And trust me, that says a lot, because I stop by this mall almost every day to browse the bookstore and for a quick bite."

I brought the strap of my purse to my shoulder. "I find that a very weird thing to say to someone. All kinds of people shop at the mall."

"Of course they do. But not women like you. You strike me as an online-order type of person. Plus, you don't have any shopping bags on you and you're already leaving, so . . ."

"I had business to tend to," I told him, raising my chin.

"Ah. So let me guess. You own this place?"

"What? You mean the mall?" I asked, scoffing.

He smirked and tilted his head, as if his question wasn't bizarre.

"No, I don't own the mall."

"You look like the kind of person who could buy this whole place out."

I sighed. "Okay, well, my smoothie is getting watery

and I have to get back to work, so if that's all—" I started to turn away, but he rushed toward me, catching my elbow. His hand was soft, and I felt a jolt run through me—something I'd never felt before. I'd been with plenty of men, but none of them were like him. So direct, so forward, so goddamn handsome. I didn't know what else to do but jump, and noticing my reaction, he snatched his hand away quickly, tossing both of his in the air.

"I'm sorry. I didn't mean to touch you—I mean, I just . . . shit." He said the last word beneath his breath and lowered his gaze. The way his lashes touched his upper cheeks and his face swam with disappointment made me feel awful. He seemed like a good guy. A terrible flirt, but still charming and funny, and he was putting forth an effort.

I turned to face him again, fully. "What is it that you want?" I asked.

And he looked at me. Really looked at me. "You," he said. "I know it's crazy and that you don't know a damn thing about this stranger you met in the mall, but I want you. Hopefully, that's not too much to ask for."

And with those words, I was a goner.

Any issues we had, we could've sought counseling to fix them. I don't want our marriage to end. I want us to be together, to travel together, have a baby, and live our lives until we're old and brittle but happy.

So pathetic.

Jocelyn was right. I do deserve better . . . but he's all I've had for years. If I let this go after so long, I'll be empty—a shell of a woman with no other purpose than silk and lingerie.

I pick my head up and hiccup a laugh at the thought that just occurred. *Jocelyn was right.* Screw her. Even if she is right and she faced me woman-to-woman, it doesn't make what she's done okay. She slept with Gabriel knowing he was married—knowing it would hurt someone else.

I shift my attention to my phone and then pick it up. After sitting back down on the bed, I dig through my jacket pocket and take out the black business card. I stare at it a moment, running the pad of my thumb over the gold-foil numbers.

What exactly would I need her help with? Does she see how much I love him? How much it pains me to even think about letting our marriage go? She seems to have her shit together—a good head on her shoulders despite being a bit arrogant. If she and Gabriel were friends . . . well, maybe she can convince him to come back to me. She can tell him to ditch Julianna, focus on our marriage, go to counseling, make things right.

I sigh, and even though I feel like I'll regret it, I start up a text to send to Jocelyn.

I want Gabriel back. I only want him to myself.

She's not quick to respond this time, and while I wait, I eventually doze off on the bed. But when I wake up, sunlight spills through my curtains and I groan, sitting up sluggishly. I check my phone, which now only has 10 percent of battery left, and a text from the number Jocelyn gave me.

I think I can help with that.

I read her message twice and I can't help but sigh with mild relief because for the first time in a long time, I feel like there's hope.

CHAPTER SEVENTEEN

Panda's hair reminded me of silk. Soft and sleek—a pleasure to comb and brush. It wasn't like mine, which was thick, coily, and unruly—especially in the mornings when I first woke up. Claudette never gave me a bonnet to wear at night and, fortunately, by the age of eight, I'd learned how to do my own hair so that it wouldn't be so matted anymore. Panda didn't need a bonnet as much as I did. Her hair hardly ever appeared messy, though it did require a good brushing here and there.

Her eyes were hazel and her lips were like those of a doll—rosy and full. She was gorgeous to me, but to Claudette, she was a monster.

Perhaps it was because he wanted her. He was never supposed to want her, but because he did, it made Claudette angry and worthless. At first it was subtle the way he lingered, the way he watched her, talked to her, laughed with her. But then it became glaringly obvious that he wanted more from her. It made him a terrible man, but it also made the girl an evil, evil thing.

CHAPTER EIGHTEEN

JOCELYN

"You're right. We shouldn't keep doing this."

I sigh, turning my head to look at Gabriel's back. His belt buckle jingles as he adjusts his pants, and he glances over his shoulder at me. We're in a hotel room again. An empty bottle of gin has tipped over on the counter, and one of the glasses is on the floor because he couldn't wait to have me and I ended up dropping it. Some of the liquid spilled, of course, but I didn't care.

"Are those your serious eyes?" I ask, fighting a smile.

"I'm being serious. Why is everything such a joke to you lately?"

"Oh—I'm sorry. Am I not allowed to laugh about the fact that I'm not just the mistress but the *other* mistress to you?"

"You've been acting weird all day." Gabriel shakes his head, buckling the belt and snatching up his shirt.

"Why can't we keep doing this?" I ask, just to amuse myself.

"Because." He sighs, finally turning to face me. "It doesn't feel right anymore."

I stare at him for a moment, watching as he fixes his

watch, then I shift my gaze to his ring finger. "Where's your ring?"

"Oh my God," he grumbles. "Are you serious?" His head shakes as he says, "I'm not doing this with you." He avoids my eyes, marching to pick up his shoes. "I'm gonna go."

"Wait, Gabriel." I climb off the bed and walk toward him before he can get to the door. Sighing, he turns to look at me, and I grab his hand with one of mine, lifting it and kissing his knuckles. "If I can be honest, I don't want this to be over."

"It needs to be. This is getting messy now."

"Well, what about the other one?" I demand. "Why don't you leave her instead? You can't just bring me into this and then expect me to let it go."

"What?" Gabriel scoffed. "You're the one who started this! I told you this was crazy to do from the beginning, but you didn't listen!"

"Of course I wasn't going to listen! I know what I want, Gabriel, and that's you."

"Yeah. Right. Sure you do."

"What's that supposed to mean?"

"It means I can't do this anymore. I don't *want* to do it anymore. Let's just let it go while the damage isn't so bad. Okay?"

"I thought this was what you wanted," I say, as calmly as my voice will allow.

"I mean, it was fun at first, but . . . it's getting out of hand now. It's becoming too much."

"So, this is it?"

"Shouldn't it be?"

He drops his shoes and bends down to slip them on. Once he collects his keys, he opens the hotel door and walks out, looking back at me once before shaking his head and walking away.

The door clicks shut on its own and I stare at it in pure

disbelief. He really has the audacity to leave like that after fucking me every which way he could? After meeting me at hotels and begging me to cry his name?

I turn in a fury, picking up my phone and reading Adira's messages again. She wants my help? She wants that worthless fucker back? Fine. I'll help her, and I'll make sure he regrets ever walking away from me.

CHAPTER NINETEEN

ADIRA

After leaving work the next day, I make my way to the parking deck to get to my car. I sit in the driver's seat for a moment, breathing slowly, counting to three, the way Dina taught me.

One.

Two.

Three.

And we breathe.

Then I open my eyes and take out my phone to read the text message I sent Jocelyn when I told her to meet me at Giotto's. This is my third time reading it, and each time I do my heart races a little faster.

I drive there and check in with the hostess, who leads me to the back of the restaurant, to the specific table I requested. It's my favorite booth—a private area where not many people can see you and your conversations won't be overheard. The last thing I need is for the whole restaurant to learn details about my husband's affair.

I thank the hostess when she places menus down on the polished brown table. A waitress approaches moments later and greets me while pouring water into my glass. I thank her as well, then place my purse on the black leather bench beside me.

Classical music pours from the speakers and my eyes shift right, to the industrial windows ahead. Pothos in clay pots hang in front of the windows, adding a pop of color to the neutral setting, and cool air blows from the vents, causing the leaves of the plants to sway. A stunning view of the city is just outside the window, along with tan umbrellas set up for outdoor dining.

"So we're really doing this, huh?" A voice rises behind me and I gasp before looking over my shoulder. Jocelyn Vann stands there, dressed impeccably in an ivory pantsuit with gold jewelry, smelling of a vanilla-scented perfume. Her hair has been brushed up into a neat, sleek bun, and her makeup is flawless.

She walks past me and sits in the booth opposite me with a small smile on her lips.

"Thank you for coming," I murmur.

"You said you needed help," she says, placing her clutch on the table. "I'm here to help."

The waiter approaches with a basket of bread rolls and butter. I thank her again, and Jocelyn immediately goes for a roll. I don't know how she can eat. After knowing what I do about Gabriel, hunger is foreign to me.

"So, where do we begin?" Jocelyn asks, unraveling her silverware from the cloth napkin. She takes out the knife and scoops up a hefty section of butter, spreading it on the top of the roll and then biting into it. "Oh my God," she groans around a mouthful. "It's honey butter. This is so good."

"This restaurant is one of my favorites," I tell her.

"Yeah. I can see why." She looks around. "It's a nice spot."

I force a smile, and Jocelyn studies my face, eyeing me carefully, which causes me to look down.

"You shouldn't do that, you know?"

"Do what?" I ask, meeting her eyes again.

"Look away." She bites into her roll again, chews, swallows, and then says, "Confidence lies within."

"Of course you can say that," I say, laughing a little. "Look at you."

She shrugs and purses her lips, fighting a smile.

I mean what I say. She's a gorgeous woman and I envy how she can just sit there, stuffing her face with carbs and saturated fats as if she knows she won't swell like a balloon the way I do when I eat too much bread. And God, what I would do for her cheekbones. They're sharp and natural. There are women paying thousands of dollars to have her facial bone structure.

"Anyway, I have a meeting in an hour, so we should probably make this quick," I inform her.

"Okay."

"You said you and Gabriel are friends. Do you still plan on staying in touch with him as a friend after this?"

"Honestly, I'm not sure. But if you're asking me if I'll sleep with him again, the answer is no." She cuts her eyes at me, plucking at her piece of bread. "We officially called it off last night."

I shift in my seat while she smirks at me. How can she be so casual about this? As if sleeping with a woman's husband and then speaking with said woman is a normal occurrence for her?

"I guess that's good to know." I sigh and twist my fingers on my lap. "I'm sorry, I'm just . . . I'm not even sure what I expect to gain from us meeting like this. When I found out there was *another* woman, I just lost it, you know?"

"I get that. And speaking of being the *other* woman." Jocelyn places a palm flat on the table and leans forward. "How long has he been fooling around with the other chick?"

"I'm not sure. I want to say for a couple of years now."

"Years!?" Her eyes stretch wider. "What the fuck?"

"Right? All this time I thought we were happy, but he's

been with her . . . and *you*. I do everything I can to make sure he's happy, but apparently, it's not enough. *I'm* not enough."

"Hey, don't you do that," Jocelyn snaps, pointing a manicured finger at me. "His issues and affairs don't have shit to do with you. Those are his own insecurities. Don't put that on yourself."

"I know. I just . . . I don't understand why I would even want to stay with him if he's cheated on me. And not once but twice."

"Because you love him. Because he makes you feel whole. Because—and let's be real—he's *incredible* in bed."

I stare into her eyes with a frown.

"Too soon. Sorry." She picks up another roll, breaking it in half. She offers the other half to me and says, "Eat something."

I take the offered half of her roll and bring it to my mouth, giving it a nibble. "There's also the fact that I want to start a family."

"You do?" she asks, her eyes stretching wide with surprise.

"Yes. I can't imagine having a baby with anyone else but him."

"Wow." She blinks twice, really fast, and pops another piece of bread into her mouth. "He doesn't really seem like the fatherly type."

"He'd make a great dad."

"Does he want a kid?"

I avoid her eyes and nibble at the bread again. "He said he's willing to do whatever makes me happy. That will make me happy."

"But does he *want* a kid?" she asks, more slowly this time.

I meet her eyes. "Look, don't worry about that, okay? That's not why we're meeting."

"Okay, okay." She raises a hand in the air. "Well, I have been thinking about what you should do." Jocelyn straightens in her seat. She starts to say something else, but the waitress appears with a notepad and smiles at us.

"Are you ready to order?" the waitress asks, chipper.

"Sure, yes." I peruse the menu and select the first thing that sounds good, grilled salmon with asparagus and a sweet baked potato.

"Anything for you?" I ask Jocelyn. "I'll cover it."

Jocelyn shakes her head no. "Since this'll be quick, I'm fine with bread and water."

The waitress looks at me for a moment and then steps away with a smile. "O–kay. I'll put that order right in for you."

When she's gone, Jocelyn takes a sip of water. "I was thinking, maybe we should start *watching* Gabriel."

"Watching him? What do you mean?" I ask.

"You know, sort of follow him around, see what he's really doing with his time? How do you know there aren't more women? What if it's not just this Julianna woman and me, but many others?"

I work hard to swallow while lowering my gaze. "There can't be any more."

"We won't know for sure unless we see for ourselves."

I hesitate. "I already did that. That's how I found out about Julianna."

"But you didn't know about me, and you wanna know why? Because we were careful until the stupid emails," she counters. "Look, you say you want him to yourself, right?"

"Yes."

"Well, that means we need to know more about him. What is he doing when he's not home? Who is he hanging out with? Where does he park his car when he's not using it, or when he's traveling? What does he get with this Julianna girl that he doesn't get with you? We figure that out and you can make the necessary changes that help you keep your husband."

"That sounds extreme. I mean, when would I even have the time? I used to go before work, but things are picking up now and he'd eventually catch onto me, I'm sure. Plus I have so much to do."

"We can start with nights," Jocelyn says. "Whenever you're off, I'll meet you, and I can drive, so your car isn't so obvious."

"But . . . what if I find out there are more women?"

Jocelyn searches my face before saying, "Then you'll know exactly what you need to do going forward."

CHAPTER TWENTY

ADIRA

The room spins above me. I close my eyes and count to three.

One.

Two.

Three.

And we breathe.

I open my eyes again. I'm still here. I sit up, gripping the fabric of the love seat in my office. I can't get the meeting with Jocelyn out of my head. I'm not even sure why I trust her. This woman was sleeping with my husband, and now that it's over with him, she wants to help me?

To anyone else, it would feel like a set up. But there was sincerity in her eyes, and it seemed she had much better things to do with her time than to waste mine. Before we parted ways after lunch, she told me, *"I still think you deserve better, but if you want your marriage to work, I'll help you."*

"Why?" I asked.

And she shrugged. *"I guess I feel guilty."*

I did deserve better—a hell of a lot better than what he gave me. But at the same time, I was curious to know what all Gabriel did when he *wasn't* with me. I've only followed him twice—once when he went to the mall to meet Julianna and the second time when he had to go in late for work. That was how I found out where Julianna lived.

I admit I want to know what he does with Julianna when they're alone, or if he gives her more of himself than he gives to me. Does he treat her the same way he treats me? Is he telling her that he loves her too? Shit, *does* he even love her? What if he does? How do I cope with that?

My work phone rings and I stand, walking barefoot across the office to catch the call.

"This is Adira," I answer.

"Hey, Adira. It's Dina."

I sit in my chair. "Dina, hi. What's going on? Why are you calling my work phone?"

"You weren't answering your cell. I called last night and this morning."

"Oh—I'm sorry, D. I had a late night, and this morning I was running behind because I had to meet someone for lunch."

"Meet who?" she asks.

"Just a work friend," I lie. There's no way I'm telling Dina about Gabriel's *other* mistress.

"Oh, I see. Well, I'm just checking in. I also wanted to tell you that I found some of your pieces in Ana's boutique in Miami!"

"Really?" I exclaim. "That's amazing! I didn't know Ana ordered them for her store."

"She did, thanks to me." I knew if I was face-to-face with Dina, she'd be winking and grinning. A car horn beeps on her end and she blows a raspberry. She does that when she's frustrated and doesn't want to explode on the person. It's one of her coping techniques. Instead of getting angry at someone else for their irritations and impatience, she blows a raspberry. "Never directly at the person—unless they deserve it," she'd tell me. It's a bit childish, but I've tried it before and, surprisingly, it works. I wish the raspberries worked when it came to my husband.

"Where are you?" I ask.

"I just left a client's house. I was crossing the road and some rude guy beeped at me."

"Oh."

"Yes. Oh, by the way, Ana and Kellan finally got moved into their new house."

"Yes, I'm aware. Kellan emailed me about it a few days ago."

"Yeah, I figured he would have. You know I did some Reiki work with Ana after she had her baby?"

"Yep." I sigh. "You told me."

"I did? Oh, well, anyway, I was talking to Kellan, and he mentioned that they're having a housewarming party at their house, but I don't think I'll make it on that date. I still want to see them, and he said he didn't mind me coming another day. He told me to try to steal you away from work for a few days to see him too." Dina laughs. "I told him I'd let you know. It's around the time I come down to see you, so maybe we can fly there together."

"Sure, that sounds nice. I have a lot of work to do, but I could use a day or two off."

"Great! I'm so happy to hear that. Okay, let me get off the phone and find my car! I swear, I'm always forgetting where I park. Love you!" She hangs up and I laugh, placing the phone back on the hook.

CHAPTER TWENTY-ONE

ADIRA

Many people take the easy way out when it comes to marriage. I know there's supposed to be trust and a solid foundation. An open line of communication is key, and let's not kid ourselves—sex is a huge deciding factor. Without the sex, the connection, the feel of skin on skin, lips locked, and fingers running through each other's hair, what's the point of marrying that person? When you have a connection to your spouse in every way, nothing should be able to come between the two of you. Not even an *affair*. You work to make it better.

However, when the affair cuts so deep that it breaks your heart, I suppose the easy way out is, well, *easiest*. Separation is a must and divorce is often imminent. Once trust has been severed, often times it's hard to salvage that trust, especially when it comes to the person you'd planned on spending the rest of your life with.

But I'm a firm believer that humans are put on earth to make mistakes. We are capable of good morals, yes, but we're also capable of fucking up too. My husband has fucked up. He's had weak moments, and so have I. That's why I'm parked in the parking lot of Jessa's Lounge, waiting for Jocelyn to come out of the back exit.

Impatient, I check the time on my watch. Light bounces off the gold edge of the clock face and I blow a breath. Why the hell am I even doing this? Why should I bother? I'm better off going home and sulking.

Because you need answers, a little voice chants in the back of my head. Another sigh escapes me and before I know it, the back door of Jessa's swings open and out walks Jocelyn. She's dressed head to toe in black. Shiny black ankle boots, black jeans, a black blouse tucked into her jeans, and a belt weaved through the loops with a gold buckle. Her hair is neat today. It's been twisted out to a thick, curly Afro, parted at the arch of her left brow.

She notices my car and waves a hand, gesturing for me to follow her. I kill the engine of my Audi, grab my Michael Kors bag, and step out of the car. Jocelyn unlocks the door of a red 2022 Genesis and the headlights flash on me. She opens the driver's door and places one arm on top of the hood of the car, leaning against it with more poise than I have in my left pinkie.

"You absolutely sure you want to do this?" she asks, watching me walk toward her.

My heels click on the blacktop road as I nod my head, meeting her at the passenger side. "I'm here, aren't I?"

"There's still time to change your mind," she says with a shrug. "We're going down a road you can't come back from, boss lady."

I watch as she sinks into the cushiony leather driver's seat, settling behind the wheel, and I draw in a deep breath before pulling open the passenger door and climbing in too.

In the confines of her car, it's strange, being so close to her. Her perfume is different today, powerful, with hints of vanilla and an undertone of floral.

She push starts the engine and clears her throat. "Just so you know, I'm only doing this because Gabriel is a jackass who tried to play me too."

"Well, I appreciate that," I say without meaning it.

"Where to?"

"Oh . . . um." I swallow hard, my face burning as I dig through my purse until I retrieve my phone. I go to the maps app on my iPhone and click one of the addresses I'd saved when I first visited it.

My hand tilts the phone toward Jocelyn, but I peer through the windshield, swallowing the embarrassment of having one of my husband's mistress's addresses saved on my phone. I steal a glance at Jocelyn as she pulls out of the parking lot of Jessa's and she's fighting a smile as she follows the directions.

We ride in silence for the most part, jazz at a low volume trickling out of the speakers. Along the way, we pass one of the shops in town that sells my robes, Beverly's. One of the lingerie and robe sets is on display on one of their black mannequins. The gold fabric of the robe shimmers beneath the recessed lighting above and I have the urge to smile, but I don't. Once upon a time it was a dream to see my items in stores— let alone in someone's display window. Now, nothing feels real and I don't feel worthy. I look ahead, through the windshield again.

"So, how long have you and Gabriel been together anyway?" Jocelyn finally breaks the silence, side-eyeing me before putting her focus on the road again.

"Seven years. Married for two."

"Damn. Only two years married and he's been messing around with two other women already?" Jocelyn scoffs, and I roll my eyes, looking away. "Oh, come on. Don't take that personally. The reason he's doing that has nothing to do with you."

"It clearly has everything to do with me. He's bored with me, or tired of me, or I'm not spicy enough. I don't know."

"Good Lord, girl. Where is your confidence?" Jocelyn huffs a breath, glancing at my phone for the next direction.

"Sorry I'm not as confident as you are," I mutter.

"You don't have to be as confident as me, but you can at least try. Come on, some girl has your husband running to her bed and you're over here moping! Do you know who you are? What you're worth? What you need to do is shut this shit down quick. That, or get rid of his ass."

"I told you, Jocelyn, I don't want to lose my husband. Yes, he's made his mistakes, but so have I. Neither of us are perfect, okay?" I pause and work to swallow. "I'm just . . . I'm worried about this Julianna girl. I think he's become *too* invested in her."

"Well," Jocelyn says, flipping the switch for the right signal and making a smooth turn. "We're about to find out."

CHAPTER TWENTY-TWO

ADIRA

As soon as Jocelyn turns into Julianna's neighborhood, she drives to the back of the complex and parks beneath a tree with branches that nearly touch the ground of the median beside us. It's a good hiding spot. Not close to the resident parking area, but close enough to see Julianna's apartment.

She shuts off the engine and sits back against the seat. "And now we wait."

"He should be in town by now. I'll text him to see where he is." The phone is shaking and I realize my hands are trembling. I can feel Jocelyn staring at me, so I draw in a deep breath and then exhale, steadying my hands to send the message.

"He says he's leaving the airport. But he's going to catch drinks with a friend."

"Hmm. Well, let's see if it's an actual friend or his infamous fuck buddy." Jocelyn folds her arms across her chest, staring ahead.

I lower my phone as the screen dims and notice another car pulling into the complex. It's entirely hard to miss, painted a hideous pink that not many would go for. The silver rims gleam beneath the lamp posts as she parks and out jumps Julianna Garcia. Her hair isn't up in a topknot like the last time I saw her. It's bone straight and hanging down to the middle of her back. It shines beneath the gold light, sways like dark, glimmering threads as she pops open her trunk and takes out a few shopping bags. She's gotten her hair done. When she takes out a Victoria's Secret bag, my throat constricts. *Lingerie? Hair styled? She's prepared for him.*

"That's her," I say, pointing ahead.

"Oh." There's a hint of surprise in Jocelyn's tone that makes my belly clench. Yeah, Julianna Garcia is no mediocre bitch. She's a *stunning* bitch any man would drop to his knees for.

With a pep of eagerness, Julianna makes her way toward the entrance of the building, greeting the security guard at the door. He smiles and watches her sashay away.

I'm tempted to ask Jocelyn what she thinks of her, but, frankly, I don't care what she thinks. Not long ago she was sleeping with my husband too. *Ugh.* I can't believe I'm even sitting next to her and doing this. Letting her see the ugly side of my marriage. She doesn't deserve that. Hell, she's part of the reason Gabriel and I are crumbling.

As tempted as I am to forget all this—to tell her to take me back to my car so I can arrange my own stakeout—another vehicle arrives several minutes later and pulls up to the front of the building.

Out of the back seat, Gabriel steps out, rolling his shoulders back and peering up at the building with a smile gracing his lips, as if he's missed the sight of it. He thanks the Lyft driver, closes the door, and walks toward the entrance with a silver suitcase on wheels.

"Gabriel," I whisper. Tears spring to my eyes and they burn, but I blink to prevent them from building up.

"Meeting with a friend my ass," Jocelyn grumbles.

I have the urge to burst out of the car, chase after him, and beg him not to do this, but I can't bring myself to. I'm shaking now—shaking with anger and embarrassment.

"Look. There." I glance at Jocelyn, and she's pointing upward, through the windshield. I look where she's pointing, and on one of the balconies—the second from the top—is a woman. *Julianna.*

She stands on the patio wearing a white robe that's loosely tied at the waist. Her hair is just as perfect as it was before, and she has a glass of wine in her hand that she's taking delicate sips from.

She stares ahead, at the cars and the Tampa skyline beyond her complex, and then a silhouette appears behind her. My gut clenches tight as I watch Gabriel step out of the shadows and onto the patio with her. He snakes his arms around her from behind and she raises the hand with the wine in the air. I imagine her giggling about almost spilling the wine on herself, and him giving a sultry apology in her ear for startling her.

And then it happens. I see it for myself and I want to snatch my own eyeballs out of my head. He takes the glass of wine from her, places it on the ledge of the balcony, cradles her face in his large hands, and kisses her.

Kisses. Her.

For the second time, my husband kisses her.

Her arms lace around the back of his neck and she sinks into his strong body, and as badly as I want to pull my gaze away, I can't. He hitches her robe up, revealing the left side of her hip and thigh, and before I know it, he's carrying her in his arms and they're lip-locked as they make their way back inside the apartment.

My throat thickens, my vision blurs, and I feel a hand rubbing my back. I realize I'm sobbing, the sounds foreign even to my own ears. This isn't like the time at the mall. At least when I saw them at the mall, they were in public, so it wasn't so affectionate, but this? It's a betrayal that stings so bad, like pouring alcohol on a gushing wound. I've been ripped wide open and there's no way to repair this ache, this pain.

"I know this isn't what you want to hear," Jocelyn murmurs, still rubbing my back. "But . . . it looks like they're *in love*, Adira."

"Don't say that!" I bark.

Jocelyn is quiet for a moment. "I hate seeing women get like this over men."

"He's my husband," I say and damn my voice for breaking. I want it to sound confident and strong. I need it to still be a fact.

"I know, but you saw what just happened with your own two eyes, Adira! You think he was thinking about you while he had his hands all over her?"

"It's not about that!" I cry. "He's mine! *Mine*, Jocelyn!" I sound delirious—on the brink of madness—but I don't care. "He belongs to me, okay? I—I gave him so much of me. He's . . . he's all I have, Jocelyn. Please. We have to do something about this."

"Well, we could find a way in and go knock on the damn door." Jocelyn pulls her hand away.

"That place is locked tight. Security guards watch the front door and the other entrance on the side; you have to have a keycard to get in."

"I can distract the guard or something." She shrugs. "Julianna isn't the only one with good looks."

My head shakes and I sniffle.

"The only way I can see this ending is you actually communicating with Gabriel and telling him that you know and you want it to end with her. Immediately."

"Yes, I could, but it's . . . it's so complicated between us right now. I feel like if I say anything or give him any kind of ultimatum, he won't choose me, and I don't want to lose him."

Jocelyn lets out a frustrated sigh. "Well, boss lady, I don't know how to help you then." She sits up in her seat and starts the engine. When she drives out of the complex, I take a glance back at the balcony, but they're not there. They're probably fucking like animals inside.

I wipe my tears away, sitting numb in the seat until Jocelyn pulls into the parking lot of Jessa's lounge.

"Why don't you come in for a drink? On me?"

"I should get home," I murmur.

"Just one."

I look into her brown eyes. They're soft and sincere, which, I'm sure, is a rare way to catch Jocelyn Vann.

"Fine. Just one."

CHAPTER TWENTY-THREE

JOCELYN

"You got a favorite?" I ask over my shoulder as I walk behind the bar. We're in my private room, where the velvet curtains have been drawn to reveal the nearby buildings and passing cars.

Adira sits on one of the stools while I stand behind the counter, fingering through some of the alcohol bottles on the top shelf. I glance over my shoulder. "Hello?"

Adira's head shakes and nothing more.

"Fine. You don't want to decide, I'll pick for you." I retrieve two cocktail glasses, pull down a bottle of top-shelf whiskey, and go to work on concocting a beverage I'm sure she'll like. Adira watches as I swish it all together in a cocktail shaker, dump the brown liquid into each glass, and then slide one across the counter to her.

"Come on. Drink up. It'll make you feel better."

She studies the brown liquid in the glass for a fleeting moment before dragging her eyes up to me. "A Manhattan. This is one of my favorites. How did you know?"

"I like to think everyone loves a good Manhattan. And

trust me, after the night you've had, there's more where that came from." With a smirk, I pick up the other glass and take a sip, then make my way around the counter to sit on the barstool next to hers.

We're quiet for a moment, both of us. I'm fingering the rim of my glass and she finally picks up her drink to take a sip. As if she likes it, she takes another sip and nods her approval.

I narrow my eyes at her, and when she looks at me, she sits up higher on her stool and asks, "What?"

"Nothing," I say, focusing on her drink again.

"No, what? Tell me. You think I'm a fucking idiot, don't you?"

"I don't think you're an idiot at all. I mean, okay, maybe I wouldn't just sit on my ass in the car while my man is walking into another bitch's place, but you're better than me—not as reckless—so you're not an idiot."

She smiles at that, and I'm glad I can help with that at least. "On a serious note, though, I am a little worried about you," I confess.

"There's nothing to worry about," she mutters.

"What are you going to do now that you've seen how they are?"

"What can I do, Jocelyn?" She sighs, pressing her fingers to her temples. "I still love Gabriel. I can't see myself being with anyone else but him."

"Even after he cheated on you? Not with one woman, but *two*?" I ask, deadpan. I don't get it, and I don't think I ever will. Here this woman is, with a net worth of over twenty million dollars, and she's whining over one man. Please. If she wants a baby that bad, I'll find her a better candidate. But . . . I suppose I should digress. After all, I'm part of the reason she's in such a fragile state right now.

Adira takes a large gulp of her drink, and I can tell by the tears lining her eyes that she wants to cry, but she won't. At least not right now. "Can I have another?" she asks. "I'll pay."

I slide off the stool and walk around the counter. After I prepare another drink and push it toward her on the sleek counter, I remind her, "Drinks are on me."

"You might want to consider letting me pay you." She laughs. "I plan on having at least three or four more of these before I go."

"And I don't blame you. You're hurting. I know I don't know you all that well, but I'd rather you hurt while around someone than go through it alone."

"You say that like you think I'm suicidal or something."

"Are you?"

She lifts her gaze to mine and realizes I'm dead serious. I'm not smiling. I am worried about the well-being of this woman, oddly enough. "Of course I'm not." She looks away, resting her back against the back of the chair.

"You want to know what I think?" I ask.

"What?"

"He's fallen too hard for her. You saw the way they were together. How he was all over her." I sip my drink. "Your only choice is to remove her from the picture. *Indefinitely.*"

"What do you mean *remove* her?"

"Well, you wouldn't have to lift a finger, that's all I'll say."

"Do you mean like . . ." She stares into my eyes and shakes her head. "No. That's—that's taking it too far. What would you even do?"

"Well, if I told you that, I'd have to kill you, my love." I toss her a wink and a smirk.

"Jocelyn, he's having an affair, that's all. It's not like he's out here kicking women in the face or something."

"Yeah, he's having an affair that's *hurting* you. Look at

you! You're sitting here at my bar, shedding hella tears over it. Seeing all of this and knowing it's happening is killing you on the inside. If we can get rid of her, we've eliminated the element of distraction. She'll be gone and he'll be all yours again. You can focus on building your family and having that baby."

She takes another gulp of her drink. "That's . . . that's dark."

"Hey, sometimes we have to do dark shit to get what we want."

"Really? So is that how you became so successful? By doing dark shit?"

Jocelyn smirks, and that smirk is answer enough.

"I . . . I don't know." Her throat bobs as she swallows. I can tell the conversation is making her uncomfortable as she fidgets on the stool and runs her finger around the edge of her glass.

Okay. Let me chill out before she thinks I'm crazy. "Let's change the subject. What's your favorite color?" I ask.

"Lilac."

"What a random favorite."

"And yours?"

"Orange." I grin. "Any siblings?"

"Uh . . . just one. And you?"

"Just one as well. A sister. Parents still alive?"

"Well, I haven't seen my mom in years and I have no clue who my dad is so . . ." She shrugs. "You?"

"You're just piggybacking off my questions," I scoff, waving a hand. "Ask me something different."

"Okay . . . um." She twists her lips. "Why aren't *you* married?"

She tosses her head back to laugh. "Are you kidding? You ask me that while you sit in here, drinking liquor from your husband's *other* mistress, right after sobbing over him being with the *original* mistress?"

"Ouch." She scrunches her nose. "Touché, bitch." She raises her glass and takes a big swig.

I smirk, amused. "I like you."

"I'm not sure I can say the same," she returns, but I don't miss the coy smirk on the edge of her lips.

We continue asking questions and answering them while I keep pouring drinks. By Adira's fifth Manhattan, I find that she may actually *like* me. She's opening up more and being honest. Sure, she may not fully trust me, but who would after what I did with her husband?

I swear, it's like that movie *The Other Woman*, where Cameron Diaz finds out that her perfect boyfriend is married, and then she teams up with his wife, Leslie Mann, only to find out that he has another mistress who is insanely stunning. Only I'm not the girlfriend, I'm Cameron Diaz, and Adira is Leslie Mann.

"Were you serious about what you said earlier?" Adira is loose now, so the questions are rolling off her tongue.

"About what?" I ask.

"About . . . removing *her* from the equation."

I straighten on the stool and feel my eyes widen. "Are you sure you want the answer to that question?"

"How would you do it?"

"I wouldn't."

"Then who?"

"I can't tell you that."

She sighs, pressing a hand to her forehead. "I do want her gone. . . ."

"Honestly, murder is much easier to get away with than people think."

"Oh my God," she gasps. "Don't—don't say the word! I—I mean, yes, I hate her, but . . . no. Shh, shh, shh." She presses a finger to her drunken lips. "Don't say the word."

I raise an innocent hand. "Suit yourself."

"What am I even saying? Ugh." She drags her palms down the length of her face and it causes her eyeliner to smear.

"Divorce or she goes," I say.

"Stop."

"I'm just saying. At the end of the day, it'll have to be one or the other."

CHAPTER TWENTY-FOUR

ADIRA

"I don't know why I want a baby so much." I pick up a cherry and roll it around in my mouth. "I guess I just think about the way I was raised—my mom wasn't the best parent. And . . . I don't know. I guess I want to prove to myself that I can be a better parent. That I can love my baby no matter what and will always put them first."

"Hmm." Jocelyn rests a fist beneath her chin, her elbow on the bar counter. "I guess that makes sense."

"Do you want kids?"

"I'm not sure. Probably not. I'm way too busy."

"You're not busy right now."

"I'm not?"

"No. You're wasting time listening to a dejected wife."

I slap a hand on the counter and laugh, and Jocelyn mutters, "Oh boy. How drunk are you?"

"No, no. You're right. I'm—I'm so drunk. I'm so stupid drunk—and that literally defeats the purpose of all the medication I have to take at home!"

"Medication?"

"Yes. There's one for anxiety, then I have the pills that

help me sleep—oh, and then there are the infertility treatments and injections. I've had to do them alone lately because, you know, my husband is too busy fucking other women."

"Good Lord, Adira."

"What? It's true."

"I didn't realize you were having fertility issues."

"I am . . . and maybe that's why I want this to work with Gabriel too. He gets it. He gets *me*. I can just imagine a little me or a little him running around. Feeding him or her fruits and veggies and taking them to the park and for walks. I honestly think I'd hand my job over to someone else for a few years, just to spend as much time with the baby as I can."

"That's some serious dedication."

I sigh, planting my elbows on the counter and closing my eyes. "It's all I want. For once, I just want to be happy, and to have whatever I want without so many problems, you know? My life has sucked, and I just . . . I just want this. I just want *him* . . . a future with him." I feel a tear fall down my cheek and I swipe it away. "Gah. Look at me."

"You're okay," Jocelyn murmurs.

"I'm far from okay." I dig my phone out of my purse to check the time. "It's getting late. I should book a Lyft."

"I didn't drink much. I can take you home," she offers.

I meet her eyes. "Okay."

Jocelyn collects her purse and keys and I stumble off the stool, collecting my belongings as well. Once we're in the car, I give her my address and she drives me straight home. As we drive, I can't help glancing at her every so often. It's strange that she'd subject herself to my drama. What I have going on at home can literally be erased from her life and yet she wants to help. And the fact that she is so willing to help me with my Julianna situation is extreme. You'd think she'd have something better to do, better places to be. If anyone should be *removing* anyone, it should be me.

"Why the hell would you put yourself in a situation like that anyway?" I ask when she's parked in my driveway. It sort of blurts out of me—but it's all I can wonder. "The whole re-moving Julianna thing, I mean. Gabriel's affair with you is over and what he's doing with Julianna has nothing to do with you, you know that right?"

"I know it doesn't."

"So then why suggest . . . *that?*"

"Because it's what you want."

"I never said that's what I want," I counter.

Jocelyn sighs. "You don't have to say it for it to be ob-vious."

I study her eyes briefly before lowering my gaze to my lap. Then I open the car door and climb out. "Thanks for bringing me home. I'll swing by the lounge to get my car tomorrow."

"Sure thing." I start to close the door, but she calls after me before I can get away. "I'll text you later, make sure you're good."

"Okay."

I close the door and stumble my way to the front door, unlocking it from the outside before locking it from the in-side. When I reach the den, I steal a peek out the window, watching Jocelyn drive away.

A breath of relief escapes me and I sink my body into the suede recliner behind me, pressing a hand to my clammy fore-head. My mind is running a hundred miles per minute, my breaths quick, my head fuzzy. The room spins and I feel like if I stand, I'll collapse, but that doesn't stop me from getting up.

A thought occurs to me and I spring out of my seat, rush-ing up the stairs and into my bathroom. I snatch open the medicine cabinet and take down my anxiety medication—the medication I'd stopped taking since finding out about Gab-riel's' affair. I fill the glass on the counter with water from the sink, gulp down the pill, then chug the water. Wrong to do it with a full belly of liquor, but I don't care. Maybe the liquor will make the effects stronger. With a sigh, I step back, grip the edge of the sink, and glare into the mirror.

I stare at myself, my hair that's all over the place, my eyes that are bloodshot red from crying on and off, my face like dark ash.

"You're so stupid. So, so stupid." The longer I stare at myself, the more Jocelyn's words ring in my head. *"Because it's what you want."*

It is what I want . . . . isn't it? And that's so fucked up.

I shove a finger down my throat, rush to the toilet, and vomit the pill back up, along with most of the alcohol I'd consumed.

CHAPTER TWENTY-FIVE

ADIRA

When I wake up, it's to the sound of running water. The sound runs through the dark, throbbing corners of my mind, and I'm instantly reminded of dim lights and clinking glasses, the continued sobs and burn of whiskey running down my throat to ease the pain. My mouth is tacky and dry and there's a dull throb in the back of my head.

I'm alone in bed. Alone with my thoughts. But the running water continues, and I conclude that I may not be alone. I sit up and turn over in my bed, looking back at the closed bathroom door. The shower is running.

I twist my legs, climbing off the mattress and going to the closet to grab a robe. After limply tying the silk tie around my waist, I go to the bathroom door and press my fingers to the cool wood. It lightly creaks open and I spot a tall silhouette ahead, behind a foggy glass scattered in clear droplets. Only one light shines, and it's the cool, recessed light above the shower.

My feet move before I can process what I'm doing, and before I know it, I'm standing in front of the shower door, stripping out of my robe and gripping the silver handle that feels like ice beneath my palm. When the door is open, I see *him* standing beneath the stream of water, in all his naked glory.

Gabriel's eyes are squeezed shut as he rinses shampoo out of his hair, and I take this as an opportunity to surprise him. I close the door behind me, allowing the tufts of heat from the water to envelope us, and when he hears it close, his eyes squint open.

"Oh, hey," he says. "Shit, sorry. Did I wake you?"

I shake my head and press a finger to his wet lips. He looks down at me with warm hazel eyes and his head cocks only slightly to the right. He's wondering what I'm thinking. But the truth is, in this moment I don't want to think.

Perhaps it's because I saw the way he kissed *her* last night and I want to show him I can do it better. Or maybe it's simply because I've missed him, despite how fucked up our entire situation is. I want our marriage to work. I want us to fall in love again. I want to be spontaneous, because isn't spontaneity an important part of marriage? Isn't that how a couple keeps the spice? I've been working hard for so long that I've been forgetting about him. I've been so consumed with everything else like work, and having a baby, and not planning enough time with him, and he found someone else to fill that void. Of course he has.

"I've been so selfish," I whisper, pressing a hand to his toned arm. I rub my hand up and down, while using my other to cup his cock in my hand. He groans instantly, his eyes becoming more intense as he looks down at me. "I want to change that. I know I've been busy with work, but I'm here now. I want to do better."

"What do you mean?" he asks, but I begin to stroke him and his jaw goes slack, his head tilting backward to indulge in the pleasure of this moment.

"Just don't ever leave me," I murmur, standing on my toes and placing a kiss on his lips.

"I'll never leave you," he rasps. He kisses me back, firmer

than the kiss I gave him, and I purposely break the kiss to lower to my knees and bring him into my mouth.

I don't care that my hair gets wet, or that I'll be late for my meeting with Vito. I can call my hairstylist, Selma, and she'll squeeze me in, and Vito works for me, so the timing is, ultimately, up to me. All I care about is right now—this moment with Gabriel. I want him to remember how good I am. How I make him feel. How good we are together. And I also want to forget what I talked to Jocelyn about last night.

It doesn't take him long to stop me. He doesn't want to finish in my mouth. He doesn't often do that. He picks me up in his arms, presses my back to the shower wall, and thrusts himself into me. Both of us gasp as the warm water streams down his back, droplets splashing onto my nose and cheek.

"You do crazy things to me, you know that?" he growls on my lips.

Funny he says that, because he's been making me do crazy things to save our marriage for weeks.

CHAPTER TWENTY-SIX

ADIRA

"Hey, so I was thinking..." I trail off, biting into my lower lip as I wrap myself in a robe. Through the corner of my eye, I can see Gabriel using a towel to dry himself off. He truly does have the physique of a god. His body is chiseled in all the right places, and I love that he takes care of himself. It helps that he has access to a gym that's open to him and his rugby team at all hours, and that he works out with the team. When he's not with the team, he goes to the gym every morning at eight and comes home to shower. It's nearing ten in the morning, which tells me that he left Julianna's, went to the gym, and then came here.

"What are you thinking?" he asks, wrapping the cotton towel around his waist.

"I'll have next weekend off and I was thinking we could go to the condo in Destin to get away."

One of his brows lifts as he walks toward the double sink and wipes away some of the perspiration from the mirror. "Destin," he repeats. He picks up a razor. "Next weekend we have a meeting with Logs about the expansion."

I drop my head. "Oh."

I can feel him looking at me as I stand near the bathroom door. My hair is a damp mess now and I'm sure it's going to shrink and turn into a ball of frizz within the next thirty minutes if I don't at least blow dry it. I could call Selma, but I'm better off moisturizing and brushing it and throwing it into a ponytail today if I plan on getting anything done.

"I tell you what," Gabriel says, placing the razor back down. "I'll ask to reschedule the meeting."

I light up, meeting his eyes. "Are you sure? I know the expansion is important to you, so—"

"It is important, but so are you. Hell, it wouldn't even be happening if it weren't for you." He walks up to me, a smile taking over his lips. His hands clutch my waist and he reels me into him, bringing the tip of his nose down to the crook of my neck. He inhales and groans, then picks his head up and licks his lip. "Just you and me in Destin?"

"Just us," I answer. "Making love. I'll be ovulating too."

He probably doesn't think I realize, but he freezes for a moment before saying, "That's good. You'll be all mine."

I smile. "I'll always be yours."

He kisses my lips slowly, passionately, then he pulls back and says, "We should get something to eat. Caraway has bottomless mimosas until two, and I know how much you love their peach schnapps version."

"I do love a peach schnapps." I step sideways. "But I'm not sure I can. I have to do a treatment today, plus I have a meeting with Vito—and look at my hair! It's all messy because I was fooling around with you!" I tease.

"You think I give a damn about the hair? You can brush it, style it real quick, and as for Vito—well, let's just say only one of us can give you that baby, right?" Gabriel winks, kisses my cheek, and turns away to get back to the razor.

"I'll reschedule with him," I say, turning around, already eager to get to my phone.

"That's my girl!" he calls after me.

"But I am booking an appointment with Selma this afternoon! There's no way I can go around with my hair looking like this all weekend."

"That's fine. I have to meet someone this afternoon anyway."

My smile falters when he says that. "Oh really? Who are you meeting?" I catch myself asking, but it's too late to stop the words from coming out.

"Just an old friend," he says, but it's not in the same confident tone he used before. It's low and curt, and it feels like a betrayal. It *is* a betrayal because I know this "old friend" of his is not anyone I want him to be with.

"It's not . . . Jocelyn, is it?"

I hear his footsteps coming in my direction and he appears in the bedroom. "What?"

"Nothing," I mutter.

"You just mentioned Jocelyn," he says.

"You were sleeping with her," I say without looking at him.

He's quiet for so long that he leaves me no choice but to look up, and I can't believe it, but he's smiling. "What are you smiling about?"

"Nothing. I just—" He shakes his head quickly, then drags a hand down his face, as if physically wiping the smile away. "Look, I don't know what you're talking about, Adira, but I'm getting hungry, so can we just finish getting ready, please?" He returns to the bathroom, sighing. I shift on my feet. I should keep going. Hell, maybe I should even mention Julianna too because he wants to pretend there is no Jocelyn. No. No, no, no. We have brunch and I don't want to ruin a good morning with the mention of her too.

My phone buzzes in my hand and a text from Jocelyn appears. *Speak of the devil.*

Off tonight at 7. Is another stakeout happening or was last night too much for you?

I ignore her text. If I can convince Gabriel to stay with me the rest of the day, there'll be no need for another stakeout. We'll be together, and that bitch Julianna won't be a problem.

At least that's what I think, until I return to the bathroom with my phone and catch him texting. Aware of my returned presence, he immediately lowers the phone and places it face-down on the marble counter.

"Get in touch with Selma?" he asks, putting on a broad smile.

I shake my head and smile. Because that's all I can do right now. Smile. Fake it. Pretend all is well. He thinks I don't know about her, but the truth is I know *everything*, and that leaves me no choice but to work harder at keeping him away from her.

CHAPTER TWENTY-SEVEN

There was something off about Bower. I wasn't sure if it was the way he stood, or how lanky he was. Maybe it was his fingers and how thin and bony they were. His smile seemed to be wider than his face, almost breaking it in half anytime he revealed it, and his teeth were small and sharp on the ends, like miniature shark teeth.

He was new to the church because the previous pastor—Pastor Herald—had colon cancer. I'd seen Bower around before, but he was a visitor most of the time. Just a man who lingered in church and spoke every time Pastor Herald asked if any visitors wanted to speak. I'm assuming Pastor Herald reached out to Bower when he'd gotten sick and Bower assumed the role.

And because Bower was a man in a suit on Sundays, he was a good man—a great man even. He sat in his chair on the pew, sang gospels, clapped his skinny hands, smiled at the church members and even wider at the guests, and when it came to tithes, he made sure everyone pitched in, even if it was a penny. Apparently to him, a penny was worth more than we assumed.

Panda and I had a habit of finding pennies in Claudette's car, in her cupholders or between the cracks of the seat. We eagerly waited for our turn to drop our coins into the wicker tithe basket, and the usher, *dressed in white polyester, would smile at us, then wink at Claudette for having such well-behaved girls.*

Church wasn't always so bad. Panda really enjoyed Sunday school, and even though I wasn't a huge fan of it, I went with her. We learned the basics of the Bible, like Adam and Eve and Moses, Jonah and the whale and Noah and the ark. Panda loved Sunday school because she was younger, and the youngest always got treats for behaving well afterward. I was in the older kid group, so we didn't get treats. We just got pats on the back for attending, despite being in the same room as the younger kids. It sucked seeing them eat cinnamon rolls or sugar cookies while we stood and watched, but to the church, the older kids didn't need them. We'd had our turn for treats when we were their age and now that was over. It was time for us to mature, get serious about the word of God.

As I said, church wasn't so bad. At church, everyone was always on their best behavior, so I only ever saw the good in people.

But then one day I heard Claudette laughing loudly at something Pastor Bower said. I was standing with Panda near the door, ready to go home. Panda was licking away at a lollipop she'd earned from one of the nice church ladies for being so well-behaved.

My eyes locked on Claudette and Bower—the way she touched his chest and the way he laid a skinny hand on her shoulder. She was grinning from ear to ear and he was nodding and smiling and giving her a look that didn't seem appropriate for church. There was something about seeing them together that made my heart sink.

And when Claudette took us to the car, humming church hymns in between telling us to buckle our seat belts, I realized that sinking feeling I had was for a reason.

"Pastor Bower will be coming over for dinner next Sunday," Claudette said. Panda said nothing. She was still working on her lollipop. But I heard every word, and deep in my gut I knew none of what she was saying was good news for any of us.

CHAPTER TWENTY-EIGHT

ADIRA

Our favorite restaurant is called Caraway. It's a Mediterranean restaurant that serves the best cod and makes a mean peach mousse to top off any meal.

It feels nice to be out with Gabriel. It's been weeks since we've done anything like this, and I have to wonder why. Of course there's the tragedy of his affair (and I plan on getting to that subject with him in regard to Julianna eventually), but I also wonder if it's because I've been consumed with work.

Business had increased a lot this past year, which took me to my office more often, and had me working late into the evening. I suppose Gabriel and I didn't have much of a chance to arrange lunches. He knows my work is important to me and that, without my income, we wouldn't live the lifestyle we have, so he doesn't complain about my hours, or gripe, or make it seem like my job is an issue.

To be honest, I wish he would complain if that's truly what's bothering him. If there's going to be an issue in our marriage, I'd much rather argue with my husband about working hours than an affair.

"This is nice," Gabriel says after the waitress has taken our orders. He takes a sip from his glass of water, eyeing me.

"It's very nice. When's the last time we did this?"

He laughs. "Hell, I couldn't even tell you. We've both been so busy." He reaches across the table to grab one of my hands. Bringing my knuckles to his lips, he kisses each one lightly. "We have to work on that. Good thing we have the Destin trip coming up, huh?"

"A very good thing. I'm excited to try for a baby."

Gabriel frowns. "Let's not make that the primary focus, baby. We need to put ourselves first. Right?"

I nod. "Yes. Right."

"We should try Emilio's while we're there," he suggests. "I know how much you love their salmon."

I force a smile. "Don't tempt me."

Gabriel's phone buzzes and he releases my hand to retrieve it from the tabletop. I notice his features tighten as he checks the screen, and I don't have to ask to know who it might be.

"I'll get that later," he says, placing the phone facedown on the table again. I glance at the back of his phone. He doesn't usually put it facedown. The only reason he would is if he has something to hide. "You sure you don't want a mimosa or anything?"

"No. I'm okay with water," I tell him.

The waitress returns with the garlic butter Gabriel requested for the artisan bread. He slices into the bread and slabs some butter on, takes a big bite, and I'm instantly reminded of when I met Jocelyn at Giotto's.

"Gabriel?" I call.

"Hmm?" His eyes swing up to mine.

"What made you call it off with Jocelyn?"

He stops chewing briefly, looking me in the eye. "Oh, um . . ." He begins to chew again, then dusts off his hands and straightens up in his chair. "Well, I just thought it was becoming too much. And I'm sorry if what I've done has hurt you, Adira. I really am. . . . I just . . ." He sighs, clearly at a loss for words. "I just know that I love *you*. It wasn't right what I was doing with Jocelyn. But when I'm with you, everything is always right."

I lower my gaze, nodding.

"Are you angry about her?" he asks in a soft voice.

"A little."

He reaches across the table to grab my hand and I lift my head to look into his eyes. "I'm sorry, Adira. You know you mean the world to me. I don't want you upset over this."

"I just feel like we haven't really been on the same page lately and that's probably why it happened."

"How do you mean?" he asks, using his free hand to take another bite of bread.

"Well, I know I've been working more, and you have rugby things to take care of—and with the expansion of the stadium, I'm sure that's adding to your already full plate. . . ."

He mulls it over, chewing the bread in his mouth slowly before swallowing. "Yeah, things have been busy lately, but all for the greater good."

I force a smile and, as if he notices, he says, "Oh, come on, Adira. Don't lose faith in me, okay? I love you, woman. You make all my dreams come true. Without you, where would I be?" He's leaning forward, his forefinger now resting beneath my chin.

I look into his brown eyes and think this is the moment. This is when I tell him that I know about Julianna too and that, if he loves me like he says he does, he'll let his affair with her be history and focus on us.

But I don't get the chance to because his phone buzzes obnoxiously on the table again and he sighs, retracting the hand he has on mine to pick it up.

"Shit. I'm sorry, baby. I really have to take this. It's work. They don't call twice unless it's important."

I force a smile and nod. "Okay."

I watch as Gabriel stands and leaves our table, weaving his way through the others until he's at the door that leads to the patio. He presses the receiver of the phone to his ear as he steps out, and he probably thinks I don't notice, but he keeps his back to me while speaking.

I watch him closely, the way he's hunching his shoulders, the way his head tilts to the side when he speaks. The way he smiles as he turns a fraction.

Work doesn't have him smiling like that. It's *her*.

At the sheer thought of it, I feel raw inside—all sinew and bone and blood. My chest aches, my throat is dry, and all I want to do is go out there and snatch the phone away from him to curse her the hell out.

I watch him several seconds longer before grabbing my purse and fishing my phone out of it. In the thick of my cocktail of emotions, I open the last text I received from Jocelyn—the one where she followed up about the stakeout—to start a new one.

I've been thinking about what you said last night and you're right. I want her gone. How do we do it?

CHAPTER TWENTY-NINE

JOCELYN

I truly thought Adira would never ask. See, I knew she had it in her.

I smile as I walk up the stairs of the lounge, deleting the message she sent me an hour ago so as not to leave a trace on my end.

When I enter the private room, I sit at the bar, where the TV is playing above. There are contracts left here from Paloma, the lead manager at Jessa's, and I sign off on them as I listen to two talk show hosts in a heated debate about a woman recently released from prison.

"Let's not forget this girl pretended to be someone she's not just to get in good with Lola and Corey!" one of the hosts says at the round white table where they're seated. "She lied and manipulated the crap out of them. I don't care what y'all say or if there is new evidence, that girl is crazy, and if she isn't going to be locked up in jail, she needs to be locked up in a mental-health facility real quick."

I lower my pen for a moment, watching the next host speak, a Black woman with long brown hair and a terrible pink scarf around her neck. "Sure, you have a point about the lengths she went to. But you have to think—this woman suf-

fered as a child for years. Her parents are gone and it was because of Lola, mind you. Lola covered up that dirty little deed
for years, so it's understandable that she'd suffer mentally because of it. This young woman was lost and on her own for a
while, and I get it—some people react differently to what life
tosses their way. Sure, this Ivy had an extreme reaction, but
there's a reason she's out, right? There's more to this case, and
I'm glad we're finally getting some light on it."

The hosts continue going back and forth before the show
cuts to a commercial break, and I pick my pen back up again,
rolling my eyes.

See, that's the problem with people like Ivy Hill. I heard
all about that case. It was unfortunate for Lola Maxwell and
her husband. That Ivy girl took way too much to her advantage. If she'd played her cards right, she wouldn't be in the situation she's in. Personally, I don't think she killed that couple,
but if she did, she went about it the wrong way.

I won't be like her. I'll be smart with my cards and with
what I tell Adira to do. She's beginning to trust me, and once
the trust has been instilled, there's no going back.

CHAPTER THIRTY

Panda looked up to me, and I took pride in looking after her. I was a much better person to her than Claudette, and Claudette knew that. It made her quite jealous. Whenever she saw us together, she'd stew about it, and sometimes she'd stare, as if trying to find ways to split us apart. She'd tell us to get on our knees and pray if we laughed together too loudly or got along entirely too much for her liking.

"Close your eyes."

"Sit up straight!"

"What's so funny? You think the Lord would appreciate you laughing while you're talking to him?"

At first, Bower would take up for us. When he came to the first Sunday dinner, he was dressed down in khakis and a tucked-in, white button-up shirt. Claudette had set up the table with her nice china plates and the good silverware we weren't allowed to use. When we were about to sit and pray over our food, Panda knocked over her cup of sweet tea and I gasped. I saw the anger cloud Claudette's eyes instantly, and through clenched teeth, she said, "Go get some paper towels. Now!"

I hurried to the kitchen with Panda and returned to the table with the paper towels, and Bower stood and said, "Let me help you girls."

He smiled at us and then at Claudette. "Don't worry, Claudy. It's just a little spill. Accidents happen. Right, girls?" He revealed those sharp teeth at us, and I found it hard to return a smile, but Panda eagerly returned one to him, bouncing on her toes and helping clean up some of the tea with her own section of paper towel.

"You're right, Pastor," Claudette said, sighing. "I just wanted tonight to be perfect."

"Oh, don't worry about perfection. We're all humans. We're flawed. The dinner still goes on."

We resumed eating and after we were finished, Claudette shooed us off to our room while Pastor Bower stuck around for another three hours, drinking sweet tea and eating cookies.

I want to say it was after the fifth or sixth dinner that Bower felt more comfortable in our home. When he'd once taken up for us, he now allowed Claudette to pass her snide remarks. And Claudette wasn't a fool. She gave her comments with kindness, but I could always see in her eyes how serious she was.

Then Bower began to spend the night. And at first it was fun. Bower would bring movies and we'd have movie nights with popcorn and sugar-free candies from the dollar store (sugar free because Claudette didn't like us eating a lot of candy). Me and Panda would watch movies until our eyes burned and we were tired. Claudette would insist that we go to our room, but Bower would tell her to let us fall asleep on the sofa—that it wasn't the end of the world—and at first that was fine. We had our pillows and blankets and we slept on the couch. Claudette and Bower would go to the bedroom, leaving us in the living room with the movies playing loudly while they did whatever they did in Claudette's bedroom.

But there was one night in particular when I felt myself being pulled out of my sleep by whispering.

I lay sideways on the sofa and opened my eyes. The TV was still on and a pale white light was spread across Panda's body beneath her blanket. Bower was sitting on the couch next to her and his hand was beneath her blanket. His hand was moving, and Panda moaned in her sleep and turned.

"Be still, girl. Be good," Bower whispered.

I refrained from gasping, from screaming. There was no reason his hand should've been under her blanket, it was late, and Panda looked uncomfortable.

Panda kicked a leg and Bower grunted, and I took that as my sign to pretend I'd been woken up by Panda's noise and sat up.

"Bower?" I called with squinty eyes.

"Hey, there," Bower murmured. He stood up and walked to me. "You go on back to sleep now. I was just checking to see if you two were okay."

Bower pulled the blanket over me and smiled that sharp smile, then he walked around the corner to go down the hallway. I heard a door click shut, even though my rapidly beating heart was in my ears, and I sat back up, rushing to Panda. I pulled her blanket off of her and her pajama pants had been pulled just below her hips. Her white panties were showing, and I looked toward the hallway again before shaking her awake.

I didn't wait for her to fully wake up. I wrapped one of her arms around me, pulled her pants back up with one hand, then carried her with me down the hallway to our room. I laid her in her bed and when I locked the door, I lay in bed with Panda and didn't sleep for the rest of the night.

CHAPTER THIRTY-ONE

ADIRA

I took up dance when I was twelve and never went back. Dina figured I needed an outlet—a place to channel all my confusion and rage—so she enrolled me in a hip-hop class. I took to the class right away, and by the end of the first season, I'd taken home second place during one of the competitions.

I'm great at dancing, and I love how my body feels so free and alive when I move. While I dance, I don't have to think or try to control my thoughts because I don't allow myself to think, really. I just flow with the music and allow my limbs and joints and heart to follow their own beats.

Gabriel knows I love to dance. He used to take me to a salsa class every Thursday night, before he became heavily invested in his rugby team. I'm currently at one of the salsa classes without him for the first time and, of course, the first thing my dance instructor, Miranda, asks me about is him.

Miranda greets me with a kiss on each cheek. "Where is that darling husband of yours?"

"He's working tonight. Big things are happening for him right now," I inform her.

"Really? That's so wonderful to hear!"

I smile.

"Well, I'm so happy you could make it tonight. I know how much you love class and, fortunately, Tommy is here. You two can partner together."

I force a smile. "Thanks, Miranda." Tommy is Miranda's brother. He and Miranda opened the dance studio five years ago, but it never made sense to me that Tommy got involved because the man has two left feet. Don't get me wrong, he's cheerful and his personality is amazing, but he can't dance worth a damn.

As if on cue, Tommy bounces toward me on the tips of his toes, grinning from ear to ear while sporting a tight white T-shirt and leather capris, because that's his thing—leather. When the music starts and I'm forced to be with my partner, I can't help wishing Gabriel was with me.

After we left Caraway and he took me back home, he said he had a meeting to attend. I didn't ask questions, and despite how tempted I was to follow him and see who he was actually meeting, I didn't. I didn't because I knew exactly who he was going to see. And not only that—I needed to get my car from Jocelyn's lounge, so I booked an Uber to take me and was relieved that I didn't see Jocelyn's car in the parking lot. I wasn't ready to face her yet after my manic text.

After the partnering, Miranda turns up the volume of the music and gives us the chance to dance solo. Solo is my favorite. Everyone tunes the other out and focuses on their own moves, even the married couples.

I drown in the music and move my body this way and that, my feet staying in rhythm, my hips rocking to the beat. For a moment I close my eyes and remember that after this, I'll be meeting Jocelyn to discuss our plans for Julianna. God, I need her gone. I want her gone so that Gabriel can stop running to her every fucking day.

I dance harder, faster, as the tempo increases.

Seriously. Can't he see that I love him?

Can't he see that I'm hurting?

Doesn't he know that I've always been happy, but now that this is happening, it breaks my heart?

What's so wrong with me that he needs *her*? What makes him look her way? What am I doing wrong?

WHAT'S WRONG WITH ME?

The music comes to an abrupt stop and my eyes pop open. Everyone is staring at me.

"Adira, sweetheart, are you okay?" Miranda stands in front of me, and when I look up at her, I find that I'm on the wooden floor. My face is wet and I'm on my hands and knees.

"I, uh—oh my gosh, Miranda. I'm so sorry." I swipe at the tears on my face. I've stopped dancing to fall down and cry. *How fucking pathetic.*

"You said something was wrong with you? Did you hurt yourself?"

"No—I . . . I didn't mean that. I . . ." *Shit.* Did I really say that out loud? I look around the room and the others are whispering among themselves and giving me concerned glares.

"Come with me." Miranda has my hand and tugs on it to bring me to a stand. "Everything's okay, everyone! Tommy, resume the music and pick up where we left off, please!" Miranda reaches the door to her office and swings it open. She lets me in and I sit in one of the chairs in front of her desk. After closing the door, she walks to the minifridge against the wall, pulls it open, and takes out a bottled water to offer to me.

"Thank you, Miranda." I accept the bottle, cracking it open and taking a big chug. Taking a seat behind her desk, Miranda watches me cautiously.

"Adira, are you sure everything's okay?"

I nod. "Everything's fine. I think I'm just a little tired. Long hours at the office lately."

"But not too tired to come dance, I see?" She laughs, but the smile doesn't reach her eyes.

I laugh with her anyway. "I suppose not."

Miranda exhales and sits back in her chair. "Should I call someone for you?"

I mull that over for a second, taking a sip of water and sloshing it around in my mouth. I come to the realization that there is no one she can call. If she calls Gabriel while he's with Julianna, he probably won't answer, and Dina won't be in town for another week and a half. There is Jocelyn, but . . . no. I can't have her knowing *everything* about me . . . or how pathetic I really am.

"I'm okay. I promise." I give Miranda a smile to prove I am. "I should probably go home and get some rest, though."

Her lips press into a smile. "Okay, love." She fixes her mouth like she wants to say something else, but then clamps it shut.

"Is something wrong?" I ask.

"Well, it's just that. . . . I've noticed you and Gabriel don't come together anymore. And then you showed up tonight . . . alone . . . without your wedding rings on."

"Oh." I drop my eyes to my ring finger. There's a light strip of skin there, created from years of wearing the rings. My eyes find Miranda's again and I'm tempted to tell her to mind her own business. But this is Miranda—she's always been nice to me. She even gave me a discount to take her class, even though she knew I didn't need the discount. I insisted on paying the full amount, but she declined and graciously embraced me, welcoming me into her class.

"Well, the truth is, Miranda, that . . . um . . . Gabriel and I are going through a really rough patch right now—but . . . we're fine, really! I'm fine. I came here tonight because I felt like I really needed to let loose, and you know dancing is one of my outlets, so . . ." I shrug.

"Oh, I'm so sorry to hear that," she says, her face saddening.

"It's okay."

"Well, I'm glad you came here for the outlet, at least." She pauses, and I find she does that a lot—pauses or hesitates, as if she isn't sure whether she should continue asking questions or let it go. "Is there anything I can do to help?"

"Yeah, there is, actually."

She perks up in her white leather chair. "Okay, sure. What is it?"

"Make sure this conversation stays between us."

CHAPTER THIRTY-TWO

ADIRA

I'm glad no one is in the elevator when I ride up for work. After completely embarrassing myself last night during dance, I went home and drowned myself in whiskey. Now I have a hammering headache that won't go away, the sun feels too bright, and for some odd reason I'm hungry as hell and could use a greasy meal, but I have work to do. I've postponed with Vito for way too many days. If I go another, he'll probably end up leaving me, and the last thing I need is to lose a talented designer like him.

When the elevator doors spread apart, I'm glad to see Alaina hasn't arrived yet. I've beat her today. I start up the coffee machine and prepare myself a mug, dump some cream and sugar in, and carry it to my office, closing the door behind me.

Placing the mug down on the desk, along with my bag and phone, I sit in the cushioned chair and sigh, taking in the view ahead of me. This is nice. Really nice. And it's quiet, and the sun is shining. It's a beautiful day and I should be happy about it. I should go out and frolic in the sun, act like a normal human and bask in it.

Sometimes I sit and think Dina is right. Life shouldn't be all work and no play . . . but if I don't work, what do I have? If I hadn't built this, what would I be doing with myself? I don't trust anyone enough to run this company yet, and even when the time comes, I'm certain I will still be involved. Sure, I'll probably have more vacation days than now, but I'll still come into work. Because my life needs purpose. Without purpose, I doubt I would survive, and if Gabriel isn't fully set on giving me a baby, Lovely Silk will always be my baby.

My phone vibrates on the desk as I sip my coffee and I glance at it. It's Dina. *Speak of the devil.* I sigh and let it ring. *I'll get back to her later.*

Heels click from a distance and that lets me know Alaina is here. She's talking loudly and my head rings from her obnoxious voice.

"Is she ready?" a man asks, and judging by the voice, I'm going to assume it's Vito.

"Let me check." Alaina gives my door three quick taps with her middle knuckle, like she always does.

"Come in."

In she walks, smiling brightly at me. "Good morning, Adira. Vito is here to see you. Do you want me to send him in?"

"Sure." I sigh, placing my mug down on the desk. "Let's get it started."

"Good Lord, woman." Alaina marches forward and grabs the lavender coaster near the edge of my desk. She places it down in a spot near me, picks up my mug, and sets it on the coaster. "You have this fancy glass desk and don't use the coaster." She rolls her eyes and I shrug. "You feelin' okay?"

"I'm fine. Just had a long night. Can you send him in, please?"

"Sure." Alaina turns to walk, but not without glancing at me over her shoulder. I dig into my purse and take out my compact mirror.

"Shit," I murmur. I see why she's staring at me. My hair has become frizzy in its ponytail, most likely because of the humidity. I didn't do my skin-care routine this morning—too tired—but I did apply a light coat of mascara. I thought that would be enough. I was wrong.

"Ahem." Vito stands at the door, dressed head to toe in beige. He's like David from *Schitt's Creek*, but where David would wear black in every outfit, Vito wears beige—and sometimes he adds a pop of gold with an accessory if he feels like it. Today he's wearing a V-neck tucked into his pants. Even the belt is beige, minus the gold buckle. I don't know how he doesn't get tired of it, but he makes it work. He's got fashion sense, and I love my Italian designer for that. "This meeting was supposed to happen *days* ago, woman," he says, walking into the office.

"I know, I know. I'm sorry—life is a little crazy right now."

"Is everything okay?" he asks, taking the seat on the other side of the desk.

"Everything's fine." I brush it off. "So . . . whatcha got for me?"

Vito goes into his whole spiel about the patterns he's choosing for the fall. I nod my head in agreement, not saying much, just listening. It's all I can do right now. His voice is just a buzz and my mind begins to wander.

Gabriel and Julianna.

Julianna and Gabriel.

What if he leaves me for her? Would he do that? Perhaps I should ease up on the baby stuff for now. Do I want it? Yes, but if he's not ready, I can't force him.

"Adira?" a deep voice sings.

I flicker my gaze up to Vito's. His brows are drawn together and his lips are pursed. "Ma'am? Are you present? I feel like I'm talking to the walls!"

"I'm present—I'm here." I stand and walk around the desk to get to his side, viewing the designs from his perspec-

tive. "And the orange and brown swirls will go on the cam-
isoles too?"

"Yes, they will." He looks me up and down. "Um,
honey?"

I glance at Vito, and he's staring down at my shoes with
utter shock. "What?" I ask quickly.

"Can you please tell me why the hell you walked out of
your house with two different heels on your feet?"

I stare down at my shoes with him, and when I realize
what he sees, I gasp. "Oh my goodness. How did I—?"

"They're not even the same color, Adira! What is going
on with you?"

I open my mouth but clamp it shut in an instant.

"Honey, do you want to reschedule? I know I shouldn't
say it, but you look horrible today. Are you sick?" At that,
Vito leans back. "Please don't tell me you're sick! There's
a fashion show I'm attending this weekend and I refuse to
miss it!"

"No, I'm not sick." I lean on the arm of his chair to tug
off my heels. Alaina walks into the office and looks down first
before looking into my eyes.

"Are those—"

"Two different heels? Yes, honey. They are. Alaina, get your
boss another cup of coffee or something. I need her to get to
one hundred so we can get through these designs already."

"Adira, I can make some tea," Alaina offers, still standing
at the door.

"Tea would be good. Chamomile, please."

Vito sighs when Alaina walks away, then stands while collecting all of his design sheets. "I can come back tomorrow.
Will that work?"

I look into his eyes, and I don't know if it's my raging disappointment in myself for walking out of my house with two
different shoes on, or the fact that my heart is crumbling to
pieces, or both, but I immediately start to cry.

Vito freezes for a split second before cooing, "Oh, Adira. What's wrong?"

"I'm sorry." I step away, pressing a hand to my mouth.

"Don't be sorry. What's the matter? Why are you crying?"

I wave a hand as he rubs my shoulder. I can't find the words, so I press my hand to my mouth again and walk to the sofa.

Alaina reenters the office, and it's clear she notices my tears too because she asks, "What did you say to her?" to Vito, to which Vito replies, "I didn't say anything! I just asked if she wanted to reschedule!"

"Adira. I have your tea. Here." Alaina sits next to me with the tea in a cup on a saucer.

"Thank you," I murmur.

"Should I go?" asks Vito.

"Please," Alaina murmurs.

"'Kay. I'll shoot you an email to set up another appointment. Maybe next week, right, Alaina?"

"That would be wise."

"'Kay." Vito is gone, and all that's left is Alaina.

"I'm really sorry." First I break down in dance class and now this? In my own workspace. Gabriel is really doing a fucking number on me.

"Don't apologize. I think I know what's going on."

I whip up my head, trying to find her eyes through my blurry vision. "You do?"

"It's your marriage."

I frown. "How did you—"

"He doesn't send you gifts or flowers anymore. I noticed it a few weeks ago, actually. They stopped coming in. You . . . also don't talk about him as much anymore. I just never said anything because I didn't want to assume . . ."

I lower my gaze, staring at my bare feet. "Wow. It's *that* obvious?"

"From one heartbroken woman to another, yes. It is." I

tilt my chin and she's giving a half-hearted smile. "Let me guess. He's seeing someone else?"

I swallow hard, then nod. What's the point of lying about it anymore? Alaina knows this feeling. She knows what this pain is like, no matter how hard she tries to mask it with one-night stands and late nights out.

"I'm pretty sure he is. I think . . . I think he's *in love* with her."

"Damn. I'm so sorry, Adira."

We're quiet for a moment. Then Alaina adjusts herself on the sofa and asks, "Do you want to find out if he is for sure?"

CHAPTER THIRTY-THREE

ADIRA

Alaina cancels all my calls and orders us lunch from one of my favorite sandwich shops. When it arrives, I dig right into the turkey and avocado melt.

"Mmm . . . I needed this," I groan.

"Okay, so to find out for sure if he's in love with this other woman, you have to download an app."

"An app?"

"Yes. You download it to your phone first, and then you can download it onto his, and pair them. Then you'll be able to read all of his messages."

I frown. "What? Won't he notice there's a random new app on his phone?"

Alaina smirks. "That's the beauty of this app. Once you install it, it hides itself within another app; you just have to select which one you think your man is using most to cheat on this other woman with. My guess is that it'll be his text messaging app. The only way he can find out that the app has been installed on his phone is if he goes to his settings and takes a look at storage or something, but who has time for that?"

"Not Gabriel," I admit.

"Exactly. So I say if you get a chance to download it on his phone while he's not around it, you'll be able to know. Not only that, but you'll have proof about his affair. Say it came down to a divorce or anything, he can't lie and say he wasn't having an affair because you have the proof on your phone."

"Wow. How did you find out about this app?"

"My best friend is an app developer. She helped the buyers make it."

"Wow. And it's a legal thing?"

"Hmm . . . that I'm not sure about. But people still use it." Alaina shrugs, then takes a slurp of her ramen. She then sets her bowl down and says, "Let me see your phone." I hand it to her, give her the code, and she unlocks it. "There."

"What'd you do?"

"I downloaded it. Now all you have to do is download the app when you have access to his phone and pair them. Once they're paired and you select the apps you most want to see messages from, they'll come rolling in." She gives me a triumphant smile, and I don't know whether to thank her or be a little terrified of her. I'm glad I like her and haven't talked shit about her via text messages to someone else. Who's to say she isn't spying on my texts too? Despite my conflicting feelings, I smile right back.

CHAPTER THIRTY-FOUR

ADIRA

It's typical of my husband to show up the following night with a hot dinner, fresh clothes, and a smile after the way he sneaks around during the day. The best thing to do would be to slap that smile off his face, but I'm not a violent woman and I need the night to run smoothly, so I thank him for the food, set it all up on plates, and we eat dinner at the table.

He talks about work and how tired he is, and how he can't wait to go to Destin. I don't tell him a damn thing about my day and fortunately, he doesn't get the chance to ask.

"Would you like a drink?" I ask him after turning on some music in the den.

"That would be great, babe. Thank you." He sighs, settling into his favorite leather recliner.

I pour his favorite bourbon on ice and carry the glass tumbler to him. He smiles up at me, guzzles down the drink, and I get up to make him another. This happens repeatedly between conversations about his expansion, his car needing an oil change, and how some kid stepped on his good shoes, until he yawns, stretches, and falls asleep on the sofa.

When he does, I carefully take the glass tumbler away from him and set it on the coffee table. I keep my eyes on him, listening as he snores, his chest rising and sinking, and dig into his pocket to retrieve his phone.

I unlock it, and of course there are no messages and no one by the name of Julianna in his phone.

I'm quick to install the app on his phone, and I pair them so I can receive his text messages. When I'm done, I replace the phone and leave his ass on the sofa so I can shower and get in bed.

When I wake up, Gabriel is in bed beside me. He does that often, migrates to bed in the middle of the night after drinking too much. He rustles around in his sleep and then his phone vibrates.

He hears it and reaches for it, keeping his back to me. Then, as if he's been zapped awake by a Taser, he sits upright. My heart begins to race as a stretch of silence swims through the room.

Oh my God. Does he know about the app? Can he see it? What if Alaina is wrong and the app *doesn't* hide itself anymore?

"Everything okay?" I ask, keeping my voice level.

"Yeah . . . uh." He clears his throat. "Yeah. Everything's fine."

"Wanna lay back down?"

"Nah, baby. Can't. I need to shower and get to work, actually."

He turns to kiss me on the cheek, but not without shutting the screen of his phone off.

When he's in the bathroom—with his phone, of course— he closes the door behind him and I hear the shower start up seconds later.

And while he's in there, I grab my phone, unlock it, and go to the sneaky app.

There's a red notification bubble there and I open it. A new message has appeared from someone named JuBoo.

I freaking miss you after yesterday. Come back to me. I'm waiting, baby.

And right below the text is an image of Julianna Garcia's breasts.

I glance at the bathroom door while gripping the phone tightly. *Wow.* He has got to be fucking kidding me right now! Is that what gave him a pep in his step? Work my ass. That motherfucker is running to her!

I sit in bed, staring at the image until Gabriel finishes his shower. My phone screen has turned black by the time he kisses me on the forehead and leaves, but not before telling me he'll see me later.

My phone chimes again with a sound I'm still getting familiar with. I check the screen, and it's a notification from the sneaky app, only this time it isn't a message *from* Julianna. It's a message that Gabriel has sent to her.

That woke me up better than a strong cup of coffee. On my way to you and I want you completely naked when I walk through that door.

"That *motherfucker!*" I chuck my phone across the room and it crashes against the wall.

CHAPTER THIRTY-FIVE

JOCELYN

I often have moments where I don't feel like I'm in my own body. I lie in bed, stare at the ceiling, and wonder if anything about my life is real. But then I pinch myself and realize that yes, I am real. I have flesh, a pulse, breath.

But even in being real, my world feels so dark. I wish I could see everything with rose-colored glasses—wish that I could enjoy life like a normal human being, but I am far from normal. I haven't felt normality since I was ten years old, and even then my life was a little fucked up.

I grew up protecting myself, putting myself first, and not giving a damn how it affected anyone else. So when it comes to Adira, I don't know why I care. I don't know why I let her get to me, or why I want her to succeed so badly. In truth, I envy her life, her success, even her looks. Hell, I even envy her love life because at least she *has* love. I tell myself I don't want a man—I don't *need* a man—but who wants to live a life alone in misery? I can be selfish, but I also know how to love and protect my own. Plead your loyalty to me and I'm as loyal as a dog. But fuck me over, even once, and I make it my mission to make your life a living hell.

Adira doesn't deserve that. In all reality, I don't deserve her compassion or understanding. If I were in her situation, I'd have slapped the other woman several times to release my frustrations, dunked her head in a filthy public toilet, then stomped on her with my Louboutins, but Adira isn't like me. She's good, and despite her naïveté, her heart is made of gold. But the thing about Adira is that she's easy to manipulate.

And, as I said before, I'm used to putting myself first. So as bad as I feel for her, I'll use her weaknesses to my advantage. In the end, I always get what I want. And what I want is to be completely free.

Will you come over? I don't think I can be alone right now.

I read Adira's text again, respond, and get dressed so I can meet her.

CHAPTER THIRTY-SIX

ADIRA

"You know he's probably still with her right now." My head turns left to look at Jocelyn. She stands next to the window in my den, fingering the sheer taupe curtain. I don't know what possessed me to text her, but after chucking my phone across the room and seeing the shattered screen, I had the urge to drop to my knees and sob. But I didn't. I texted her instead because for some odd reason, I knew she'd give me strength. I didn't know who else to be angry about this with. I could've called Alaina, but she was my secretary, at the end of the day, and I didn't want to scare her off.

"I don't need the reminder," I mutter.

"I can't believe you're just sitting here and letting that shit happen."

"What the hell else am I supposed to do?"

Jocelyn frowns as she looks me in the eye, then lifts her glass and takes a sip of the Merlot I poured for her less than twenty minutes earlier. I take a sip of my wine too, realizing I don't ever usually drink this early, but this day calls for it.

"All I know is if it were me, I'd be marching right past security and making a whole damn scene, banging on her door and everything until he came out and faced me."

"Well, that's *you*, Jocelyn. I'm not like you."

"Yeah, and look where *not* being like me has gotten you."

I avoid her eyes while taking another big gulp of wine. Jocelyn turns away from the window and walks my way and, as always, she's impeccably dressed. A creamy blouse and high-waisted jeans with a pair of black Jimmy Choo pumps. She takes the spot on the leather sofa next to me, and though I feel her staring, I don't meet her gaze.

"Are you ready to talk about why you *really* asked me to come here?"

"I don't know what you're talking about."

"You know, I found your text from the other day very interesting—especially considering how, the other night when I brought it up, you looked at me like I had two heads." She's referring to me asking her how to go about . . . getting rid of Julianna.

"That's because the idea is extreme."

"Shouldn't we all go to extremes for happiness? Hell, that shit is sacred. I say do whatever it takes to achieve it." She shrugs.

I press a hand to my forehead and groan. "I just . . . I really want things to go back to the way they were, Jocelyn. I was so much happier—Gabriel was happier. Even now, he feels like a stranger to me, and I'm pretty sure it's because his mind is constantly on her."

"Who's to say that even if something does happen to her, he won't still have her on his mind?"

"He could, but at least he wouldn't be able to go running to her." I chew on the inside of my cheek. "Maybe I can pay her to leave him alone. I'll introduce myself to her, tell her who I am, and she'll realize she's in the wrong, she'll hate Gabriel for lying and being a cheat and will back off."

"Something tells me money won't make her leave him alone if they're in love," Jocelyn deadpans.

"Ugh." I groan again and then polish off my wine. Jocelyn

picks up the wine bottle from the glass coffee table and dumps more into my goblet.

"Maybe you're onto something when it comes to talking to her, though," she says.

"What do you mean?"

"I mean, maybe not *you*, exactly, but we could hire someone to talk to her—approach her and all—and they can demand that she stop fucking with him. If she doesn't agree, then bam! The person can scare the shit out of her with a threat, shake her up a little."

"Are you serious? That's a terrible plan. She'd just run home and tell Gabriel, and then he'll know that I know about her before I can bring it up, and it'll cause a whole mess with him that I don't need right now."

"No, you're right. It has to be serious." Jocelyn taps her cheek and crosses her legs. "A threat won't be enough." She's quiet for a moment, and then, as if the greatest idea hits her, her spine seems to stack and her mouth gapes open as she stares at me.

"What?" I demand. "Why are you looking at me like that?"

"You said she doesn't know who you are, right?"

"No, she doesn't."

"Then you can use that! Use yourself to split them up!"

I frown, confused.

"Think about it, Adira. If you can get closer to her, you can find a way to ruin her . . . or a way to ruin their relationship from the inside so they lose trust in each other."

I'm tempted to tell her how ridiculous that is, but I can't bring myself to do that. Because, in all actuality, it's fucking brilliant.

"You'd have to be smart about it, of course. Don't tell her your real name. Maybe wear a wig when you meet her, so she doesn't give off any key features if she ever describes you to

Gabriel while they're together. You could literally sabotage them from the inside out. Then you wouldn't have to go the route of . . . well, you know." Jocelyn runs a finger across her throat, cocks her head to the left, and croaks.

"That is some seriously messed-up shit." I laugh.

"But you can't say it isn't some *smart* messed-up shit. Girl, if you don't do it, I will!"

I shake my head and take a careful sip of my wine. "No, no. It has to be me. I have to see the look on her face when she realizes he's not who she thinks he is."

"Is your mind churning with ideas already?" Jocelyn asks with a devious smirk.

"Yes. It definitely is."

CHAPTER THIRTY-SEVEN

ADIRA

I tuck a loose strand of real hair into the copper wig I bought from the beauty supply store this morning, then sigh as I look into the visor mirror. My glasses are big and square—a non-prescription pair I found at the pharmacy—and my lipstick is dark red.

I'm clearly out of my mind doing this—going undercover, pretending to be someone else—but what other choice is there? This seems to be the safest alternative. No one gets hurt—physically, anyway—and I'll have Gabriel all to myself again soon enough.

The worst that can happen is Julianna ending up with a broken heart and, frankly, I don't give a damn if that happens. She's young, beautiful, and, as many say, there are plenty of fish in the sea. She'll reel another one in with a simple bat of her eyelashes and be perfectly okay again. Besides, if anyone's heart is to be broken, it shouldn't be mine.

With that in mind, I step out of my car after sitting in the parking lot of Velvet's Café for well over fifteen minutes. I noticed Julianna's car park at the curb a moment ago. This time, I didn't want to be seen waiting at my usual table, watching her. No, today I have to make my presence known.

Pulling open the door of the café, I step inside and wait at the door for a split second, my eyes wandering to the front counter. There's a brunette woman taking orders behind the register, and second in line is Julianna. In front of her is an indecisive man staring up at the menu, debating over a banana cream smoothie or the banana and peanut butter shake. He's speaking so loudly, I can hear him from the door.

"I'll go with peanut butter," the man says, and the cashier nods and smiles, plugging his order into the register.

After he's paid, Julianna takes a step forward and places her order. I walk up behind her, studying her at this angle. She's wearing black leggings and a long-sleeved white shirt that's strappy in the back. I notice a lot of peach fuzz carries down her back, and I'm instantly curious if Gabriel finds that attractive. Does he stroke her back? Rub it? Kiss her spine as he makes love to her from behind, the same way he does me?

I remove the idea from my mind as Julianna pays and then turns to make her way to the pickup area. She orders the same thing every time she arrives, and it won't take long for them to make it, so I hurry and order a coffee and muffin. I snatch out my credit card to pay quickly, then hurry to the pickup area.

Julianna's back is to me as she scrolls through her phone. The man who ordered the peanut butter shake has his name called and he smiles graciously after taking the cup to go. Several minutes later, Julianna is called, and she moves to the counter to pick up her drink. She retrieves a straw from the container and starts to turn, ready to make her departure. I step in her way, pretending to grab a napkin. As I do, she gasps and stumbles backward, and some of her drinks spills onto her white shirt.

"Oh my goodness!" I gasp. "I'm so sorry! Are you okay?"

Julianna stares down at the green slush on her shirt before picking her head up and looking into my eyes. I can tell she wants to frown by the way her brows start to pucker, but she immediately draws in a breath and says, "I'm fine. Are you okay?"

"Yes. I'm so sorry. I was going for a napkin and didn't realize you would be turning in this direction."

"That's okay." She presses her lips and shrugs. "These things happen, right?"

"I suppose so." I study her face up close. There's a red pimple on her chin that I can tell she's tried to pop. I'm thinking maybe it's a sign of her menstrual cycle. Does Gabriel sleep with her while she's bleeding? *Ugh. What the fuck, Adira?* "Here." I offer her my napkin. "Let me help." She takes the napkin and I turn for the napkin holder to take more out, offering them to her.

She thanks me with a small smile and once the drink has been cleared, minus a green stain on the heart of her shirt, I say, "Why don't you let me buy you another?"

"Oh—no, that's okay. You don't have to do that. I still have some left." She lifts the cup and gives it a shake.

"Please? I feel so bad about it. You paid for that and I caused you to waste almost half of it. And between you and me, well, we know this place overcharges for the little bit they give you."

Julianna laughs and I smile with her. Her teeth are rectangular and straight. They appear to have been whitened. She has a nice smile. "Um . . . okay. But only if you're sure."

"I'm positive." And I really am because my plan is working. I return to the counter to order her another smoothie, but not without asking her what she ordered first. I know she always gets the avocado, banana, and mango smoothie with vegan protein powder, but she can't know that I know.

After I pay and we wait at the counter for her drink, I'm surprised when she asks, "Would you like to sit?" She extends an arm, pointing to an empty table.

"Oh—um . . ." I check my watch, pretending like I'm short on time.

"Please? You paid for my drink and tossed in a muffin. The least I can do is get to know your name."

"Yes, but I spilled the previous drink all over you." I laugh.

Julianna studies my eyes for a moment, tilting her head ever so slightly. The way she looks at me—it's as if she knows exactly who I am but refuses to say it. But that's impossible. She can't know who I am. And I realize she doesn't when she turns for the table anyway and pulls out a chair to sit. She places her muffin and drink down, then reaches a hand across the table to tap the empty spot. "Sit with me."

I glance around the café warily before moving forward and pulling out the seat across from hers. I place my drink on the tabletop as well and then look at her. She's smiling, clearly satisfied that she's convinced me to sit with her.

"So, who is the woman who stained my shirt and gave me this delicious muffin?" Julianna asks, smirking as she removes the paper from the blueberry muffin.

"Skylar," I tell her. It's the name Jocelyn and I agreed to use. "And you?"

"Julianna." She takes a bite of muffin while narrowing her eyes. "You seem so familiar."

"Really?" I smile and instantly lower my gaze.

"Have you been here before?"

"No, this is actually my first time here," I lie. "I kept hearing great things about this place. Of course, I had to cause a whole scene to let it be known, but here I am."

Julianna giggles, and the sound of it makes me cringe. A giggler? Seriously? Is this what he's so obsessed with?

"Trust me," Julianna says. "It's no big deal. I just came from barre class. These clothes were going to go in the wash anyway."

"I hope the stain comes out."

"A little baking soda and dish detergent will definitely do the trick."

I stare at her, confused.

"Oh—that's just a little trick *mi mamá* used to do. She was the stain master. My brother was always getting dirty, plus he played sports, so I guess she didn't really have a choice but to learn how to get stains out of clothes."

I smile at her. It's all I can do because, quite honestly, I don't care about her or her brother or her mother. "Did you grow up here, in Tampa?" I ask.

"No. I grew up in North Carolina, believe it or not."

"Oh, really? What part?"

"Charlotte."

"Oh. Interesting." I sip my coffee. "And what made you decide to move here?"

"I came here for college, but I stopped going after, like, a semester. I started learning how to do makeup, got my cosmetology and aesthetician license, and from there, everything just soared." She shrugs, as if it's no big deal, but by the stars in her eyes, I can tell she wants me to ask more about the whole drop-out-of-college-and-become-a-makeup-artist thing.

"That's incredible. Can I see some of your work?"

She's already unlocking her phone screen to get to her portfolio. She slides the phone across the table to me and it's her Instagram page. I pick it up and scroll through, pretending I've never seen these images before when the truth is, I've seen every single one of them.

I've studied her Instagram account for weeks. She has a makeup artist account and a personal account. I'm not keen on seeing her makeup account because her personal account is where she posts images of her and Gabriel. But never of their faces. It's often posts or stories of her holding his hand, or her shiny legs on top of his while lying in bed. Off guard images of his muscular back, with comments below of women saying, *Girl, I already know he's fine!* and *Damn, you are one lucky bitch.* She likes it to be a mystery of who she's with, which is strange to me because Gabriel is not the kind of man a woman should hide, but it also makes sense. He's a married man, and if any-one found out, it'd ruin his reputation—something that he cherishes very much.

"These are really good," I murmur. "Wow. Maybe you can do my makeup one day."

"I'd love that!" she exclaims. "Believe it or not, I don't get a lot of Black women, and I've been dying to do more. I could do yours and add it to my portfolio. Then maybe more Black women will feel comfortable coming to me."

"I'd be happy to help." My phone vibrates in my pocket, and I take it out to check the screen. It's a text from Jocelyn. **How is it going?**

I peer up, and Julianna takes a sip of her drink and then says, "Mmm. I'm going to run to the ladies' room really quick. Be right back."

I watch her take off, and when she's opened the bathroom door and allowed it to swing behind her, I lift my phone to text Jocelyn back.

She doesn't know who I am.

That's good. Get in deep with her. Make it all end.

That's the goal.

I shut off the screen of my phone just as Julianna returns to the table. "Ugh, I'm so sorry to do this, but I just got a call from my brother and I should probably get home so I can call him back."

"Oh—okay, no worries!" I say as she starts collecting her things.

"Hey, it was really nice meeting you today, though. I feel like I owe you now."

"Oh, please, you don't owe me anything."

"No, no. I definitely owe you. That muffin—even though

I shouldn't have had it—was fucking amazing." She steps back, looking me over. "Why don't you meet me at Emerald Golf Club tomorrow? My boyfriend has a membership there and I sometimes use it for spa days and to use their sauna. Don't tell him that, though." She winks.

Her boyfriend? She must be talking about Gabriel. He has a membership to Emerald—one that I paid for and gave to him as a birthday surprise two years ago. This bitch has been using the gift I paid for, for herself? And he's been *allowing* her?

I clutch my phone tighter in my hand and do my best to put on a smooth smile. "That sounds wonderful. I'd love to join you."

"Perfect! What's your number? I'll text you so you can have mine."

I read her off my number, she sends the text, and then she thanks me once again for the replacement drink and muffin. I watch her exit the café and saunter to her pink car, and when she drives off it takes everything in me not to scream where I stand.

I leave the café, rush to my car, close and lock the doors, and scream in there instead.

CHAPTER THIRTY-EIGHT

The first thing I wanted to do was tell Claudette about what I saw that night. Unfortunately, I couldn't tell her right away because Bower stayed over until late in the evening the following day.

It was bizarre watching him flip pancakes and scramble eggs for breakfast and then make us sandwiches for lunch. He also snuck us pieces of candy when Claudette wasn't looking. I didn't eat the candy, but of course Panda devoured it because candy was her weak spot and he knew it.

I kept a careful eye on her the whole time. Anytime Claudette walked out of the room, I sat next to Panda and distracted her with hand games like rock paper scissors and patty-cake. She hated patty-cake, but it was all I could come up with to as a distraction. It didn't stop Bower from looking, though. He'd sit on the opposite side of the room, nestled on the old recliner, his ankle resting on his knee and both arms on the armrests.

There was a sleazy look in his eyes that made my heartbeat quicken, and what was the most terrifying was how that sleazy look transformed as soon as Claudette entered the room again. He'd look calm and loving, as if he were the kindest man in the world.

When he eventually left—because he had to work third shift—I waited until he'd started his car and driven away before going to

Claudette's bedroom. She was sitting on her bed, her back against the headboard as she read from her Bible. She hated being interrupted during her Bible studies, but this was important.

"Momma," I murmured.

She picked up her head and I expected anger to flash in her eyes, but, to my surprise, she was unbothered. "Yes, Adira?"

I walked deeper into her room, wringing my fingers together. "I, um . . . I need to tell you something. About Pastor Bower."

At the mention of his name, Claudette perked up and smiled. "Oh, Adira, isn't that man something? He's heaven-sent, I'm telling you."

"No, Momma—that's not what I wanna tell you."

She narrowed her eyes and defensively squared her shoulders. "So what, then?"

"Well, last night while you were sleeping, I saw Bower sitting on the couch next to Panda."

Claudette's head tilted a fraction. "Okay? And?"

"His hand was under her blanket. I . . . I think he was touching her . . . down there."

Claudette stared at me, and for a long, long time she said nothing. I waited for her to speak, but she only stared, which made me uneasy.

"Momma?" I called, shifting on my feet.

"Get out," she snapped.

"W–what?"

"I SAID GET OUT!" she barked. Claudette climbed off the bed in a fury and marched toward me, gripping my arm tight and dragging me out of her room. She shoved me away, and when my back hit the edge of one of the walls, she said, "You're always lying! Always! God doesn't like liars, Adira!"

"But I'm not! I'm telling the truth, Momma! I saw him!"

"Pastor Bower is a man of God!" she shouted in my face. "He would never—" Claudette's head shook, and it appeared her whole body was vibrating with rage. "You're just a liar," she growled. "You hate seeing people happy. You hate seeing me happy. You're a liar!"

With that, she turned away, walked back to her bedroom, and slammed the door behind her.

I sat on the floor, breathing rapidly, my heart banging like a chaotic drum. I caught something moving in the corner of my eye and turned my head left. Panda was standing at the end of the hallway, her eyes big and glassy.

"I'm scared, Adira," she said, and all the fear that'd sunk into me dripped out and onto the floor as I ran to collect her in my arms.

CHAPTER THIRTY-NINE

ADIRA

I'd been to Emerald Golf Club once. It was with a colleague from work who invited me to join her for brunch at their on-site restaurant, and then for massages afterward. She wanted to close a deal with me for one of her boutiques in Manhattan. The deal was secured the same day—what can I say? I'm a sucker for a good massage—she was a happy lady, and I had garnered $400,000 from the deal. Not only that but I was able to create a membership for my husband so that he could enjoy Emerald Golf Club for himself too.

I can count on one hand how many times Gabriel has been to Emerald. Granted, he's busy with work, and he's not big on golfing or massages from strangers, or spending time in spas to unwind, but the fact that he allows his little *mistress* to use it instead feels like a slap in the face.

I'm here with a woman who isn't offering me anything but a waste of my time and it's taking every ounce of willpower to swallow down the bitterness and pretend I'm having a good time. We caught lunch in the on-site restaurant, where Julianna ordered a turkey sandwich with waffle fries and I went with potato soup and a sliced green apple.

"You eat so light," she teased me. "You make me feel like a fat ass!"

I had no choice but to laugh at that. I'm sure I weigh at least fifteen pounds more than she does.

After lunch, Julianna leads the way to the saunas. I watch her undress completely and pack her things in a locker. It's strange watching her get undressed, standing there completely naked, and of course it occurs to me that she's done this many, many times before with my husband.

I study the soft curves of her body. Where she has no cellulite or dimples, I have plenty of it. Her nipples are pink and erect, a complete contrast to my dark brown nipples, and she's waxed from head to toe—minus the peach fuzz on her back.

She turns away from me to slide her arms into a robe and I follow suit. I have to thank her internally for that. After seeing her naked, the last thing I want is to show her my body. Don't get me wrong, I'm proud of my body, but she's a little younger and slightly more put together, and I suppose my insecurities are getting the better of me.

I undress quickly, then slide into the soft, cotton robe. After tying it around my waist, Julianna turns to me while bringing her hair up into a floppy bun.

"Ready?" she asks once she's secured her hair.

"Yep." When she turns, I bring a hand up to scratch my scalp beneath the wig.

I follow her out of the changing room and down a long hallway painted green with gold sconces on the wall. In the sconces are flickering pillar candles that provide a soft, soothing light. Julianna grips the gold door handle and swings open one of the sauna doors.

A sigh immediately escapes her as she enters the steam room and sits on one of the wooden benches. I take a seat on the bench across from her, thankful no one else is here but us.

"So, Skylar. Tell me about you," Julianna says, pushing the collar of her robe down and revealing her shoulder. "I feel like I've been talking about myself so much since we met. What do you do for a living? How old are you? Favorite color? Tell me all the things."

"Um . . . okay." I force a smile.

"Wait, hold on. Before you begin," Julianna stops me, raising an impatient hand, "please know that you don't have to be nervous around me. I sense that you're being reserved, but I promise you, I'm the last person to ever judge anyone."

"Well, that's good to know. Sorry—I'm not really the type to make friends so quickly, so . . ."

"You're an introvert," she says matter-of-factly.

I nod. "You could say that."

"Well, it's a good thing there are people like me—extroverts who help the introverts open up."

I nod and smile.

"So? Tell me all the things."

"Okay. Well, to answer your questions, I'm twenty-nine years old and my favorite color is pink."

"Oh my God—no way! Pink is one of my favorite colors too! I mean, I'm more a rose-gold type of pink, but still . . . pink is pink, right?"

"Right!" I so badly want to roll my eyes right then.

"And what do you do for a living?"

"Oh, um I work at Jessa's Lounge right now."

"I've heard of Jessa's. It's that ritzy place with all the different chairs."

"Yep, that's the one."

"Wow, yeah, I have a couple of friends who go there some weekends. It's their hangout. I've never been, but now that I know you work there, maybe I'll have a reason to go." Julianna tucks a loose strand of hair behind her ear and her skin is glistening with sweat already.

I wipe my cheek, feeling a line of sweat drip down my face too. This damn wig isn't helping a thing. I'll have to get another one if Julianna's goal is to have me sweat to death.

"So, tell me more about you," I say, sitting up taller. "I know you're a makeup artist and that you're from Charlotte. What else?"

"What do you wanna know?" she asks, smiling.

"You mentioned being in a relationship . . ." I say, plucking at a loose thread on my robe.

"Yes, I am." She sighs. "He's so great."

"That's nice." I snatch the string off. "How long have you two been together?"

"About a year and a half now. Yeah . . ." Her eyes wander off, focused on a spot on the wall above my head.

"Are you happy?"

"Ugh. Yes, beyond. But . . . our relationship is different, you know?"

"Different how?"

"I don't know. It's hard to explain unless you're in it. As many say, it's complicated."

"Oh."

"What about you?" she asks, wiping sweat from her chin.

"Oh—I'm single," I tell her, waving a hand. I'm glad to have taken my wedding band off yesterday morning. "I don't really have time for relationships."

"You're kidding—as stunning as you are." Julianna rolls her eyes. "But I completely get that. Focusing on yourself. The right one always comes when we're doing that, right?" She gives me a smile and a wink.

"I wouldn't know."

I feel her eyes on me, but I avoid them and look at the pit built into the floor with gray stones. Julianna picks up the spoon next to the water bucket, ladles a scoop of water, and dumps it onto the rocks. The rocks sizzle and hiss, conjuring more steam, and I inhale before sitting back and resting the back of my head against the wall.

"Are you from Tampa?" she asks me, replacing the spoon.

"I am."

"That's cool. Have any family in the area?"

"Just my mom, but she travels around a lot. We talk pretty much every day, though."

"That must be nice—talking to your mom every day." I look into her eyes, which have saddened.

"Is your mom not in the picture anymore?"

"She passed away the year I got my aesthetician license." She's wearing a smile, but it doesn't reach her eyes.

"I'm so sorry to hear that."

"Fucking cancer," she says, huffing a laugh. "Fuck it, right?"

"Yeah." I swallow hard. "Fuck it."

Julianna crosses her legs. "You know, despite her being gone now and having a shitty father who didn't want to be a part of my life . . . I grew up pretty good, you know? I always had everything I needed—my mom made sure of that while she was here. We had running water, a roof over our heads, food in our bellies. We were great. She always worked so many hours though. That's why I went to college—so I could eventually get a job that could help her work less, cover her bills, all that." She pauses and twists a silver ring on her fore-finger. "Now I can do all that, but she's not here, so . . ." Julianna sighs and looks into my eyes. "Sorry—I don't mean to bring down the mood."

"You're fine. I'm glad you feel comfortable telling me."

"Yeah. Anyway," she says, sliding her robe down more. Both of her shoulders are bared and I can see her cleavage. How can she be so comfortable in her own skin? I love my body, I do, but I'm not comfortable enough to show it off around someone who's practically a stranger.

Perhaps it's the way she grew up. She and I clearly had different upbringings. She was happy in hers and I wasn't. Nor was I comfortable enough to be who I truly was. That must be it.

Julianna catches me off guard by sliding closer to me. She grabs my left hand and places it in hers, palm down. "You're lying to me about something, Skylar," she says. Her eyes slide up to mine and a faint smile is on her lips.

"What do you mean?" My heart begins to race as I pull my eyes away.

"You have a tan mark here," she says, rubbing my ring finger. "From a ring. Am I right?"

I look down, noticing some of the foundation I applied to my finger this morning has rubbed off on my robe.

"You got me." I laugh.

"I knew it." She giggles. "Were you engaged?"

"I was . . . for a short time. It didn't last, clearly." The lie rolls right off my tongue.

"Meh, there are other people out there," she declares. She releases my hand and sits back. After crossing her legs again, I glance at her through my peripheral vision.

"The reason I say things are different with my boyfriend and me is because . . . I'm not sure what I really want, you know? I mean, I *love* the unlimited supply of dick, don't get me wrong. But I also love my freedom."

"Oh."

"That's inappropriate, right? I know." She folds her arms and laughs. "Why is it such a taboo thing for women to talk about their desires?"

"I don't know."

"Sometimes I think I'm supposed to be with him. I'm so happy with him . . . but I also think that sometimes . . . he's not completely happy with me, so I hold a lot of myself back from him." She grabs my hand again and touches the tan line on my ring finger. "We as humans weren't built for this. Being monogamous. Maybe that's why it didn't work out for you and your ex."

I fight the urge to pull my hand out of hers. *He's not my ex, he's my husband, and it's not working out because of you!* I can feel her looking at me, so I find her eyes and she's staring at me with so many questions in hers. Utterly confused and mildly uncomfortable, I pull my hand out of hers and sigh.

"Oh—shit! Wait—what time is it?" she asks.

"I'm not sure. I left my phone in the locker."

"Me too. Damn it—I forgot I have to let the cable guy in to switch out my router." Julianna stands and pulls her robe on completely. "Do you mind if we cut this spa day a little short?"

"No, of course not."

"Okay." She grins and walks to the door to pull it open. I walk out with her and let out a refreshing sigh when I feel the coolness of the air-conditioning in the halls.

When we return to the locker room, she says, "Actually, do you want to follow me to my place? I'll just let him in and then we can go to the mall. Grab some froyo or something? My treat?"

"Oh, Julianna, I'd hate to intrude—"

"Nonsense. You wouldn't be intruding. I'm inviting you!" She takes a step closer to me. "To be honest, I lied to you too. I don't really have friends here. The friends I do have aren't really friends, just fake bitches who want their makeup done for free."

I laugh.

"Don't laugh, okay?" She giggles. "Those bitches can kick rocks. With you, I feel like there's a possibility of something real. At least you gave me a free muffin. So? What do you say? Follow me there? We'll hit up a mall?"

"What about your boyfriend?"

"Please. He's out of town. He won't be back until tomorrow night."

"Okay. But only if you're sure."

Julianna grabs my hand, squeezes it, and says, "I'm positive."

CHAPTER FORTY

ADIRA

I would've been a fool to pass up the opportunity to get inside Julianna's apartment. For months I'd been trying to figure out how I could get past security and get to her door, and now it was happening without so much as a hiccup.

The security guard waves at her from his desk as she enters and cuts an eye at me before going back to scrolling through his phone. When we're in the elevator and riding up, Julianna digs through her purse for her key.

"I know it's in here somewhere. Ah! Here it is!" She wrenches it out with a smug smile, and the elevator spits us out onto floor seven. Walking to the end of the hallway, she stops in front of apartment 712, unlocks the door with her key, twists the doorknob, and steps inside.

I draw in a shallow breath as I step into the dim confines of her home. Her curtains are drawn together, but she flips a switch to turn on the recessed lighting in the kitchen, then she makes her way across the room to open the curtains, revealing a stunning water view out of the floor-to-ceiling windows.

"Make yourself at home. Cable guy should be here within the next ten minutes or so. Once he's done, we can go. I'm going to take a shower, if you don't mind."

"That's fine. I'll wait here."

"Okay." She walks around a corner and disappears, and I take slow, methodical steps after her to see she's entered a bedroom. The bed is large, with a pink duvet and pillows to match, a canopy elegantly draping above. A light gray recliner is against one of the walls, with a fuzzy pink-and-white bunny pillow on top of it. A gold chandelier also hangs from above, the crystal-like droplets shimmering from the sun.

So much pink. I roll my eyes and turn to take in the details of her living room. There's a TV mounted on the wall, set up beneath an entertainment system with a built-in fireplace. Her sofas are ivory leather, with two pink Sherpa throw blankets tossed over the backs. The accent pieces and mirrors on the wall are brushed with rose gold. It's vomit-inducing, really—how much pink and rose gold there is. Her floors are marble and polished so well, I can see my reflection.

I run my hands along her square glass dining table, which seats four, and wonder how many dinners she's had with my husband here. A portrait is on the wall across from me—rose-gold marble, and beneath it is a built-in wet bar with drinks neatly lined up on a clear shelf. It's all so high-end and luxurious, and I'm curious how a mediocre makeup artist can afford any of this.

Something in the corner of the room catches my eyes. It's a coatrack. A gray, pleated jacket hangs on it, and my eyes broaden when I realize whose it is. At the bottom of the rack are a pair of dress shoes, placed together neatly and in pristine condition.

I work hard to swallow as I move toward the rack, lifting the sleeve of the jacket to smell it. *God*, it smells just like his cologne. Just like his skin. And it's here . . . in *her* home.

I squat to pick up one of the shoes I bought him when I traveled to Miami on a trip. They're a pair of black Versace that I'd shopped for and given to him for his birthday, along with a set of gold cuff links with his initials engraved.

I stand up straight, clearing my throat as I hear Julianna start up the shower. I make my way to her kitchen, where there are bubble lights hanging down like mini balloons, and open the refrigerator. There's not much—some wine, old takeout, heads of lettuce, eggs . . . and a to-go box from Caraway. I take it out, open the container, and there's a sliver of baked chicken breast and sweet potato casserole, along with a half-eaten side of creamed spinach.

"His favorite meal," I whisper. Are these the leftovers he took with him when we had lunch together? I replace the container and close the fridge, leaving the kitchen to enter her bedroom. Her bathroom door is cracked open and, based on the echo as she hums, I can tell she's already in the shower.

I shift my gaze to Julianna's nightstand—primarily focused on the one on the left. There's a gold watch placed there, as well as a *GQ* magazine. *His side.* I walk ahead, where the closet doors are, and draw them open. The closet is huge. Not as big as mine, but it's big enough to be another room.

One side is full of feminine clothing—lingerie, robes, gowns, shoes, and heels—and on the other are the masculine clothes and shoes. Suits, ties, belts. All seemingly the size of my husband. My heart beats harder, faster, as I try to process the fact that he's made himself at home here. He has a life here—one could almost assume he's been leading a double life. Only now I know all about it and I'm going to rectify it.

I shut the closet doors, then turn to finger through the perfumes and lotions on her dresser, stopping at a picture frame close to the edge. It's a photo of Julianna with her arms wrapped around him on what looks like a boat. The wind is whipping at her hair, which is strewn all over the place, even flying in his face, and they're laughing and kissing. He looks undeniably happy with her and it makes my belly clench with jealousy. I run my fingers over the glass encasing the image, wanting so badly to break it.

Julianna hums a little louder and I hear something vibrating. Turning around, I notice her phone on the bed in a pink case. I take a step closer, and the caller ID says Lil Bro. Well, at least it's not Gabriel. That would have been the icing on the cake and a clear sign for me to destroy everything before leaving.

Julianna's humming comes to an end and I realize that if I don't act now, I may not ever get the chance again. I take my purse off my shoulder and walk to Gabriel's side of the bed. Opening the purse, I dig into the inside pocket and retrieve a condom.

So, here's the thing: Gabriel is allergic to latex. And the condom I'm planting is made of latex. If he's been with Julianna for a year and a half, like she says, she'd know by now that he's allergic to it.

The only reason Gabriel would have this kind of condom in her apartment is if he had someone else there and she brought her own protection. And not just any condom—a cheap one he'd never use. Perhaps she dropped it by accident and he forgot to pick it up. Who knows how it happened?

Knowing this, I rip the condom open just a little to reveal the lubricated rubber and place it on the floor beneath his side of the bed so it sticks out. She'll see the foil before the day is over, I'm sure.

There's a distant knock and I gasp, hopping up and leaving the bedroom. Julianna still has the shower running, so I walk to check the peephole of her front door. A man stands on the other side, dressed in a blue uniform. He rubs his nose, sniffs, then knocks again.

I swing the door open and in a gruff manner, he says, "Here to fix the Wi-Fi."

"Of course." I let him in, and he walks deeper into the condo. He looks around, then frowns and says, "Gonna lead me to it or what?"

"Oh—I don't live here. This is my friend's apartment. She's in the shower."

The man rolls his eyes and grumbles, "Jesus Christ." A door creaks on its hinges and Julianna waltzes out of the bedroom in a pink robe—and not just *any* robe. A silky pink robe by Lovely Silk. My fucking brand!

"Hey—sorry! The Wi-Fi box is right over there," she says, pointing at the shelf built into the wall beside the entertainment system.

The man grumbles again and makes his way toward it.

"Why didn't you come for me?" She laughs. A whiff of her body wash runs past my nose—a fresh cucumber melon.

"You weren't done. I didn't want to bother you."

She points her gaze to the man. *He's an asshole,* she mouths.

I laugh and mouth back, *Yeah. He is.*

She walks past me in her robe to stand a few steps away from him, answering his questions about the Wi-Fi. As she does, I continue staring at her. I have no idea why it bothers me so much that she's wearing the robe. I've seen plenty of women wearing my robes. I take pride in seeing people in them . . . but not when it comes to her.

I can't help wondering if Gabriel gave it to her. Did he purchase this robe for her? Give it to her as a gift? Or did she buy it herself, simply because she loved it? No, it can't be. She has the floral pink robe—which is exclusively sold online. Sure, she could have seen it herself, but what are the odds of that? He had to have seen it while I was doing designs, knew she'd like it, and ended up ordering it for her as a gift.

"Where did you get your robe from?" I ask when the man stops his questions.

"Oh—my boyfriend bought it for me!"

"It's beautiful. I love it." *I fucking knew it.*

"Yeah, I've been in love with this brand for ages." *Good thing you don't know who the owner is,* I think to myself. "Their quality is amazing and the silk is so soft. I think this one was shipped from an online order, but maybe you can snag one at the mall today when we go."

"Maybe."

When Julianna lists off a few more tech issues about her router, she goes back to her bedroom and returns moments later wearing a yellow sundress, her damp hair pulled up into a slick ponytail.

She hands me a bottled water as we wait for the Wi-Fi man to finish up. He double-checks his work and then has the nerve to ask her to leave him a good review when the company calls for a survey.

"Yeah, sure, bud. Will do," she says, then she closes the door in his face and huffs a laugh. "The audacity of that jerk." She picks up her purse from the coatrack. "Come on. Let's go shopping."

CHAPTER FORTY-ONE

ADIRA

"Wow. I didn't think you'd have the balls to do it." Jocelyn is seated at my dining table with a glass of wine in her hand and a smile gracing her lips.

"I had no choice," I mutter, chopping a rinsed head of lettuce with a knife. "It was that . . . . or your *other* plan. This one was safer." Some of my hair gets into my eyes and I move it away with my pinkie. I went to get my hair done by Selma after leaving my mall trip with Julianna. That wig was horrible—so horrible I tossed it in the nearest trash bin when I arrived for my hair appointment. I feel like myself again with my silk press. I even got gold highlights as a form of victory.

"I wonder if she found it yet," Jocelyn laughs.

"Why are you so amused?"

"Because the bitch deserves it."

"You hardly know her, Jocelyn. And let's not forget, *you* were fucking my husband too."

"Touché." Jocelyn sighs, uncrosses her legs, and stands up, making her way across the kitchen. She watches me dump some of the chopped lettuce into a bowl while planting her elbows on the marble countertop.

"You know, if you want me out of your life, just say it. You did what you had to do, and now we've clearly settled our differences."

"What makes you think we've settled our differences?"

"Um, the fact that you've invited me into your house twice says enough." She laughs.

I press my lips together, resisting the urge to smile.

"Besides, there's no way she won't find it if you put it there. Gold is hard to miss. Their little thing will end, you'll have him back, and I'll go on my merry way." She stands up straight to sip her wine again. "You're welcome, by the way."

I stop chopping. "What is that supposed to mean?"

Jocelyn smirks and nothing more. I move to rinse off the tilapia. "Don't you hate tilapia?" she asks me.

"I used to."

"Ugh." She scrunches her nose. "Tilapia. That cheap-ass fish. Reminds me of my mother."

I take the fish to the counter to season it. As I do, my phone rings on the counter. "Who is it?"

"The husband," Jocelyn mumbles. She puts her wineglass down and I wash my hands quickly before hurrying for the phone.

"Hi, baby," I answer.

"Hey. I'll be home in thirty. Have you had dinner already?"

"I'm making dinner now. It should be ready by the time you get home."

"Perfect. I'll see you then."

"'Kay."

I hang up and Jocelyn inhales before exhaling. "I guess that's my cue."

"Yes, it is," I tell her, fighting a smile.

"I don't get why you're so happy that he called you." She walks to the dining table to pick up her Jimmy Choo purse.

"He's been playing you right in your damn face. But, hey, who am I to judge? He makes your heart drum happy little beats and that's more than I can say for myself." The strap of her purse is on her shoulder, her car keys in hand. "I guess after tonight I won't be hearing from you for a while, huh?"

I turn to look into her eyes, clinging to a confidence I didn't possess before knowing about Julianna. "No. After today, me and Gabriel should be much, much happier."

CHAPTER FORTY-TWO

ADIRA

Gabriel isn't happier. He comes home in a sour mood. We eat dinner at the dining table, and I take out a pricey bottle of wine I've been saving as a form of my own quiet celebration. Gabriel eats his food quickly, then dismisses himself from the table, informing me that he's tired and wants to shower and relax for the rest of the night.

I clean up the kitchen and once I'm finished, I go upstairs. I enter our bedroom but realize he isn't there. Then I hear the floorboards creak and turn to walk out of the bedroom. The door to the guest bedroom down the hallway is cracked open, light seeping through and illuminating the end of the hallway.

Walking to the door, I peek through the crack. His back is to the door. He turns at an angle, and I realize he's rapidly texting someone with a heavy frown. I step away from the door, knowing he's most likely texting *her*.

I make my way back downstairs for another glass of wine and when I come back up, Gabriel is in the shower. I change into a nice set of lingerie and wait for him to come to bed, but when he steps out of the shower, he goes straight to the closet. When he walks out of it, he's dressed in a T-shirt and boxers.

Plugging his phone into the charger, he places it facedown on his nightstand and then turns his back to me.

"Really?" I ask.

"What?" he calls, glancing over his shoulder.

"I wore this for you," I tell him, smiling and leaning toward him. I press my breasts against his back and he sighs. "It's new lingerie."

"Oh. Nice," is all he says.

I walk my fingers down his biceps. "You don't wanna . . . ?" My voice trails off as I wait for him to turn and face me, but he doesn't. Instead, he lifts the duvet higher over his shoulder to cover himself.

"Not tonight, babe," he mumbles. "The flight drained me. I need some sleep." And that's that.

Not even ten minutes later, he's snoring. I have the urge to check the sneaky app on my phone, but I don't. Even if I wanted to, I couldn't because I deleted it shortly after I planted the condom in Julianna's condo. I figured I wouldn't need it anymore—that the plan would work and Julianna would kick him to the curb. I didn't want to read messages of my husband groveling, begging her to listen and trying to plead his case. I go to the closet, change into something more comfortable, then lie in bed next to him, annoyed by the way he dismissed me, but then smiling as I close my eyes, pleased to know he's never going to go back to her.

CHAPTER FORTY-THREE

ADIRA

When I wake up, I turn over and realize Gabriel's not in bed. Cabinets slam closed downstairs, pots clang, and silverware rattles. I make my way to the closet and take down a robe, slide into the slippers on my side of the bed, and make my way down the stairs.

When I enter the kitchen, Gabriel is standing next to the stove, reading the back of a box of pancake mix. I stand at the mouth of the kitchen a moment, watching him. This life is good to him. He has it all. The fact that he's standing in such an exquisite kitchen, with floors that sparkle and are waxed weekly by the housekeeper, touching clean, white cabinets with gold-finished knobs and farmhouse windows that overlook a freshly cut lawn—which he doesn't have to worry about cutting, mind you—you'd think he'd never risk losing this.

"Shit," Gabriel curses under his breath when some of the pancake powder misses the clear bowl he's dumping it into and sprinkles onto the floor.

"You're rushing the process," I finally say.

He turns quickly and a smile spreads across his lips. "How long have you been standing there?"

"Hmm . . . . maybe a good minute or two."

"Watching me?" he asks, smirking, amused.

"Oh, absolutely. I'm always watching you."

He laughs at that. "Oh, I bet."

I walk to the fridge, taking out the milk and bringing it to the counter he's at. "You're normally pretty good at this whole breakfast thing. You okay?" I ask.

"Yeah, I'm good. Just a little tired, you know?"

I nod, then pour two cups of milk into the mix. The kitchen is quiet now, and Gabriel grabs a whisk, ready to whip the batter. As he does, I move to the built-in music player to turn it on, but his hand touches it just as mine does. We both freeze, then laugh as our fingers entwine. Gabriel steps back, slowly releasing my fingers. "I'll let the queen pick the music this morning."

"Thank you." I smile at him before taking out my phone and connecting the Bluetooth. Elton John belts out a tune and I sing along with it, going to the fridge to take out a new pack of turkey bacon.

"I like this," Gabriel says, whisking the pancake mix.

"What?"

"Making breakfast with you. It isn't the same when I do it alone."

"Aww." I stand on my toes to kiss his cheek and he grins. That's a one-up for me. I'm sure Julianna doesn't help him make meals.

When the pancakes, bacon, and eggs are ready, Gabriel gently commands me to sit at the dining table while he sets it all up. He brings over some pomegranate juice for us to wash it all down and when we're both nice and full, he sits back in his chair. "Homemade is better than anything at a restaurant." He chuckles.

"It is."

"Listen, I'm sorry about how I was acting last night."

I sit up straighter in my chair, giving him my complete attention. "I figured you just needed some space."

"I did . . . but I shouldn't have taken my frustrations out on you."

I pause. "What were you frustrated about?"

"Just . . . life. You know? And work is kicking my ass."

"Oh." I force an understanding nod.

Gabriel leans forward and reaches across the table to grab my hand. "What do you say we go to Destin a couple days sooner? I could use the vacation right now, and I'm sure if I call Tray, he'll handle things for me."

"Oh. Uh . . . are you sure?"

He squeezes my hand and kisses my knuckles. "I'm sure." He pauses. "You wanna know something?"

"What?"

"I'm so lucky to have you. Without you, I'd have nothing, Adira. I'd be *no one*."

"Please." I laugh as he kisses one of my knuckles again. "You're just saying that."

"No, I really do mean it."

"Well, if we do go early, that means you can't make a bunch of calls on our getaway. Or texts," I add for good measure.

"All right. I think I can do that."

"Yeah sure." I huff a laugh and take a sip of juice.

"Wanna shake on it?" he asks, releasing my hand to hold his out.

"Fine." I put down my juice and place my hand in his. We shake on it and then he jerks me forward and kisses me. "The bet is on as soon as we land."

"Okay," I breathe.

He kisses me once more, then something vibrates. I didn't bring my phone downstairs, so it has to be his. He pulls away and sits again, taking his phone out of his pocket. He unlocks it and reads something, then sighs and says, "You mind if I make a quick call? It's for work. It won't take me long, I promise."

I hesitate and immediately lower my gaze. *It has to be work. It can't be her.* "Sure. I'll be here waiting for you."

He already has the phone to his ear as he pushes away from the table and plants a kiss on my forehead. I put on a smile for him as he winks at me, then watch him leave the kitchen in a hurry, turning a corner and disappearing. When he's gone, my smile disappears and I get up from the table to follow after him.

He's making his way to the back deck. From just a few steps out of the kitchen, I can see him through the window, standing next to some of the outdoor furniture. His phone is pressed to his ear, his back to the glass. I clench a fist because he only talks with his back to doors or exits when he's talking to *her.*

I return to the kitchen, my heart sinking to my stomach. All that shit he says about how lucky he is to have me, yet he doesn't act like it. I know—I know. It'll take a while for him to let her go, but I have to say, what he's doing right now is fucking *rude.*

I pour myself another glass of juice from the glass pitcher, and just as I take a sip, Gabriel returns to the kitchen, but not in the good mood he was in when he left.

"Everything okay?" I ask as he sits down at the table.

"Yeah." He starts picking up things at the counter, throwing trash away. "All good. I'm gonna go to the office and look for flights, see if I can find anything for us for today or tomorrow."

"Okay," I murmur, but he's already leaving the kitchen. I clean up the rest, load the dishwasher, and then make my way upstairs to start up the shower. While it runs, I go to pick up my phone, and there's a text from Jocelyn. **Good mood or bad?**

I respond with: **I can't tell. I think good. He just has to let her go. We'll be going out of town, so the trip should help.**

Jocelyn returns: **Ugh. You make it too easy for him.**

Gabriel enters the bedroom and says, "I found two first-class tickets for today at three," he says, showing me the screen of his laptop. "Are those okay?"

"That's fine. Book them. I'll start packing after my shower."

"On it."

When he's gone, I go to the shower and start to think Jocelyn is right. I do make it too easy for him.

CHAPTER FORTY-FOUR

ADIRA

Bags are packed and stored in the trunk of Gabriel's Range Rover within two hours of breakfast and we make it onto a last-minute flight in the nick of time. When Gabriel and I are settled into our seats, I let out a long sigh.

"You need this just as much as I do, don't you?" he asks beside me.

"I do," I admit.

"You've been working hard lately. Longer hours at the office." He lifts a slice of my hair. "Selma did good."

I smile, thankful for the compliment on my hair, but I don't speak about work. Truth is, I hadn't been working *enough*. In fact, I had to text Alaina and let her know I wasn't going to be coming in for a few days and to move my schedule around. I'd been too preoccupied with Gabriel and Julianna to work overtime, which was costing me.

I was backed up on paperwork and contracts, all of which Alaina had reminded me of via text, and all the late-night meetings with her and Vito are starting to become questionable to them. It isn't like me to reschedule so much, and yet I've changed my Zoom meetings with them three times already, just so I can get home and either text Jocelyn or *not* go home so that I can lurk on my husband and his mistress. I'm sure Alaina understands, but Vito . . . he's probably over my shit.

"We need this," I say, sighing.

"We do." He grabs my hand and squeezes it as he looks ahead.

"Do you want to tell me what's really on your mind?"

His eyes swing to mine again and with a smile I know is forced, he asks, "What do you mean?"

"It seems like it's more than work that's bothering you. Is everything really okay?" I'm pushing it, I know, but maybe this will be when he confesses something now that he knows it's over with her.

"Ah, well, you know the expansion is a time suck. Then there are the team meetings, practices, and everything." Gabriel shrugs. "It's all become a little overwhelming, if I'm being honest."

Not the answer I was expecting, but okay. "Well, maybe this getaway will refresh your mind. Prepare you for the workload afterward."

"Yeah," he murmurs, smiling. "I hope so."

As soon as we walk through the door of the beach house in Destin—a three-story home with windows as walls and a contemporary interior—the first thing Gabriel does is kiss me.

"Look at that," he murmurs, pointing to the stretch of windows ahead. Outside the windows is a stunning ocean view. The water shimmers like crystals and the sun is setting, showering the living room and all its ivory furniture in a warm, orange glow. "Beautiful." A kiss to the bend of my neck from behind. "Just like you."

He insists that I take off my clothes and that we make love as the sun continues to set. "You want a baby," he growls on my lips. "I'll give you a baby. I'll give you whatever you want." At first, it's such a thrill that I forget myself for a moment, as well as all my insecurities, and let him take me. Our bodies are pressed against the glass, the rays of remaining sunlight bathing our skin. The glow makes Gabriel's skin appear warmer and I have the urge to kiss him all over, but because I can't and he's buried within me, I kiss his neck, his cheeks, his chin—anything I can get my greedy lips on.

But then I realize he's only saying all this because he can no longer have her. And if he doesn't have her, he only has me . . . for now, anyway.

He's *hate*-fucking me. He's thinking about her and taking it out on me, and that makes me freeze beneath him like a dead fish. When he's reached his climax, both of us somehow ending up on the floor, I lie there for a moment, staring up at the wooden beams in the ceiling and the dangling, gold chandelier in the center. Gabriel groans as he flips a switch and turns on a fan, then he shouts to our voice-service device, "Turn on the music!"

A song by Frank Ocean fills the room, and Gabriel marches to the built-in bar of our Destin home and pours himself a drink.

"Come on," he says, standing above me and offering a hand. "Let's get our vacation started."

CHAPTER FORTY-FIVE

ADIRA

After we shower together, Gabriel and I go out for dinner to a seafood restaurant on the water. I do my best to smile and be present with him, but I'm realizing this isn't an escape we're taking as a loving couple. This is an escape for him to drown himself in liquor and try to forget about his strain with Julianna.

We share buttery garlic knots and expensive red wine at the restaurant, and after I've had a few glasses, I find myself lightening up, only a little, because he's giving me his attention. He's asking me questions about work—which he usually doesn't care too much to talk about—and he's complimenting how I look tonight. I went with a black dress with gold trim and tall black pumps. I admit I look amazing tonight, but that was the goal.

See, when it's just us, he's *my* Gabriel. The one who can take a joke or even crack one himself. He's the Gabriel who showers me with attention and affection—the Gabriel who loves every part of me, the same as I do him.

When we're like this, I find myself forgiving him all his mistakes, ignoring all his flaws, and just loving him as a human being. Or maybe it's because I know the story of how he was raised, and I only know it because when he got the call that his mother had passed away, he cried on my lap. He told me he was the child of a single mother who truly didn't care about him and never indulged him. His father was absent and all he had was her, but she hardly gave him any of her heart. He craved love like a junkie craved his next fix, and I sometimes think maybe that's why he messes around with different women—because he was never properly loved. I can love him properly, wholly, and he knows it. I won't let go of him because there is a nurturer inside me so fierce that she forgives and loves constantly. After the day he cried on my lap about his mother, I saw how raw and vulnerable he really was, and I saw exactly who he was and what he needed. He was just a lonely boy deep down, who needed to be taken care of. Loved. Cherished. And I was willing to give him all that.

But it's also hard because I desire his respect. And if he respects me, he'll never go back to Julianna again.

We finish off dinner with a sweet, chocolatey dessert and then take off, hand in hand, walking off some of the food at the harbor.

"Can I ask you something?" I squeeze his hand as we stop by the railing that overlooks the ocean. My head is fuzzy and I'm tipsy, but I find myself looking into his eyes anyway.

"Anything," he murmurs.

"Do you think we're becoming stale?"

"Stale?" he repeats.

"Yes. Do you think that one day we won't be together . . . like this?"

"Of course not," he says hurriedly. He takes my hand in his. "I need you, Adira. I can't live my life without you. We're in this forever, you hear me?"

So why sleep with her and another woman?

I nod, looking into his eyes.

"Why do you ask that?" He brings me closer to the railing and out of the way of passersby.

"Just curious."

He studies me for a moment. "You know, sometimes I think it's you who who'll become tired of us."

"Never."

"Come on, Adira. I'm a man who came from nothing. Everything I have was bred through you."

"Not true," I say, shaking my head. "Your ideas were your own."

"But without you, those ideas wouldn't be a reality." He gives me a weak smile, then turns and exhales, leaning against the rail. "Sometimes I think you deserve better than me. Than *this*." He gestures between us.

"Gabriel." I step forward, clasping his face in my hands and making him look at me. "Stop thinking like that. If it weren't for you, I wouldn't be who I am either. You make me so happy, don't you see that? Being with you and sharing a life with you is all I want. It's all I need."

He drops his gaze to me. "You mean it?"

"Yes." I kiss his lips. "I mean every word."

His mouth twitches and then a slow smile spreads across his lips. Wrapping me in his arms, he takes charge and kisses me passionately—so passionately I'm sure my toes would curl if I weren't in these damn heels. I laugh as he leans me backward, as if we're dancing, and then brings me back up, close to his chest. He smells like sandalwood and a little bit of the rum from the drinks he had after dinner and I bask in it.

"You're an incredible woman," he whispers on my lips. "I don't know why you love me the way you do."

The following morning, after we share a delivered breakfast in the kitchen, I go shopping while Gabriel spends time at the pool. We were in such a rush, I only packed one set of lingerie, so I figure it's best to shop for more, surprise him for a second night. We're having a good time and I need that to continue.

I drive the rental car to a boutique at the outlet called Vienna's. The store is quiet and there is only one employee working inside. I appreciate the serene atmosphere that allows me to shop peacefully and decide to pick out a burgundy red lingerie set, as well as a blue set. I ask the employee, by the name of Lacy, if I can try it on and she escorts me to the fitting rooms.

I try on the garments quickly, and when I'm satisfied with them, I turn to open the door. But as I open the door, someone is standing outside it.

I gasp when I realize it's Jocelyn.

CHAPTER FORTY-SIX

ADIRA

"Jocelyn?" I scan our surroundings with wide eyes. Lacy is on the opposite side of the store, casually placing a dress on a velvet hanger. "What the hell are you doing here?"

"I was at the pretzel stand and saw you come in here," she says, smiling.

"What?" I work hard to swallow.

She lowers her gaze to the lingerie sets tangled between my fingers. "Wow. Doesn't this look familiar." She scoffs and then smirks.

"Jocelyn, what are you doing here?"

She peers around with a dip between her brows. "Where is he anyway?"

"Why?" I counter.

"I'm just asking. I figured he'd be close by—never leaving your side after the whole condom thing."

"Jocelyn," I say, more seriously this time. "Why. Are. You. Here?"

"Relax. I just left a space that was for lease across the street to see if I can open another Jessa's."

I press my lips. I don't know if I can believe that. What are the odds that she's in Destin for work while I'm here? I told her I was going out of town, but I didn't tell her *where* I was going.

She smirks again, then studies her reflection in the mirror behind me, and I try to control my chaotic heartbeat. She bounces a floppy curl in the palm of her hand, springing it back where it belongs. "I sent you a text last night, but you didn't text me back. What's up with that?"

"I was out for dinner with Gabriel."

"Did you guys have fun?"

"Jocelyn." I pull her away from the mirror. "I really need you to leave."

Jocelyn takes a step closer to me, tipping her chin. "I was just stopping by to check on a friend," she says.

I avoid a frown. "Okay, well, thanks for that, but I'm fine. Really."

She looks me hard in the eye several seconds longer before stepping back and putting on a smile. "Okay, well, don't be a stranger. Text me when you're back in Tampa. Or don't. Your choice." With that, she's walking through the boutique and out of the door.

"Were the lingerie sets okay?" someone asks. I look left at Lacy, who is smiling broadly with her hands clasped together.

"Yes," I tell her, glancing at the door again. Jocelyn is gone, but something in my gut tells me she may not be gone for good. "They're perfect. I'll take them."

CHAPTER FORTY-SEVEN

ADIRA

I don't hear from Jocelyn for the rest of the trip, which brings much relief. Not only that, but I had an amazing getaway with Gabriel and life seems to be getting back on track for me again. I got what I wanted and that was my husband back. I haven't seen him sneaking text messages or calls, as he promised, and he places his phone face-side up while sleeping, which proves to me that he doesn't have anything to hide anymore.

He and Julianna are done and that alone is enough to make me proud. I did that, and all with a fake run-in and a latex condom.

What is it they say about long-lasting love? That people fall in and out of love all the time, right? Perhaps Gabriel and I had fallen out of love and he sought Julianna and Jocelyn for attention that I wasn't able to give. Now that we're back on track, there shouldn't be a need for him to go back to either of them ever again.

I still find it strange that Jocelyn showed up in Destin, and I have to wonder if maybe Gabriel told her he was going out of town or something. And sure, she said she was there for work, but what are the odds that we run into each other in the same place at the same time? For all I know, it could be a big coincidence. Or maybe Jocelyn truly was worried and took it upon herself to check on me . . . in person. Wow. That sounds completely insane.

Gabriel and I are on our way back home after leaving the airport. He's behind the wheel of his Range Rover and I'm settled into the passenger seat, scraping my cuticles, still thinking about that run-in with Jocelyn. I glance at Gabriel as he sings along to a song by Pharrell and Snoop Dogg. He sits behind the wheel, so confident, and I have this nagging inside me—something begging me to just ask the damn question already and get it over with.

"Hey, Gabriel?" I call as he turns on his signal to get in the right lane.

"Yeah, babe?"

I chew on my bottom lip for a moment, lowering my gaze to the rings on my finger. I put them back on for the trip—and so he wouldn't notice that I'd taken them off.

"Why don't you talk about *her* with me anymore?"

Gabriel turns his head a fraction to look at me and his brows draw together. "Talk to you about who? What are you talking about?" He narrows his eyes and, sensing the defensiveness in his tone, I adjust in my seat.

No, no, no. You've said too much.

"Nothing," I say quickly. "Never mind. It's nothing."

"No," he says, laughing now, but it's a nervous laugh. A laugh full of questions. "What do you mean? Talk to you about who?"

"It's nothing," I tell him, looking out of my window.

"Clearly it's something," he pushes.

I don't say anything, and he groans. "Typical."

"What?" I ask, looking at him.

"You always do this. Start shit, then clam up when I ask you to explain yourself."

"Okay, fine." I sit up in my seat and glare a hole into the side of his head. "Why don't you talk to me about Julianna?"

"What?" he spits. His jaw drops and I notice him grip the wheel tighter. "What the hell, Adira?"

"Don't act like it's a stupid question. I–I know you've been fucking her behind my back, Gabriel. I know every-thing, okay?"

"Wow. Wow, wow, wow. Adira, do you realize how fucking crazy you sound right now?"

"Oh, I sound crazy? Is it really crazy of me to hate the fact that you're sneaking around with her?"

Gabriel's eyes stretch wide, a look of pure shock and dis-belief on his face. "Holy shit, Adira. Are you fucking serious right now?" Gabriel runs a hand down the length of his face. "You're fucking crazy. This is fucking crazy. Wow."

"Yeah, okay. I'm the crazy one." I fold my arms and press my back against the seat.

"I don't even understand where this is coming from!" Gabriel shouts. "We had a good time in Destin! Why are you even bringing this shit up?"

"You know what? Forget about it," I mutter." I don't even know why we went on that trip in the first place. I know you only wanted to go because you can't be with her any-more."

I turn away, staring out the window, and realize the car is slowing down. Gabriel is pulling to the side of the road, but he doesn't stop with ease. He slams on the brakes, causing my body to jerk forward. When I look over at him, he growls, "How the fuck do you know *anything* about that?"

I stare him in the eyes, refusing to back down. I've had enough of pretending I don't know about her. Enough of him walking all over me. "Because it's obvious," I say evenly. "You only come home to me when you can't be with her."

He matches my stare, and for a moment I see remorse in

his eyes. He's feeling guilty. As he should. But of course that guilt doesn't last long. He puts the car in Drive again and pulls back onto the road, muttering, "Un-fucking-believable," beneath his breath.

When we make it back home, Gabriel unloads the truck while I order myself pizza for dinner. Yes, for me. Not him. I'm still pissed at him.

After I've ordered the pizza and pulled out a bottle of wine from the wine fridge in the kitchen, I hear Gabriel's phone ping and watch him walk out the back door to get to the deck.

I step around the corner, sneaking a glance at him. His phone is pressed to his ear and his back is turned to me. He's talking to her.

I take a step away, not wanting him to see me, then rush upstairs to our bedroom to get to the balcony doors. I twist the knob and open the door quietly, then sit in one of the chairs as his voice carries.

"But what if it was?" I hear him ask in a whisper-hiss.

He's quiet for a moment.

"No, listen, Julianna. I'm heading your way now. We'll talk more about this in person, okay? I promise you, I would never do that to you."

Is he fucking serious? After all we did in Destin? After all he said to me, he's just going right back to her like that? I get it, I confronted him in the car, but why is he *running* to her? Did I push too hard?

Shit. My heart nearly fails me when I hear him reenter the house. I walk back inside and draw in a deep breath while taking out my earrings, bracing myself for the moment he calls my name to hand me some lame excuse about needing to leave, like business he has to tend to or a run to the pharmacy for some bodywash or some other shit.

"Hey, Adira?" Gabriel calls from down the stairs.

"Yeah?" I answer, walking back into the bedroom.

"I have to make a run. You need anything?"

"Where are you going?"

"To the pharmacy. I used the last bit of my deodorant at the beach."

He's such a fucking liar. "Oh, okay. No, I don't need anything."

"'Kay." He's quiet for a second, as if debating whether to say anything else. "Uh, text me if you do, I guess."

I hear the front door shut and when I go downstairs to look out of the window, his car is gone. It's almost evening, nearing five p.m. when he goes. He doesn't return until after midnight, and he doesn't join me in the bedroom to sleep with me.

Instead, he sleeps in the guest room, like he always does when he's upset with me but has spent a night with *her.*

CHAPTER FORTY-EIGHT

ADIRA

The following morning, I wake up and pretend I didn't hear a single word Gabriel said to Julianna on the deck yesterday. I shower, get dressed in a powdery pink maxi dress—which irks me to no end, considering it's Julianna's favorite color, but pink is good to wear around Dina—apply a little makeup, and go downstairs to the kitchen. I pick up a menu from the basket next to the fridge that's stuffed with catering company cards and menus.

Today is an important day and everything must run smoothly. I call to place my order for brunch, which will be delivered in two hours—just in time for Dina's arrival.

Gabriel comes downstairs about an hour after me. I notice he can hardly look at me as he enters the kitchen. He's fully dressed in jeans and a crisp button-down shirt and a pair of shoes I selected with him at the outlet we shopped at while in Destin. He's trimmed his goatee and put on cologne that I can smell from across the kitchen.

"I should get to work," he says.

"Do you think you can go in late today?"

"For what?" he asks.

"Dina is coming. She should be here within the next hour."

"Oh." He presses his lips, then checks his watch. "Well, I guess I can go in after she arrives."

"Good," I say, walking up to him and patting his chest. "Cause I ordered brunch for all of us."

I leave the kitchen to go to my office, pretending I don't feel Gabriel watching me walk away. I could bring up the fact that I heard his conversation last night, but that's adding more fuel to the fire and, as I said before, today needs be perfect for Dina. She has to see that I'm okay.

It's typical of Dina to show up exactly twenty-seven minutes *after* the time she said she'd be arriving. Dina is never on time—I've come to terms with that after spending nineteen years of my life around her. When she says she'll be somewhere at a certain time, I know not to expect her for at least thirty minutes afterward, which is why, if I have an event or if I plan to meet her somewhere, I always tell her to arrive an hour before the time I'm planning. It saves my sanity and allows her to still be herself.

As soon as I see Dina step out of the back of her Lyft, I can't help feeling a sense of relief, especially as she walks up to me and embraces me in her thin arms. She smells earthy, like cinnamon and the outdoors and adventure, and her lips are always brushed with a light tint of nude gloss, as well as her nails. Her hair, which is a beautiful, peppery gray, is pulled up into a fuzzy ponytail, a terra-cotta-colored scarf loosely tied around the edges. Dina is known for wearing baggy clothes— today it's baggy, khaki-colored pants, tan sandals, and a long white tank-top beneath a reddish-orange kimono. Ask anyone who knows her and they'll tell you Dina Holloway is the definition of peace and comfort.

There's something about her personality—her presence.

You're left with no choice but to smile, to feel at ease, and to not feel judged. I feel that as she hugs me longer than the average hug and groans while saying, "Ooh, I've missed you so much, my beloved."

"I've missed you too," I say over her shoulder.

She finally releases me from the hug to hold on to my upper arms. "Let me look at you." Her smile continues as she looks me all over, from my crown to my feet. "You look good. So, so good. This pink dress is so beautiful with your complexion."

I force a smile, and as I do, Gabriel appears in the doorway, smiling at Dina.

"Gabriel! Hi! I'm so happy to see you!" She gives him a huge hug and a side kiss on the cheek, and Gabriel chuckles while hugging her back.

"It's great to see you too, Dina."

"Come on in," I insist. "I have brunch waiting for you. Gabriel, will you take her bags to the guest room?" I eye my husband, letting it be clear to him that the guest room will be occupied and that he can't hide in there anymore after his late-night scandals.

"Of course." Gabriel avoids my eyes as he goes for Dina's luggage, and while he does, I walk to the kitchen with Dina, distracting her with a question about the flight. Because that's the thing about Dina. She can sense tension from a mile away, especially when it comes from me, but one thing Dina loves is talking about herself. Don't get me wrong, she's a terrific listener, but . . . well, there is no one she loves more than herself. After all, without self-love, she wouldn't be able to help and love on others.

"So, how is work?" I ask her as we put food on our plates. The restaurant with our catering order set up brunch on the island and there's a lot of food, ranging from pancakes to French toast, fruit, and bagels—entirely too much for three people to eat.

"Oh, please, Adira," she whines. "I didn't come all this way to talk about work. I came here for you. You should be telling me how *your* work is."

I laugh. "Well, work is good. We have a lot of new designs we'll be launching this fall and next year."

"Oh really? And do I get to try them on first? Be that influencer thing they call it these days? You know I have about twelve-thousand followers on Instagram now because of the Reiki practice. Turns out people love learning about that kind of stuff and getting behind the scenes on it."

"That's more followers than I have, so hey—congrats to that. But I thought you hated social media."

"I do hate it, but I can't deny that it's a good tool. I want to spread my word on healing, not hide it. I suppose social media is good for that and that alone. It connects me to people around the world who can't access me personally in Florida."

"Hmm."

Gabriel walks into the kitchen and grabs a bagel. "I'm gonna head to work now," he says when Dina and I are seated at the table. He kisses my cheek and Dina smiles at us. "See you tonight."

"Okay." I smile and watch as he leaves the kitchen, biting into the bagel and turning a corner to leave. My eyes linger, and I wish he'd come back, but it's also a good thing he's leaving now. It'll spare us any arguments in front of her.

"How was vacation?" Dina asks, grinning from ear to ear.

"It was good," I say, nodding and picking up a strawberry. "We bonded so much. I didn't realize how badly we needed that alone time together. Work has been killing me."

Dina puts her fork down and frowns. "*Killing* you?"

"I don't mean it like that."

"Adira, I told you, if work becomes too much, you need to take breaks. Humans aren't meant to—"

"*Work themselves to death,*" I mutter, before she can. "I know, Dina. I know."

She reaches across the table and grabs my hand. "Promise me that if your soul cries for a break, you'll take it. Not just from work, but from *anything* in your life that may be a stressor."

I cling to her hand and provide an assured smile. "I promise I will."

"Good. Now hurry up and eat so you can pack."

CHAPTER FORTY-NINE

ADIRA

Before boarding the plane, I sent Gabriel a text to let him know I was heading out of town with Dina and would see him in two days. However, when I landed, there was no text back from him. I figured he was busy with work, but hours passed and still no return messages.

By then, Dina and I had checked into our hotel, caught lunch and dinner, and it wasn't until Dina was in the shower that I thought to call him. His phone rang once, then sent me to voice mail.

"What the fuck, Gabriel?" I grumble. Just as I feel the urge to chuck the phone across the room, an alert pops up on my phone, a notification from my home-security system.

I open the app to get to the live camera, and Gabriel's car is parked in front of the house. He's walking to the door with his keys, and I watch as he unlocks the front door. Dina is still showering, so I nestle myself on the center of the bed, studying the screen and turning on the speaker to hopefully hear something.

I don't hear anything but steps and commotion, but what I see within the next few minutes catches me by total surprise. Gabriel walks out of the house with three stuffed duffel bags.

Clothes hang haphazardly out of them, and one shirt even falls on the ground. He slings the bags into the trunk of his vehicle, goes back to snatch up the shirt, and then returns to lock the door. He then hustles to the driver's side and starts up the Range Rover to leave.

It takes me but a moment to process what exactly just happened. Three bags packed. He's in a rush. He's either going out of town for a work trip or he's taking those clothes to spend time with *her*. He knows I'm out of town—that I'll be gone for days.

"Adira!" Dina screams my name and I gasp, whipping my head up and locking eyes with hers. She's standing in one of the robes I gave her—a turquoise one with a koi fish design, but even after her shower, she doesn't look relaxed. Her eyes are stretched wide, her mouth slightly agape.

"You're bleeding," she says, walking up to me.

"Huh?" I look down as her eyes fall to my forearm. Scratch marks have formed on the inside of my arm, pierced by my own nails.

"Oh . . . shit." I climb off the bed and go to the bathroom to rinse it under the sink. It stings a little beneath the warm water. When it's rinsed, I study the scratches, realizing I went a little too deep in my own skin.

"Is everything okay?" Dina asks, standing between the frames of the bathroom door.

"Yeah—everything's fine. I really think the new body-wash I'm using is causing an allergic reaction or something. I've been so itchy lately."

"You're probably using one with too many chemicals and fragrances in it," she says, then turns to open her suitcase. "Use mine when you shower. It's all natural and organic, and it's made by a Black-owned business I really love. One scrub of their wash and you'll be in love too. Trust me." Dina grins over her shoulder.

"I'll take a shower now," I tell her.

I close the door as she gives me her back to pick out a set of pajamas. I start up the shower, but I don't get in. Instead, I pick up my phone, which I placed on the bathroom counter and check my messages again. There is nothing new from Gabriel.

How can he do this? How can he go back to her so easily? And how the hell can she be so quick to forgive him?

I wait until Dina falls asleep before picking up my phone and sending the text I've been contemplating.

Hey. We need to talk when I'm back in town. The plan didn't work. He's with her again.

CHAPTER FIFTY

Bower didn't show up for three days afterward. Claudette was quieter—practically avoiding us—but I was satisfied with that. It'd been three days, so I'd assumed she'd spoken to Bower, found out the truth, and was done with him.

Boy, was I wrong.

On the fourth day, Panda and I got off the school bus and walked home, and my heart sank to my stomach when I saw Bower's car parked in front of our house. I gripped Panda's forearm and she hissed "Ow" before peering up at me.

"Sorry," I whispered. "Sorry—I, um . . . how about we go for a walk?"

Panda frowned. "But I wanna go home and take a nap."

"You can take a nap at Mrs. Stein's. She—she has those short-bread cookies you really like." I forced a smile. I couldn't show Panda I was worried. She'd catch on, and the last thing I wanted her to do was cause a scene.

"Yes, cookies! Let's go!" Panda dragged me away from the house and I breathed a sigh of relief. Mrs. Stein's house was half a mile away from ours, but we didn't mind the walk. It was a quiet stroll we took, and we often found rocks we liked on the side of the road. There

was also a trail not too far off and we'd go there to see the toads after rainy days.

Mrs. Stein's house wasn't like ours. It was nicer, quieter, and not as gloomy. Her house was lakeside, and she owned two boats. Her home was built like ours, a one-story cabin, however Mrs. Stein's was a cherrywood, while ours was more a dark oak. Mrs. Stein had rocking chairs on her porch and lots of plants. We didn't have anything on our porch because Claudette found gardening inconvenient. "We don't own the place anyway. If anyone should be gardening, it's the landlord," Claudette would grumble.

Mr. Stein died three years before, so Mrs. Stein was often lonely. Claudette had taken it upon herself to cook a meal of lasagna for Mrs. Stein around the time he died and we went with her. Mrs. Stein spoiled us with cookies she'd baked while we visited. "You're welcome here anytime," she'd told us, and I took her word for it.

When we approached her doorstep, I felt my chest become heavier, as if I were lying down and an elephant's foot was on top of me. Claudette would be curious as to why we were late, but I didn't care if it meant protecting Panda from Bower. I gave the door a quick knock and heard Mrs. Stein yell, "Just a minute!"

The locks clicked and the door swung open, and there stood Mrs. Stein, dressed in a green robe. She wore pajamas beneath it and had a green face mask painted over her sable skin.

"Oh, hey, girls!" she sang out.

"Hi, Mrs. Stein. Sorry—did we come at a bad time?"

"Absolutely not. Get in here." She ushered us in, and I smiled as I entered her home. It was warm inside—she often kept it warmer than usual, even if it was nearing eighty degrees outside—and it smelled like lavender and cookies. It always smelled like cookies. She baked for the local library sometimes and left cookie snack bags for the visitors or the homeless to have. Her home was cozy, with suede brown furniture, bookshelves built into the walls, and little antiques that filled the nooks and crannies.

"You'll have to pardon me. I used to have self-care days once a week with my daughter. She's moved out and doing her own thing now, but I still continue the tradition. Oh, you know what?" Mrs. Stein said, pointing at us and smirking. "I'm actually glad you two stopped by. I tried my hand at macarons today and I could use a few guinea pigs who can give them a taste before I send them off to the women's shelter." She grinned and patted us on the shoulder. "Is everything okay?"

"Yes, we're okay." I smiled at her, keeping strong. "I mentioned your cookies and Panda got excited and now we're here."

"Hey!" Panda shouted. "That wasn't—"

I bumped her with my elbow to shut her up.

"Well, don't you two worry," Mrs. Stein said. "You came just in time. I pulled them out of the oven not too long ago—all I have to do is fill 'em. I have caramel and vanilla fillings. I also have a green tea flavor, but y'all are too young to know anything about that." Mrs. Stein laughed at her own joke, trotting her way to the kitchen.

"Why did you lie?" Panda asked when she was out of earshot.

"You want the cookies, don't you?"

"Yeah, but I didn't really wanna come here."

I sighed and grabbed her hand. "I'm sorry. I didn't mean to use you in a lie. I just . . . I think we should stay here for an hour or so. Hang out with Mrs. Stein. She's really lonely. Remember I told you about Mr. Stein?"

Panda nodded with sad eyes.

"Plus, she loves hanging out with us."

"Yeah, I know. Welp." Panda slid out of her backpack and dumped it onto the middle of the floor. "I'm ready for macarons, Mrs. Stein!" she shouted, running to the kitchen.

I laughed and picked up her bag, placing it in a corner, out of the way, but my smile didn't last long. I hated lying to Panda. I really did. Sure, I could've told her the truth—that I didn't want to take her home because Bower was there and he creeped me the fuck out— but she wouldn't have understood. And she also didn't remember *what he'd done to her. As long as I could make sure he never did it again, I was fine with lying, and maybe Panda would forget all about what I talked to Claudette about.*

We would have to go back home eventually, but if I could prevent him from being around her as much as possible, I would, even if consequences lay ahead.

CHAPTER FIFTY-ONE

ADIRA

I'm used to putting on a façade for the sake of others—hell, for the sake of myself. For everyone to think I'm a decent human being—one who is seemingly perfect—I wear the smiles the world expects of me, I give to charities, and I pretend that when I see someone after a long time, I've been eager to see them for weeks.

It's all bullshit, of course. I'm not much of a people person, but when it comes to my life, I *have* to be a people person. If I'm not, I always fall . . . and I can't afford to fall right now.

That's why, when I'm in Kellan and Ana Wilder's home, I laugh at their jokes, drink their mimosas, dig into their food, and tell my own made-up stories when I need to.

"I'm so glad y'all could make it," Kellan says, topping off my mimosa for me.

I nod and smile.

"Please don't give her too much," Dina says to him.

"That's the last pour, swear on it." He crosses his heart and Dina laughs and waves an oh-stop-it hand at him.

I avoid rolling my eyes at the whole thing. She only says

that because she thinks I've taken my medication today. I didn't. As a matter of fact, I haven't taken them in two weeks, and I've been completely fine with that. I want to have a baby. This cocktail of pills will only hinder my chances of conception.

We're standing on Kellan and Ana's brand-new deck, which has an ocean view. String lights hang on the wooden banisters and the furniture is made with wicker and ivory cushions. Plants are in every corner and hanging from the railing. A swimming pool is just off to the right, four lounge chairs neatly lined up outside it. A firepit is built into the deck as well, but it's covered for baby Tia's safety. Tia is their daughter. The entire deck and pool area is beautiful, modern, simple, and practical, just like Ana. I know for a fact Kellan didn't pick out a damn thing. None of it suits him. He's not a go-big-or-go-home sort of person, but Ana is.

It's interesting to see the upgrade Kellan has made with his life, though. When I met him, he was just the intern of a well-known publicity rep. Now, he's running his own company, has a beautiful wife, and a one-year-old daughter with eyes as bright and brown as his.

I met Kellan at a college party my dormmate dragged me to. It was off campus, and there were people from other colleges attending. I didn't want to drink and smoke and do a crazy number of shots, so I went outside where a firepit was burning. There were a group of people there. I liked to think of them as the people with a little common sense. Each of them had one drink they nursed all night, but each conversation was raw and honest—all swirling with big goals and dreams, ambitions, student loan debts, and what we wanted for ourselves after graduating college.

When I heard Kellan speak about what he wanted, I knew I wanted to be his friend, just to pick his brain a little more.

He was an ambitious creature. The way he spoke so elo-
quently, proving to everyone and himself that he wasn't your
typical Black dude who came from nothing, on the streets,
gunning or hustling. He was book smart—had gotten an aca-
demic scholarship and all—and he was proud of it. I admired
that about him—how proud he was to be himself.

He had no clue who I was. We were both strangers who
told each other our dreams that night and somehow it bonded
us—but not in a sexual way. It was all emotional, mental. He
felt like a best friend—one of those friends you can bond with,
stop talking to for weeks or months and then speak again as if
no time had passed.

I wanted to launch a company that sold silky robes and he
wanted to work in the PR field because he found the work
fulfilling and always evolving. When I told Dina about him,
she said nothing happened by chance and that when people
like that come into our lives, they're meant to be there—that
they're with us for a reason. He said he was great at adapting
and seeing as he's living in an oceanfront home with a wife
wearing a designer dress that I'm sure cost over $2000, I knew
that to be true. Such a risk for her to take while holding a
baby, who could vomit all over her at any minute, but I also
got it.

"So, what's it like being the owner of such a luxurious
company, Adira?" Ana asks me. She has her daughter on one
hip and a drink in her free hand. She's clearly tipsy by the way
she wobbles on her heels, continuously reminding me that her
baby is no longer breastfed because she wasn't getting enough
milk. "It was such a sad time," Ana said earlier. "I cried for
two days. I would have nursed her until she was two years old
if I could. Isn't that right, boo-boo?" And like the good person I am, I smiled in awe as she kissed her daughter on her
chubby little cheek and then tickled her. A pinch of envy
coursed through me as she did, that I couldn't deny. I wanted

what she had—the dutiful husband, the gorgeous child, the happiness at home.

"It's not *that* luxurious," I say, laughing a little.

"Adira is always modest," Dina interjects.

"That she is," Kellan says, smirking. "She's always been that way, but I gotta say, a lot of your ideas are stellar, Adira. Remember when I was telling you about that company that sells sheets who wanted my help? You gave me the idea for them to do bundles and now they're thriving. They've opened up two stores since."

"Really?" I exclaim. "Wow, that's incredible, Kellan."

"Why do you downplay your success anyway?" Ana asks, and now I really know she's on the verge of being drunk because that's a deep question, and one I don't feel like answering.

As if Dina senses my unease, she says, "Adira has always been humble about what she does. I think it's part of the reason she's so successful."

I nod and smile.

"Well, let's give a cheers to that, huh?" Ana raises her glass, and we all follow suit, clinking ours with hers. Tia giggles on her hip, then claps her hands to the clinking noise, and Dina coos at her before extending her arms. "Oh, look at her! Let me cuddle that juicy baby!"

As Dina plays with Tia, Ana walks over to me and asks, "Do you plan on having kids one day?"

"Hopefully one day," I murmur. "We've actually been trying," I add in a whisper, so Dina won't hear.

Ana frowns while giving me her full attention. "Why are we whispering?" she asks in her own subtle whisper. I turn away with Ana and walk toward the railing that overlooks the pool. It's far enough that Dina won't hear.

"Because I want to surprise Dina with the news once I am pregnant."

"Ah, okay. That makes sense."

"But sometimes I think motherhood may not be right for me."

"Why? Because you're too busy as a businesswoman?" Ana asks, then sips from her glass with a smirk. "We're all busy, Adira. We just have to make time for what we really want." She may as well roll her eyes while she's at it. There's a snarky touch to her tone that I don't like, and I don't know what it is about this moment, but it reminds me of something Jocelyn said to me once. *"Boss up, boss lady."*

"That's precisely why, actually," I tell her. "If I were to have a baby, I'm not sure I'd be able to spend all my time at home with him or her. Even if I decide to take some time off, I won't really have anyone to provide for me the way Kellan does for you."

Ana side-eyes me. She does this often. She thinks I'm her competition. Kellan talks highly of me and she hates that he does. Hell, she's jealous of his damn sister. She pretends to be intrigued by what others have to say but throws shade the entire time. She has issues, but that's her problem. Fortunately, I know how to dismiss her insecurities.

"Why didn't you tell Gabriel to come?" she asks loudly now, turning to face Dina and Kellan. She really wants to ask why I don't tell Gabriel to step up and provide. And if she had, I'd tell her that Gabriel and I have already established our roles. There's nothing wrong with the woman being the breadwinner and having a husband support her in that. But Ana is old school. You can't really change her mind on the matter.

"He had to work," I say as Dina and Kellan glance my way.

"Hmm. For someone who can't provide stability for you, he sure does work a lot, doesn't he?" *Ah. There it is.*

"Ana, why don't you go check on the pie?" Kellan steps up to us, giving her a stern look. She purses her lips, polishes off her wine, and then trots away to go through the back door, flipping her blond hair over her shoulder on the way into the house.

"I'm sorry about that," Kellan says. "She's been a little off lately. Her therapist tells her it might be postpartum depression. I don't know. All of it's been so confusing. My life is a damn mess," he says, laughing, but there's hardly any humor in it.

"It'll get better, I'm sure." I pause, looking him over. "Have you spoken to Samira lately?"

"Nah." He pauses for a moment and swings his eyes over to Dina, who has Tia on her lap and is giving her small pieces of a sugar cookie. "Ever since Roland lost his cousin, she's been focused on him. They went through a lot, you know? I call, but she doesn't answer as much as she used to. But when I text to check in, she'll respond. Granted, it takes her hours, but she does hit me back, so I guess that's good enough to get from a sibling, right?"

"Yeah, that whole thing with Roland Graham was crazy, wasn't it? I remember reading about it all. Who would've known something like that could happen?"

"It was crazy and it almost got Samira killed," he mutters, clearly agitated by the subject. "I sometimes wonder if that's why she's been so distant. Maybe she's going through something mentally after that, you know?"

"Yeah, but she's still alive," I tell him. "Give her the space she needs. She'll come back around, I'm sure."

"Sure, she's still alive, Adira. But at what cost?" Kellan grumbles, then sips his beer. "You know I'm Roland's PR consultant now?" he asks, laughing.

"Really?"

"Yep. Samira convinced me to do it when that whole shitshow happened, and I felt bad for thinking he murdered his first wife, so . . . I look out for him now. Send opportunities his way. But it's not all for him. Mostly for Samira. There's still something about that motherfucker I don't trust."

"Wait—aren't they making a movie about him and his case or something?"

"Yeah, supposedly." Kell runs a hand along the length of his face. "It's going to be interesting, I tell you that. Samira doesn't do well with attention."

"Just keep looking out for her," I say. I'm not sure what else to add to that, so I sip my mimosa to fill the void instead.

Ana returns to the deck with another drink, wrapping an arm around Kellan's waist, and he slinks an arm around her shoulders, reeling her into his body. My husband should be here with me right now, doing the same thing. Holding me close, chatting with my friends, sacrificing some time from work to spend it with his wife. *Ugh.*

"Dina, whenever you're ready to do my session, we can start," Ana says.

"Oh, absolutely!" Dina pushes to a stand with Tia in her arms. She hands Tia to Kellan, who nuzzles her neck and makes her laugh as soon as he has her in his grasp.

I smile at the father and daughter and feel a pang in my stomach when I realize that that may never be a reality for me. I've been struggling to conceive for months, and now that Gabriel is sneaking around with Julianna again, I fear he may leave me. Sure, there is the option of going the sperm-donor route, but I want a baby with a man who loves me—someone who will help and gladly build a family with me. I work so much that it'll be hard to find someone to fill the space Gabriel has created. I need him. I need our marriage to work. If not, I'll never get the chance to see him hug or kiss *our* baby—a baby we share, a mixture of our DNA and blood and love.

Dina walks into the house with Ana and Kellan follows suit, and while they do, I pull out my phone to send Gabriel another text that I really hope he'll respond to.

Are you upset with me?

It isn't until Dina is deep in her Reiki session with Ana flat on her back, candles lit, and soft meditation music playing quietly through the hidden speakers, that I get a text back from him.

As Dina presses her palms to Ana's chest and tells her to inhale and exhale, I read his message, and my gut tightens into knots.

CHAPTER FIFTY-TWO

ADIRA

I've guzzled down three more drinks by the time Dina finds me. She spent nearly an hour talking to Ana after the Reiki session, then Tia became fussy and Ana had to put her down for bedtime.

Once that happened, Kell took it upon himself to show Dina his home office, and of course she oohed and aahed, which I find funny because Dina doesn't care about material things. But for the sake of uplifting other people and elevating their happiness, she pretends to care.

I don't realize Dina is in the kitchen until I'm topping off my wineglass with the remainder of the Zinfandel.

"How many?" Dina asks. I spin my glass around slowly and watch as she picks up a strawberry from the fruit tray.

"How many what?"

"Don't play the fool."

I sigh. "Five total."

"Seems like a lot, beloved."

"I'm fine, Dina."

Kellan and Ana enter the kitchen and I'm grateful for the interruption. "How about a game of Scrabble?" Kellan asks.

"Oh my God, Kellan. What are we, in a retirement home?" Ana blurts out.

I laugh harder at her remark than I intended, and I can feel Dina staring at me.

"Dina, would you like more wine?" Kellan asks, picking up the bottle I just emptied. "I can get another from the wine fridge."

"No, I'm okay, Kellan," she murmurs. "Thank you."

Ana's phone chimes in her hand and she lifts it up. "Aww! Oh my goodness! Look at this!" Ana turns her phone around and practically shoves it into my face. I wrap my fingers around her thin wrist and pull her arm back a bit but keep a smile on my face. Why the hell did I agree to come here? I love Kellan, but I can't stand Ana. And now I'm realizing the drinks are getting to me and I'd better calm down before I say something I regret.

"Aw, whose baby?" I ask, staring at the adorable brown baby on the screen. Her hair is full and curly and her eyes are bright from the flash of the phone on which the image was taken. She's wearing a pink onesie and is so, so tiny. If I saw her in person I'd be nervous holding someone so small.

"My friend Celeste. She and I go *way* back—like college days. You'd love her, Adira," Ana says, placing a hand on my arm. "She's a businesswoman, like you. Her husband owns a few island resorts. Her baby is three months old now. Such a beautiful girl."

I smile and nothing more.

"How long until catering arrives with dinner?" Kellan asks Ana.

"They should be here soon."

And, fortunately, they do arrive—within the next thirty minutes, to be exact. The caterers set up the kitchen counters with delicious seafood and sushi, and Ana sets out her "famous" chocolate pie and whipped cream for dessert. Never in my life have I had a chocolate pie, but whatever.

We eat at their six-seater dining table, Ana talking about mom life and raising Tia, Dina chatting about her traveling Reiki work, and Kell going on about his sister and her husband, which is the more interesting topic of all to me.

"I should FaceTime her," Kellan says after we've finished eating. "She'd answer a FaceTime. Maybe if I tell her you're here in a text, she'll pick up. She's always liked you, Adira."

"Oh yeah, go ahead and use me to get ahold of your sister." I laugh, swatting at him.

"Hey, it's worth a shot." Kellan picks up his phone and unlocks it, then pauses when his phone chimes with, what I assume is a notification. "Oh, shit."

"What?" Ana asks quickly, her brows drawing together with confusion.

"Y'all remember that girl they said killed Lola Maxwell and her husband?"

"Oh, yes! I remember hearing about that story!" Dina says. Her intrigue is apparent, her elbows on the table and her fingers clasped together. Her hands are holding her chin steady. "What about her?"

"I just got a notification from TMZ that says she's been released from prison."

"Seriously?" Ana exclaims, her jaw dropping.

"Yep—look." He turns his phone toward Ana so she can see, then turns it toward Dina, and then me. On the screen is an image of a woman dressed in gray. Her hair appears stringy and she has on a pair of dark sunglasses to shield her eyes. People with cameras surround her as a man holding her arm moves them out of the way while escorting her.

"I remember hearing about that. Why is she being released?" I ask.

"Says here that new evidence has been found." Kellan

scrolls down further and murmurs some of the words out loud. "The investigation has been opened again. A woman— who apparently was Ivy Hill's therapist—said she was paid to give Ivy information about Lola *by* someone who worked closely for Lola."

"What? Does it say who?" Ana inquires.

"Nah. Not yet, but I'm sure it'll turn up soon. People in Miami are nosy as hell. See, I knew that girl didn't do it! Something was off about that whole case."

"Yeah, right!" Ana blurts out. She's doing a lot of that— blurting. "Baby, you have to be kidding. She dropped her whole life just to be in Lola's. She stalked her way in." Ana looks from Kellan to me and Dina. "I mean, that's some pretty psycho-stalker shit, right?"

"Yeah, it is. But stalking someone to ruin their life— which in my opinion was sort of justified, considering Lola basically committed a hit and run on her parents—and mur- dering the person are two different things," Kellan argues. "Everyone serves revenge differently. That poor girl just got caught up in it all. I mean, think about it, Ana, if she wanted to kill her, she'd have done it as soon as she met Lola. That Ivy Hill girl was misguided, but I can't say I blame her for what she did. She was mentally ill. It was bound to happen."

"Still a fucking psycho. I could never accept someone being a stalker," Ana grumbles.

I straighten in my seat. Ana using the word "stalker" is making me feel nauseous. I turn my eyes to Dina, and as if she's noticed my discomfort at the subject, she narrows her eyes at me with a slight tilt of her head. It's her way of asking if I'm okay.

"I'm gonna run to the bathroom," I say to no one in par- ticular, but Ana and Kellan don't hear me. They're too busy debating over the mental health of this Ivy Hill woman.

I get up from the table and try my hardest not to stumble.

My head is spinning and my mouth is tacky from sticky soy sauce and sushi as well as wine, but I'm fine. I'm completely fine.

When I make it to the bathroom, I turn on the faucet for the cold water and run my hands beneath it. Then I bring some of the water to my neck, which feels hot. I want so badly to splash some on my face, but I'm wearing makeup and don't want it to smear.

I turn off the faucet and feel the burning weight of my phone in the back pocket of my jeans. Pulling it out, I unlock it and read Gabriel's message again—the one he sent earlier that I've been terrified to respond to.

No. But you need to stay away from Julianna.

CHAPTER FIFTY-THREE

ADIRA

I read my husband's text several more times, trying to figure out how he knows I was ever near her. Did Julianna tell him? But how the hell would she have known who I was? I was careful. I made sure . . .

One.

Two.

Three.

And we . . .

"Fuck that." I don't know what I'm thinking, but I sit on the toilet seat and FaceTime Jocelyn. She answers after the first ring.

"And she calls! What a surprise," Jocelyn exclaims.

I try to roll my eyes, but I can't. I'm drunk. There, I admit it. I don't drink much and when I do, it's normally limited to two glasses. I've had six tonight.

"Are you in Tampa?" I ask.

"Yes. Why do you ask?"

"Okay . . . do you remember when we snuck to Julianna's neighborhood to watch Gabriel?"

"Oh, Lord," Jocelyn groans. "Of course I remember. How could I forget?"

"Can you do that for me tonight?"

"Tonight? You must think you're the only busy person in the world," she scoffs.

"No—I know, I'm sorry. I know you're busy, but . . . listen. Gabriel knows, okay? He knows I was around Julianna."

Jocelyn's face stiffens. "How does he know?"

"I–I may have slipped up after our vacation. He left that same night, and I think he confessed and told her who I was and all about me to get her back. Men do dumb shit like that. Get all honest and lay it all out."

"Okay, but even so, why would he tell you to leave her alone?"

I blink several times, hesitant. "W–what?"

"I just mean why can't he let her go?"

"How did you know he said that?" I ask, staring at her through the screen.

"What do you mean?"

"You just said he told me to leave Julianna alone. How do you know he said that? Have you been talking to Gabriel?"

"What? Are you serious? Do you know how you sound?"

"I never told you that, Jocelyn!"

Jocelyn looks away and nods at someone off the screen. "Look, I have to go."

"Wait—Jocelyn, how—" She hangs up before I can get my question out.

I lower the phone and stare at the screen. What the hell? How does she know? Gabriel must've spoken to her. Maybe he thought to check in on her since he hadn't heard from her in a while, and that's the thing about Gabriel. He knows how to charm his way back into a woman's good graces . . . or back into her panties.

"Shit," I hiss, standing and sliding my phone into my back pocket again. I wash my hands for no reason other than to think about this some more, dry them off, but when I open the door, Dina is standing on the other side.

"Oh, shit!" I gasp, pressing a hand to my heart. "Dina, you scared me!"

"I'm sorry. I didn't mean to. Just wanted to check on you. Everything okay?" She looks me all over, her head slightly tilted.

"Yes. Everything's fine."

"I thought I heard you talking to someone in there," she says.

"Oh—yeah, I was just giving Gabriel a call." I wave a hand and start to walk past her, but Dina catches me by the wrist before I can go and stops me. "Adira." Her voice is careful yet stern.

I turn my head just a fraction to meet her eyes.

"Tell me what's going on."

"Nothing's going on, Dina."

"If nothing is going on, why are you drunk-talking to Gabriel in the bathroom?"

My head spins some more as I try to think of a lie, but I'm no good at lying when I'm drunk. However, I do get agitated when I drink, and when I realize her hand is still locked around my wrist and her eyes are hard and judgmental, it triggers something in me.

I snatch my arm out of her hand and frown. "For the last time, I told you I'm fine, Dina," I snap. "I will be fine, so please stop treating me like I'm a child."

Dina stares at me, but her face doesn't change. Mostly because she's used to this. When I'm triggered, she knows to back away, retreat, and so she does. She raises her hands in the air, a guiltless gesture, then takes a step back, tipping her chin. "Okay. If you say you're fine, I believe you." She turns to enter the bathroom, but before she closes the door in my face, she says, "After I use the bathroom, we're leaving."

CHAPTER FIFTY-FOUR

ADIRA

After we leave Kell and Ana's and catch a Lyft back to our hotel, I can feel Dina watching me. The thing about Dina is that she's subtle, but after spending over eighteen years of my life around her, I know her ways. I've adapted to them . . . and she has to mine. That's why I'm not surprised she's giving me the eye. She knows when something's off, and I really need her to ease up, so I play it cool.

When we make it to our hotel room, I begin to pack my things. I turn on the TV and stream old '90s cartoons I used to love. Dina giggles here and there as she tunes in to them as well, but she can't fool me. She's still checking me out, looking through her peripheral vision. Watching me whenever I check my phone.

There's only one way to get her to take a step back.

"Fine," I mutter after I've taken a shower and am dressed in pajamas. I've cracked open my laptop to check some emails. There aren't many, fortunately—then again, my staff knows I'm out of town and not to be contacted unless it's urgent.

"Fine what?"

"I'll tell you what's up with me, and why I drank so much at Kellan and Ana's."

Dina sits up straighter on the bed, keeps her face calm, but I can see in her eyes how eager she is for me to feed her details. "Okay. Only if you're in the mood."

I cross my legs on the bed and run the pad of my forefinger over my manicured fingernail. I had them painted orange, as well as my toes. I don't even know why. I've never really been a fan of orange.

"Work has been a lot lately."

Dina nods and waits for me to continue.

"It's just—okay, so we have these new designs to turn in for production, right?" I lean forward, really getting into the conversation.

"Right."

"Well, Vito has sent a few that I don't really like, but everyone else thinks the designs will sell. I don't know if maybe I think old school or what, but the designs are too much. Too colorful, too artsy. I love the minimal look."

"People love artsy things these days. The more colorful and artsy the better, I'd say."

"Of course you'd say that. You're Dina the Unicorn." I laugh and she laughs too and I'm glad.

Dina sighs and pushes one of her locs behind her ear. "There's nothing wrong with trying new things, Adira. Yes, it's an investment and a risk, but sometimes risks are good. After all, if you hadn't taken the risk with your online store, where would you be now?"

"That's true."

"And as I said before, if work is starting to feel like too much, take a longer break. Allow someone else to take the lead on decisions. Do whatever makes you feel comfortable, but also take care of yourself and your headspace. Too much stress isn't good, you know that."

"I know." I focus on my lap.

"Are you feeling triggered?"

"No." I shake my head carefully. Not too slow or too fast, but in between. Too fast and she'll assume I'm hiding something. Too slow and she'll think I'm hesitating.

Dina is quiet for a moment, studying my face carefully.

"Do you remember when you destroyed the painting I got from Blair?"

"Oh gosh, not that again," I mutter, conjuring a laugh. "I barely even remember that."

"I'm just asking," Dina says with her own flutter of a laugh. "What about when you punched that Shakayla girl in the face?"

"Dina," I groan, rolling my eyes. "Please."

"When I heard you on the phone in the bathroom at Kellan and Ana's, you sounded on edge, Adira. It sounded like something was wrong. And before you decided to destroy my painting or punch Shakayla in the face, you lashed out at me. Just like you did earlier at their house."

"Nothing's wrong, Dina, I promise you."

"I just don't want whatever is truly bugging you to turn into something else. These episodes when you lash out and get distant are dangerous." Another pause. "Have you been thinking about her?"

"About who?"

"You know who," she deadpans.

I shrug. "I've had some nightmares about her lately. Nothing too serious."

"What happens in your nightmares?"

"The same things that always happen."

Dina sighs, observing me. She wants me to elaborate, but I'm not in the mood to talk about her. "You're still taking your medications? I know you hate me asking, but I need to know you're leveled out."

"Yes, Dina. I'm taking them," I lie.

"Let me see them."

"Seriously?"

She raises a brow, clearly not joking. I climb off the bed with a sigh and go for my toiletry bag. I pull out the pill case and open each one to show her the pills inside. "Happy?"

"Yes. Are you meditating?" she asks when I replace the pill case.

"I've been kind of busy with working, but I've been doing it when I can at the office or at home at night, as a way to unwind."

"That's good." Dina sits against the headboard and brings the duvet up to her chest as I climb back on the bed. "I just worry about you, Adira. That's all." Her throat bobs up and down as she swallows. "Have you met anyone new? Made new friends?"

"Not really." I avoid her eyes. "Like I said, work is consuming me."

Dina doesn't say anything, but I can feel her glaring a hole into the side of my head.

"Okay, well, whether you're telling me the truth or not, I hope any new people in your life are good people. You remember the last friend you made. That didn't end well, and we don't want that again."

I nod in response, and Dina slouches down in the bed. "I'm gonna get some sleep. We have an early start tomorrow."

CHAPTER FIFTY-FIVE

ADIRA

Dina and I catch brunch before our flight back to Tampa. Relief swirls within me when the plane lands and I realize the countdown is on for her to leave.

She's mentioned having other clients she needs to see and one of them she's meeting for a consultation tonight in Tampa while she's here. She'll be in town for another week, but she'll mostly be working, which means she won't have as much time to hound me.

"I'll be calling you as soon as the consultation is over, okay?" she says over my shoulder as she hugs me.

"Okay."

"And remember, work is just a means to get by. Don't let it control you."

Easy for her to say. She travels, drinks herbal teas, manifests, and heals people for a living. My own little hippie.

Dina gives me one more kiss on the cheek before taking her bags with her and getting back into the Lyft that dropped us off. I watch her leave from my doorstep, and when she's out of the driveway and out of eyesight, I turn to go back into the house, locking the door behind me.

I rush straight to the den, where I drop my bags and fetch

my purse to dig out my phone. I didn't text Gabriel back after what he said about Julianna. Not because I didn't want to, but because if I had and he'd said something further to upset me, I wouldn't have been able to hide it from Dina.

To my surprise, there's a text from Jocelyn.

He's with her. He went back.

I text her back immediately. **Meet you at Jessa's?**

Sure. I'll be here for a couple of hours.

I grab my purse and keys and rush out of the house.

I walk past the customers at Jessa's and up the stairs, past the bar on the second floor, and to the private room Jocelyn led me to last time. I give the door a hard knock, then swing it open, and Jocelyn spins around from behind the bar.

"Fuck, Adira!" she hisses.

"Sorry—I didn't mean to barge in."

"Really? Cause I can't tell." She picks up her drink and takes a casual sip. "Gin and tonic?"

"No. Look, I don't have time for this anymore. Do you remember what you said the first time about Julianna? About . . . getting rid of her for good?"

Jocelyn narrows her eyes at me, slowly placing her short glass tumbler down on a coaster in front of her. "You mean . . ."

"Yes—I mean, no. I don't know."

"You mean yes," Jocelyn states firmly. "I thought you weren't about that life."

"I'm not."

"But now you are? After finding out he went back to her like a worthless dog after a bone."

"Stop talking about him like that."

"Why? You know it's true."

"Ugh." I charge forward, snatching up the gin and tonic from the counter and guzzling it down. Some of the liquid spills on the counter and my hand, but I don't care. I also don't normally like gin and tonics, but right now I'll take *anything* to ease the turmoil inside me.

With a smirk, Jocelyn prepares two more and slides one across the counter to me. I sit on the barstool, picking up the drink, nursing this one.

"I don't get it. What am I doing wrong?"

"Stop that."

"Buy why, Jocelyn? Why? Why can't he just choose me?"

"Why can't you choose yourself?"

I take a big chug of my drink.

"You said something on the phone," I state. "About what Gabriel said. How did you know?"

"Oh, Lord."

"Tell me."

"Because you told me, Adira."

"I . . . I don't remember telling you that."

"Well, you did, so . . ." She shrugs.

"Gabriel was with Julianna the night you texted me. And I only know because I hired a private investigator to go check it out for me. Consider it a favor," she says with a wink. She pulls something from beneath the counter and places it on top.

"What is this?" I ask, glaring at the white envelope.

"Open it and find out."

I stare up at her a moment before lowering my gaze and picking it up. My fingers tremble as I open the envelope, and I dig inside, pulling out three photos.

I place them flat on the counter, staring at each one. There's a twist in my stomach so tight I have the urge to vomit.

"He fucked her on her balcony," Jocelyn says.

"Oh my God," I cry.

"He was with her last night, ignoring your calls, your texts—ignoring you completely because he was too busy *fucking* her."

"Stop!" I shout. I shove the images away, feeling nothing but pure rage course through me.

"Why should I stop? Doesn't it make you angry?" Jocelyn demands.

"Of course it makes me angry!"

"Then why haven't you done anything about it?"

I push off my barstool and it crashes down on the floor. "What am I supposed to do, Jocelyn? He knows that I know about her now and he's probably going to leave me! That's why he's not home right now, waiting for me! It's why he's with her!"

"If that's what you want to believe." Jocelyn smirks behind the sip she takes from her drink.

"What is that supposed to mean?"

No words. Just a continued smirk.

"I'm going to talk to Julianna," I say. "Let her know what's going on and why I did what I did."

"That's the dumbest idea I've ever heard."

"How? I talked to her before and you said it was brilliant."

"Yeah, while you were in disguise and before the mistress found out who you really were!"

"I don't care." I chase down the rest of my drink and slam the glass on the counter. "I'll talk to her and clear this all up."

"Adira, you're making no damn sense right now."

"I–I'll text her first." I whip out my phone and start up a new text, but Jocelyn is around the counter in a flash, knocking the phone out of my hand. "Hey!"

"You're going to text her while she's probably lying right next to your man? Really? Are you that fucking pathetic?"

"Stop," I whimper, waving my hands as I step away from her.

"No. I won't stop, Adira. What you're trying to do is really fucking stupid."

"Fuck. I feel sick." I shake my head, moving away from Jocelyn some more. The lighting in this room is awful. It's gold and too dim and it's making my belly churn.

"Adira," Jocelyn calls. "Just tell me to help you and I will."

"No." My head shakes again, my pulse louder in my ears. "I—I'm leaving. I have to go." Before Jocelyn can call my name again, I'm out the door and out of Jessa's Lounge without a single look back.

CHAPTER FIFTY-SIX

ADIRA

I'm anxious for my meetings to be over and to sign off on the last of the contracts I have. But of course work doesn't end because I want it to. There is too much paperwork to sign, more designs to look over, and I have to force myself through a lunch with a woman named Kathy who literally complains about every meal she orders no matter where we are, but she's a primary investor in my company, so I suck it up and deal with it.

A slipper company and a Belgian chocolate company want to collaborate with our products for subscription boxes, and then I have the dreaded meeting with Vito, where I have to agree to the new designs. If there's one thing I know, it's to trust what Dina says. Half the time I choose to ignore it, but this time I will because she's right. The world is changing, and people want more color, more vibrancy, more life. People want things to show off, things to give, things that are unique. We've always chosen subtle, simple colors at Lovely Silk, and that's gotten us through for a while, but I can't lie and say our competition isn't high. Perhaps it's time to switch it up, give the world something new to talk about. Or, in the words of Jocelyn, it's time to *boss up*, even if that means taking a huge risk financially. With designs like what Vito has in mind, it'll cost us a pretty penny.

Despite it all, I get it finished and am fortunate to make it out of the office by four thirty. I drive through Julianna's neighborhood to check if her car is there. It isn't, so I park in the Trader Joe's parking lot across the street and open Instagram to find her account.

Her last post is an image of her and her dog with the caption, **Sunny skies and dog walks are the best. Love my sweet baby.**

I roll my eyes but notice that she posted it only two hours ago. I view her stories, but there isn't anything about a location. Just quotes and more pictures of her dog. Reposts of some of her makeup designs done on women with puckered lips and narrow noses.

I sigh and lower the phone, lifting my gaze to the storefront. A pink car to my left catches my eye and I do a double take when I realize whose it is.

"Shit." That's her car. Julianna's. I can't be mistaken. No one else around here would have a pink vehicle. Is she here right now?

I search the front of the store, where customers are walking in and out.

You should go in. Just go in and speak, I tell myself. *Clear it all up.*

Yes. That's what I'll do.

I grab my purse and push out of the car, marching in my heels to get inside. I've only been in Trader Joe's twice. Both times were with Gabriel. I scan the front, where cashiers work to check customers out. Flowers are stuffed to the brim in a wooden stand ahead of me, and there's a perfumed smell in the air that entices me.

I stroll through the store casually, bringing the strap of my purse over my shoulder. I pass the wine section, where a couple is perusing the shelf, and then move past the freezer sections. It's when I reach the dairy section that I see her.

She stands with her back to me, her long brown hair down the middle of her back, hiding those fuzzy hairs that I want to wax off of her. She tosses her hair over her shoulder and turns a fraction, and I watch as she chooses between two brands of mozzarella.

"This is stupid," I mutter to myself.

Just do it. Get it over with.

I draw in a breath, and without giving it much thought, I allow my feet to guide me toward her.

"Julianna?" I call, and she spins around quickly. At first she smiles, as if eager to see someone she knows in public, but when she sees that it's *me*, her smile drips away. Her eyes become frantic, bouncing around me, and then she takes a step back.

"Skylar."

"No—I, um. I know you know about me," I say, laughing a little. "Just call me by my real name. It's Adira."

She nods, then folds her arms. "What do you want?"

"I came to talk to you. About Gabriel."

"There's nothing to talk about."

"I know you're sleeping with him."

She scoffs and her jaw goes slack as she looks around to see who may have overheard.

"I came to talk to you woman to woman. I want you to stop being with him. I love him more than anything and I know he loves me too, but you're standing between us and I'm not sure why he can't let you go."

Julianna stares at me, a stunned expression on her face. "Wow. Gabriel was right."

"Right about what?"

Julianna doesn't respond. Instead, she turns to replace the

cheese and then grips the handle of her shopping cart. "Look, Adira, I want you to leave me alone, okay? You should be glad I won't press charges on you for stalking me."

"I wasn't stalking—"

"Look—just fuck off, okay!?" Julianna barks in my face. Her voice is loud, harsh, and it causes others to look our way. Her face has turned beet red, her grip tighter around the handle of the shopping cart. "If you come around me again, I will call the police and I fucking mean it." With her threat lingering in the air, she rushes away, leaving me standing in the middle of the store, unsure how to react.

When I make it back to my car, my heart is nearly beating out of my chest. I slam my hand on the steering wheel repeatedly, causing the horn to beep and people in the parking lot to stare and gawk, but I don't give a single fuck in the moment.

I'm so angry. So, so angry.

I scream in the confines of my car, then drop my forehead to the top of the steering wheel. Retrieving my phone from my purse blindly, I bring it to my lap with a sniffle. I sit up and wipe the tears away with exaggerated force, then bring the phone to my ear after clicking the name I want to call.

When she answers, I rest my forehead on the steering wheel again and tell her, "I want you to help me." I swallow hard, rage and despair pumping through me. "I *need* you to help me, Jocelyn."

CHAPTER FIFTY-SEVEN

"So, tell me what's really going on."

I whipped my head up, focusing on Mrs. Stein's face. She was seated in the chair across from mine at her dining table, her eyes slightly narrowed, causing soft wrinkles to form around them.

"What do you mean?" I asked.

She glanced sideways, toward the living room, where Panda was stuffing her face with more macarons while watching Powerpuff Girls. *We didn't get the luxury of watching cartoons at Claudette's. As a matter of fact, she didn't have satellite. Just three or four channels, two of which only showed the news. The other was PBS, and we were lucky if we ever got to watch that.*

"There was a look in your eyes when you showed up. You looked worried. Is everything okay at home?"

"Yeah, everything's fine." I had to lie. What else was I to do? Sure, I couldn't stand Claudette, but if anything ever happened to her, or she was reported, I knew Panda and I would be separated. And I only knew that because Claudette constantly reminded us of it.

"Don't lie to me, child. I can see right through it." I met her eyes again, but they were gentle and understanding. "You forget I have a daughter of my own." She smirks.

I work hard to swallow, glancing at Panda again and then back at Mrs. Stein. "If I tell you, it might separate me and Panda."

"Nothing will separate the two of you." She reached across the table. "Adira, if you're in trouble, I need you to let me know. I want to help you."

My bottom lip was trembling. Affection was a foreign thing to me when it came from adults. I only ever showed and received affection with Panda. It felt strange from Mrs. Stein, yet comforting, and it made my chest feel fuzzy and my belly swim. I met her eyes again and she nodded. "It's okay," she whispered.

And that was all it took for me to break down into tears. She brought her chair to my side of the table and sat right next to me, rubbing my back and allowing me to let it all out. I was a ball of emotion—sadness, anger, fear. But it was like Mrs. Stein understood it all and allowed each emotion to run its course.

"How can I help?" she asked in a soft voice.

I lifted my head and wiped my face. "If the time ever comes, or if anything ever happens, will you make sure we're safe?"

Mrs. Stein's eyes widened a moment before softening again. And with a nod, she said, "Of course I will."

CHAPTER FIFTY-EIGHT

ADIRA

"You really want to go through with this?"

I look up at Jocelyn beneath my lashes as she stands on the opposite side of my island counter. Her arms are folded, her chin tipped, that confidence of hers so damn high. She's happy that I've asked her for help. It makes her look stronger than me. Right now I don't care.

My eyes fall to the gleaming knife on the counter below me, where half my face reflects on it. It's large and sharp, a knife I bought when Gabriel and I cooked together and had a date night in because I was recovering from having the flu.

He hasn't answered my calls or any of my texts since I returned from Miami. I know he's with Julianna and I need to separate them. Next to the knife is an empty prescription bottle. The pills to ease my anxiety and soothe my mind have been dumped down the drain. I officially don't need them anymore. I'm better off.

"There's no turning back now," Jocelyn had said earlier. *"What's planned will be done."*

"We have to go through with it," I tell her.

Jocelyn walks around the counter and her hand touches mine. I can't look up at her. I'm too afraid to face the god-awful truth. But I feel her. And in this moment, she's all that I have. "Consider it done."

CHAPTER FIFTY-NINE

ADIRA

I spent all night bracing myself for what lay ahead.

My husband doesn't want to come home? He wants to spend his time with her? *Fine.* But he won't do so peacefully.

Jocelyn and I talked all night—back and forth, back and forth. She knows what's best from this moment on. I keep acting normal. I go to work, handle my meetings, answer Dina's texts and FaceTime calls, putting on a big, bold smile to assure her I'm okay. I'm on a roll and I'm proud of me, damn it. All I have to do is push through until tonight.

After all my meetings, I change into a maroon dress in my office bathroom suite, apply a fresh coat of makeup, a virgin hair wig with bangs, and then slide into the black stilettos I snagged out of my closet. I leave the building and drive through Tampa to get to Le Méridien.

After finding a spot in the parking deck and making my way down to the entrance, I enter the lobby of the hotel, where the ceiling is high and there's a stunning gold chandelier above, with little crystals that beam kaleidoscopic lights.

The lobby is a hum as people walk back and forth, dressed to impress. All of them making their way toward the ballroom

to my right. There's a banner posted above that says WEL-
COME, TAMPA MUA!

Tonight is the official Tampa Makeup Artist awards. It's
glitzy and fancy and everyone is practically pretending to be
on the runway. I blend right in with the dress I selected from
my closet. My cleavage is revealed just enough, the wig is
straight and neat, and my makeup is flawless.

I walk down the hallway, retrieving the ticket I was able
to get from a colleague—thanks, Daniella from Nordstrom—
out of my clutch and handing it to the woman checking
passes.

"Welcome, Adira, we're so happy to have you tonight."

"Thank you." She smiles at me and I return one, then
make my way down the long hallway. Music is playing and
the sound builds up the closer I get.

Then I make it to the ballroom, where it is dimly lit.
Strobe lights flash, a damn disco ball that is in poor taste spins
from the ceiling, but I ignore it and make my way to the bar,
ordering a drink.

As I wait for my request, I scan the crowded room. I blend
right in and I'm thankful for that, but I know to keep my distance if I see *her*.

I search the room thoroughly, knowing she's here. And
then I find her. She's standing next to the stage with a silver
sequin dress on. Her hair is styled half up, half down, and her
lips are a rosy pink.

Of course her makeup is flawless. It has to be for the occasion, and it stands out so much more than her dress. Silver
rhinestones are used over her eyeliner and her eye shadow is a
dramatic pink. Rose gold blush and big diamond drop earrings.

She laughs at someone, tossing her head back ever so
slightly, and it takes everything in me not to charge across the
room and wrap my hands around her pretty little neck.

"Your drink, ma'am." I turn to face the bartender, who

has placed my drink on the counter. I thank him, leave a tip, and then sip the gin and tonic as I maneuver across the room. I keep a careful eye on Julianna as she mingles with the crowd. There's a wineglass in her hand because she's delicate and fancy and wants everyone to know it.

A man approaches her. He appears to be slightly older than her. He touches her shoulder and she forces a smile and I roll my eyes. When the MC walks onto the stage to begin the night, Julianna turns her back to me to face the speaker, and I make my way a little closer to her—but not too close that she'll sense it.

The night carries on. I watch as she sips from the same glass of wine, then goes to the bar for another with a petite woman with pale blond hair. They laugh boisterously as they drink, and then it's time for everyone to take their seats as the awards begin.

The awards are the most boring part. Loud applause and fake sincerity. When that part of it is over, Julianna hasn't won any awards, and I laugh inside at the thought of that. Little Ms. Perfect can't be good at every damn thing.

The music from the DJ resumes and the event switches from a formal occasion to an after party. The room grows darker and begins to glow with lights. The atmosphere becomes thicker and I become sweatier in my wig. I lose Julianna a couple of times, so I make my way near the door, standing with a drink. I take out my phone, scroll through old emails to blend in, and then I hear her voice.

"Yeah, I'll be right back! I have to go pee!" Julianna prances out of the ballroom alone, making a hard right turn.

Bingo.

I leave the room too, taking careful strides behind her, but she's rushing to the bathroom with urgency. When I see her enter the restrooms, I wait outside of them for a moment. I take a quick look around, then go inside. The door doesn't creak—it's a well-maintained hotel—and I'm grateful for that.

I hear the trickle of urine, a toilet flush. A woman exits one of the stalls with an awkward smile at me. I don't smile back.

When she washes her hands and departs, I squat to check if there are any people in here other than me and Julianna. I only see the silver of Julianna's shoes and the lacy fabric of her thong draped around them.

Standing by the sink, I open my clutch, digging through it as if I'm searching for something I lost. When Julianna is finished, she walks to the sink next to mine and sighs. I keep my head bowed, still riffling through the bag as she washes her hands, then goes to the dryer to let them dry.

It's when her back is to me that I wrap my fingers around my pocketknife, realizing it would be the perfect opportunity to take my shot. I could stab her right here, right now, leave her bleeding in the middle of the bathroom floor. I have the urge within me. It's vicious and throbbing and so hungry, but as I begin to withdraw it from the clutch, the bathroom door swings open and I drop it back inside.

"Julianna! There you are!" a girl shouts. I look through the mirror, and it's the pale-haired girl Julianna was sharing a drink with. "Come on! They're about to announce the raffle winners for the Fenty bags, bitch!"

"Oh, shit! Let's go!" I watch the girls leave with nothing but the lingering scent of fruity perfume. When they're gone, I stare into the mirror. My skin is glistening, my hand tight around my clutch. I take out my phone as it vibrates and answer it.

"You're rushing it. Wait until after the event is over."

"Okay," I say. Then I leave the restroom to return to the ballroom.

CHAPTER SIXTY

Mrs. Stein sent me and Panda off with a container of cookies and two bags of veggie chips. "Come back anytime," she said, watching us go. I thanked her and waved, then grabbed Panda's hand to walk the half mile back to our house.

With each step, I could feel my heart beating louder and louder, and when we approached the driveway, I swear it felt like my heart had failed me when I saw Bower's car still parked there.

What was I going to do now? I couldn't go back to Mrs. Stein's. Then she'd really worry, and she'd probably call the police. And if the police got involved and it was my fault that I couldn't be with Panda anymore, I didn't know what I would do.

So I drew in a breath and continued ahead. We were three hours late getting home, but I had my excuse prepared. Gripping the doorknob, I twisted it open and walked in.

The house smelled like fish and boiled vegetables. Gospel music was playing and I heard dishes clinking and tinkering, being moved around.

"Dira? Jessa? Is that y'all?" Claudette popped around the corner, but she didn't look like Claudette. She wore a maroon dress and her hair was wrapped in a cheetah-print scarf. She had lots of makeup on and her lipstick was a dark red. When she smiled, I noticed some *of the lipstick staining her teeth.* "Where have you two been?" *she asked, walking up to us.*

"We had an after-school event," *I told her.* "It was spirit day."

"Really?" *Claudette placed a hand on her hip.*

I felt Panda fidget beside me. That was the second time I'd lied in front of her in one day.

"Well, all that matters is that you're here now. We've been waiting for you two." *We? Just as she said that, Bower walked around the corner from the kitchen, using a hand towel to dry off his hands.*

"Hey there, little ladies." *He smiled hard. Too hard.*

"Why is he here?" *I asked.*

"Adira!" *Claudette snapped.* "He is our guest! Stop being rude and apologize right now!"

"No, no. That's okay. It's okay, Claudie." *Bower stepped beside her, wrapping an assuring arm around her shoulder.* "I believe Adira has lost a little trust in me, but that's something I'm sure I can fix."

Claudette forced a smile at him while I took a step back with Panda's hand in mine.

Bower removed his arm from Claudette and dropped to one knee. "Adira, your mother told me all about what you said."

I looked away, my chest growing painfully tight.

"I just want you to know it was nothing like that at all. I saw your little sister shivering when I came to the kitchen for some water that night. Her blanket had fallen off, so I put it back on her, and I rubbed her arms and legs so she could get warm—you know, transferring my own body heat."

I felt Panda look up at me, then at Bower again.

"I would never do anything like that," *he went on.* "I am a man of God. My words and my actions are all I have."

I pressed my lips and glanced at Claudette, who tilted her chin and smirked. Bower stood up and smiled, saying, "To restore your faith in me, I figured I'd cook you all a meal. How does tilapia, rice, and vegetables sound? And right after, we can make some skillet s'mores."

I don't remember much of the details after that. We all ate dinner. Bower laughed. Claudette giggled. Panda ate so many s'mores. But what I do remember is that on that same night, I couldn't sleep. I slept in the bed with Panda, and when it was well past midnight, I heard our bedroom door creak open.

I saw Bower's frame between the doors, and then I saw him enter the room. I pretended to be sleeping but had my eyes slightly open to watch what he did next.

He bent down in front of Panda's bed, clasped his hands together, looked up at the ceiling, and said, "Lord, please absolve me of my sins." Then he sighed, unclasped his hands, and lightly pulled Panda's blanket down past her chest. He rubbed her immature breasts while leaning forward and kissing her on the lips.

And just when I had the urge to demand that he stop, Panda sprang up and screamed at the top of her lungs.

CHAPTER SIXTY-ONE

ADIRA

Julianna wins one of the Fenty bags and eats up the attention she receives from all the other makeup artists. Big deal. It wasn't like she won it from Rihanna herself.

I don't know when she plans on leaving, but I know I'm getting tired of waiting. She dances. Drinks more with her pale-haired friend, who I realize is named Nicole, a makeup artist in training, after doing some light research on her Instagram stories. The blue light of Julianna's phone glows on her face as she seems to be texting someone back, and I can't help but wonder if it's Gabriel.

He sent me a text not too long ago, asking where I was and telling me he needed to talk to me. I didn't respond. If he knew where I was, he wouldn't be pleased. And it's not like he really gives a fuck. He hasn't been home in days, pretending to be out of town working, but I know he isn't. He's working in town and going home at night to her.

The thought of it angers me just as the DJ transitions the song to a Missy Elliott throwback. My eyes swing to Julianna across the room. The pale-haired girl had left her nearly fifteen minutes before to join the others on the dance floor, and

Julianna now stands in a corner with her gold prize bag in hand, texting away.

It's nearing midnight when she lowers her phone and goes to the dance floor to say something in Nicole's ear. Nicole makes a pouty face, murmurs something, then hugs Julianna, and Julianna turns to leave the ballroom moments later.

I put down my drink and follow her. She sashays through the lobby, her dress twinkling beneath the golden light, and out of the hotel. I keep a safe distance but continue following after her.

She walks to the parking deck and I hide behind the cement blocks, listening to her heels click and a car horn beep. She's in her Mercedes and I know if I don't get to my car, I'll miss my opportunity.

I rush to parking deck C and crank up my car, leaving the deck after paying and spotting Julianna's car at a red light.

Gripping the steering wheel, I glare through the back window of Julianna's hideously pink car, watching her head bob to whatever music she's listening to. I follow her along the freeway, and it's when she takes an exit that I realize she's going home.

She parks in her space. I creep in and park two spots away from hers. To my dismay, right in front of me is a familiar silver Range Rover. *Gabriel's* Range Rover. I can tell by the rugby team sign hanging from the visor mirror.

"Yeah, I made it home," I hear her muffled voice outside my car. "Yep. He said he has a surprise for me." Her joyous, shrill laughter makes my stomach coil.

I climb out of the car and march toward hers.

"Julianna," I say just as she ends her call. Her eyes swing up to meet mine and she narrows them for a fleeting moment, probably unsure of who I am because of the wig, but then her eyes broaden as recognition slithers across her face.

"Oh my fucking God!" she shouts. "I told you to *leave me the fuck alone!*"

I move closer to her as she raises her phone in the air and threatens to call the police, but there is no time for her to do so.

Clutching the side of her head, I slam it into the side of her car and watch her limp body fall to the ground.

CHAPTER SIXTY-TWO

I sat up in the bed with Panda and stared at Bower.

"Girls," he said, raising his hands in the air. "Jessa? Calm down, now. I was just checking on you."

"You were kissing her!" I shouted at him.

"What?" he hissed.

Footsteps thundered down the hallway and Claudette charged into our room, wrapping her robe around her. She flipped on the light switch and then looked at Bower, who was still bent in front of the bed—in front of Panda—and then at us. "What's going on?" she demanded.

"He—he was kissing me!" Panda screamed. "He was touching me, Momma! I felt him touching me!"

"Don't be silly!" Bower barked, standing up. "I had my hand on her arm and was praying for her. I was praying for both of 'em. That's why I was on my knees!"

Panda slid away and moved closer to me. I wrapped an arm around her and tossed a pleading look at Claudette.

"Claudette, you know who I am. I'm not that kind of man. These girls—they're no good. I don't know why they keep lying on me when all I want to do is help and heal them. And you said it yourself—they need healing. That's what I'm doing. Using my divine gift to heal them."

Claudette's throat bobbed as she looked from Bower to us again. "It's late, Bower. Why do you have to pray for them so late?"

"When it's the devil's hour, that's when they need it most."

Claudette lowered her gaze and nodded, and while she was in her vulnerable state, Bower moved toward her, clasped her chin between his fingers and said, "Look at me." And she did. "I would never hurt you or your girls."

"Momma," I crooned as Panda buried her face into my chest. She had to believe us. We were her daughters. "He's lying."

"I am a man of God!" he shouted, turning to look at me. "I don't lie! Y'all are the liars! Got the devil swimming all through you! You know, Claudette," he said, swinging around to face her again while waving a finger, "when I walked into this house, I could feel a dark presence lurking. But I tried to ignore it—I tried to bring the good light in this place and cast it out. But these girls?" He shook his head hard, still pointing that finger at Claudette, who was clutching the lapels of her robe. "These girls have something in them—especially that young one! And you told me all about how she came to be and how you had her! She needs to be cleansed!"

"Cleansed," Claudette repeated, eyes wide.

"Yes, cleansed! I don't know how you're raising them, but what I do know is that you need to get the devil out of them, otherwise I won't ever be coming back to this place!"

And with that, Bower charged around Claudette to leave the room.

"Wait—Pastor Bower," she called after him, rushing out of the room and down the hallway. But I don't think he waited. Keys jingled, the front door slammed in an instant, and I heard a car engine turn over.

After several minutes, Claudette returned to the room, her eyes wide and her lips pressed so thin it looked painful. She met up to the bed and yanked on Panda's arm, and Panda screamed.

"Momma, stop!" I wailed, tugging on Panda's other arm.

"I never should've kept you!" Claudette barked in her face. "I kept telling myself you were worth keeping—that God wouldn't want me to get rid of an innocent soul—but I should've known by the way you were conceived that you wouldn't be innocent! That was the devil whispering in my ear, telling me to keep his demon child!"

Claudette released Panda, only to point a stern finger in her face. Her eyes were red and lined with tears, her lips chapped and tight. "You've done nothing but cause me pain," she cried, her voice breaking. "Whenever I look at you, all I see is him. All I see is that white man who pinned me down and had his way with me! You were never supposed to be here!" She swiped at the angry tears rolling down her face. "But I'll tell you one thing. Bower is right. You need to be cleansed again because one time clearly wasn't enough for you."

Claudette glared at Panda with her dark, wet, angry eyes, and then she shifted her gaze over to me. For a split second, I saw nothing but raw pain. I saw a woman who was damaged and afraid and lonely, because I knew who the white man was who she was talking about. He was my father's coworker—but my father was dead. And the white man—whose name I couldn't remember, and Claudette never said—had decided to step in and help her out, try and raise me. But he didn't raise me and he didn't help. He drank a lot. Cursed a lot. Claudette denied his advances all the time, until one night he got angry. I knew he was angry because he threw a glass at the wall, and it shattered.

Claudette didn't know what to do, so she sent me to my room and closed the door, but when she went back to him, I heard her begging him—pleading. She asked him not to "do this," but whatever it was, he did it. And then, a few months later, Claudette was wobbling around with a big belly and the white man was nowhere to be found.

I felt for Claudette. I truly did. All the anguish, all her pain, everything she wanted rinsed away still lingered and I saw it in her eyes. But that split second ended before I could even react.

Claudette's eyes darkened all over again and she grimaced, turning away to storm out of the room. Before slamming the door, she said, "You can't protect her forever, Dira. And you shouldn't. Her evil will only seep into you."

CHAPTER SIXTY-THREE

JOCELYN

It's a struggle getting Julianna's body into the building. She and I are about the same weight. I stumble a lot as Adira helps me and we manage to get her inside. Julianna is still unconscious, fortunately, so we drag her to the middle of the floor in Jessa's basement.

I'm grateful we have a separate space where we store the liquor and supplies. No one ever comes here unless they're told to by me, and if they want to get in, they need a key—which also must come from me. I have all the keys right now. I'm the only person who has access to it, and I take delight in that as we lay Julianna's body on the middle of the floor.

"We fucking did it!" I laugh.

I rush to the shelf where I left the duct tape and rope and go to wrap Julianna's ankles. It's as I rip the duct tape when her eyes pop open and she starts to scream.

"Don't you fucking do it." I clap a hand around her mouth and she shakes her head back and forth, still trying to scream. "Stop screaming or I'll grab that knife on the shelf and you'll leave me no choice but to stab you with it."

Julianna hears my words. I know she does, despite how calm

they are, because her screaming stops immediately, though her eyes remain the same. Wide. Delirious. Full of fear.

"Good. Now stay quiet." I release my hand from her mouth slowly and continue ripping the tape. She breathes raggedly, staring up at me.

"Adira, please," she begs.

"Don't beg her," I grumble.

"What?" she gasps. "I–I don't know what's going on. Please, if this is about Gabriel, I'll end it, I swear! I'll be done with all of it!"

"You know what, Jocelyn? I think we've taken this too far," Adira says, and I turn my gaze to her. She's standing next to the shelves with her arms folded while I do all the work. "I never should've hurt her in the parking lot."

"Oh, please," I mutter. "Stop trying to take all the credit. You and I both know you wouldn't have had the balls to do that. *I* felt your rage and did it for you."

"We shouldn't have." Adira holds herself tighter and a tear slides down her cheek.

"What the hell are you crying for?"

A phone rings and, startled, we both gasp, dropping our gaze to Adira's pocket.

Adira pulls it out and says, "Oh, God."

"What? Who is it?"

"It's Gabriel."

I march toward her. "Give it to me." I take it out of her hand and answer. "Well, look who it is."

Gabriel is quiet for a moment before saying, "Who the hell is this?"

"Who do you think?"

"What?" A pause. "*Jocelyn?*"

I smirk. "Your poor wife is hurting, Gabriel. What is wrong with you?"

"What the fuck are you talking about? Where's Julianna?"

"I'm not sure, but she left her phone with us and I don't think she wants to be with you anymore. I'll let her know you called, though."

"No—wait!" I hang up before he can get another word in.

"Jocelyn, are you sure about this?" Adira asks.

"Why wouldn't I be?"

"I–I don't know. I think I should call Dina before—"

"No!" I shout. "If you do that, you'll defeat the whole purpose of us bringing Julianna here! Wasn't it *you* who said you wanted Gabriel to yourself?"

"Please, Adira . . . I–I didn't know it was like that with you and Gabriel," Julianna pleads. "I didn't realize how you felt. I–I thought it was just . . . Oh, God. Please, don't kill me! Please don't kill me!"

I watch Adira look at Julianna, and of course there are tears in her eyes. She's always ready to fucking cry for someone, no matter how badly they've hurt her—no matter how much pain she's in—and why? What's the damn point?

"She has to go. It will make you feel better. I promise."

"No, Jocelyn, let's just . . . let's take it back a step. We should let her go."

"Let her go? Are you stupid? She'll run straight to the police!"

"Then let her! We assaulted her and now we're threatening to *kill* her! There's no way we'll be able to get out of this, so let's just—let's face the consequences and be done with it!"

I sigh, bored with her. "Okay, you know what? I think it's time for you to go."

"What?"

"Yes. Go and hide, please. Your voice is no longer needed."

"But you can't do that! You're not the one in charge!"

"Really?" I sneer. "Because, if I can be frank, Adira, I've always been the one in charge. You've done everything I told

you to do. Hell, you brought her here, just like I told you to
do. Deep down, in the dark, dark depths of your soul, you
want this to happen . . . so I'm going to give you what you
want. Why? Because I love you, and I always want what's best
for you."

"Jocelyn, you can't do this!" Adira screams.

"I'm sorry," Jocelyn quips. "I can't hear you. Your voice
is fading, sweetie."

Adira is shouting now, but I can't hear her . . . and soon
enough, I can't see her either.

Just like that, she's gone, hidden in the darkness, and I'm
the only one left standing.

Me, and the home-wrecking bitch who caused her heartbreak.

CHAPTER SIXTY-FOUR

"Get up. Get up now." A voice hissed at me and I gasped, looking into bloodshot eyes that belonged to Claudette.

She yanked on my arm to sit me up, then moved across the room to dig some clothes out of one of my drawers. Tossing a shirt and sweatpants my way, she said, "Hurry up and get changed."

"Where are we going?"

"Stop asking questions and come on." She left the room in a flurry, and I climbed out of bed, listening as she bustled around. It wasn't until I'd changed clothes that I realized Panda's bed was empty. Her blanket was strewn across the bed haphazardly, and I don't know if it was because of how abruptly Claudette woke me up, or the fact that it was the middle of night, or the fact that Panda never left the room without me after what happened with Bower, but my heart sank to my stomach.

I rushed out of the room and down the hallway, and Claudette was in the kitchen, riffling through the drawers.

"What are you doing?" I asked. "Where's Panda?"

"Stop calling her that!" she shouted.

I vibrated with fear as I turned to check the living room. Bower wasn't there, thank goodness, but neither was Panda. I turned back to the kitchen and Claudette whispered, "This," with a roll of duct tape in hand. My eyes swung to the clock on the wall. It was five in the morning.

"Where is Panda?" I asked again, my voice firmer this time. Claudette turned around and smiled, and it was an eerie smile that made my skin crawl. Something had gotten into her ever since Bower left.

It'd been three weeks since he was gone. We stopped going to church because she was ashamed of how we'd acted and didn't want to face him. Around the house, she was quieter, and she lurked.

She watched us closely, especially Panda. She'd sip her drinks, narrow her eyes. Scoff whenever me and Panda made up jokes or found something funny. Claudette was always a little unhinged, but this was a different side of her—a side that terrified the hell out of me.

"You wanna know where she is? Fine. I'll show you. But you have to promise to keep it a secret, okay?" She grinned, like she was going to surprise me with a present. I didn't know what kind of game she was playing at, but I sensed Panda wasn't okay, and to get to her sooner, I needed to play along, so I nodded obediently, and Claudette walked past me to get out of the kitchen and to the front door.

I walked after her and was submerged in a thick fog. The clouds were lower than I'd ever seen them before and it was hard to see much of anything other than the skinny, dark branches of trees. The day was gray and muggy and my heart was in my throat as I tried to keep Claudette's white shirt in view.

She took the trail that led to the lake and stepped onto the rickety dock, and that's when my blood ran cold. I halted and spotted a boat ahead as Claudette kept going toward it. Claudette hardly ever used the boat. The last time she had, it was during one of her bad days. One day when she didn't get a job she applied for and resorted to drink—just once, as she told us. Was this day a bad day?

I ran ahead, not giving a damn that the wooden slats were shaking beneath me and on the verge of breaking in half. It wasn't until Claudette jumped onto the boat and I reached the end of the dock when I realized this was much, much worse than I ever could have imagined.

CHAPTER SIXTY-FIVE

DINA

Dina picks up her phone from the kitchen counter after a forty-five-minute meditation. It's been hours and Adira still hasn't responded to her text from earlier. She's worried, but she doesn't like projecting her worries onto Adira because she knows Adira can sense it.

Adira has always been a tricky person to understand, Dina knows, and lately she's been more of a challenge to grasp. Normally, Adira is the one to send Dina a text or give her a call to check in, provide an update, and to let her know everything is going well. She hasn't done that in months, and the Adira she was with at Kellan and Ana's house—that wasn't her Adira. That was someone else.

Dina bites into her bottom lip when the call goes straight to voice mail. At this point she doesn't care if she's bugging her. She's all for personal space, but she also trusts her gut and something with Adira isn't right, so she follows up her call with a text: **Hey, beloved. Give me a call when you can please.**

She's probably working, Dina assumes. The girl is always working. She's like the walking contradiction of everything Dina stands for. While Dina loves her free time, her meditation periods, and floating where she needs to be, Adira is about routine and pressure and restrictions. She'd accepted a long time ago that that is just how Adira is and what she needs. When she follows routine and sets restrictions, she is her best self. But when she falls out of it, or when something triggers her past, Dina worries.

Dina goes to the bathroom of the Airbnb she's booked to take a quick shower. After her shower, she dresses in a skirt and a loose T-shirt. It's as she's styling her hair that she receives a call.

"Gabriel?" She frowns at the name on the screen because he's never called her. And the fact that he's calling and Adira hasn't been answering must mean *something*, so she answers it quickly.

"Hello? Gabriel? How are you, love?"

"Hey, I'm good." Gabriel pauses, then sighs. "Actually, not that good."

"Well, don't beat around the bush. What's going on?"

"Okay . . . um . . . I'm calling because I'm really worried about Adira."

"Why? What's happened?"

Gabriel clears his throat. "My girlfriend didn't come home last night."

That causes Dina to frown again, and confusion tickles every part of her brain. "Your *girlfriend*? Gabriel, what are you talking about?"

"My girlfriend, Julianna."

"You're *married* to Adira, Gabriel." Dina does her best to control her reaction. "What are you talking about? You can't have a girlfriend."

"No, Dina. I'm not married to Adira. I've *never* been married to her." Hearing those words are like bullets to the soul. Dina takes a step back, breathing hard through parted lips.

"W–what are you talking about?"

"I've been pretending to be married to her."

"For how long?"

"For two years now."

"So all this time—all the meetings before? You introducing yourself as her boyfriend when we met?"

"It wasn't real," he murmurs, and she can hear the defeat in his voice.

"Why the hell were you doing that?!"

"I don't know. It's what she wanted. It's . . . it's all she really asked of me. We, um . . . we hooked up one night, right before I met Julianna. We just made it a habit to be there for each other if Adira had events or needed a plus-one. I took her up on it because it seemed like a fair deal. And I had nothing, Dina. *Nothing.* Adira was willing to help me. It only seemed fair."

"Oh, God."

"Then I met Julianna and I knew she was the one. We moved in together and everything. I told Adira that it was getting serious between us, but she didn't want me to go. And Adira was providing for me, Dina. She helped me get the rugby going. She bought me my car so I could get around. She's done so much for me. It would've been wrong to just quit on her, you know? She kept saying she needed me. But I– I think now she's really convinced herself that we're married and . . . I–I don't know. Things have gotten so weird now."

"Weird how?" Dina demands.

"Um . . . she's been doing a lot of pretending and wanting me to pretend with her."

"What do you mean, pretending? What kind of pretending?" Dina's heart is racing now. Because she knows. Deep in her gut she knows what's happening, but she never thought she'd have to face this again.

"A couple of weeks ago she told me to meet her at a hotel she booked. She told me to call her Jocelyn for the night—to pretend we were old friends who have always had an undeniable attraction and are finally getting the chance to do something about it."

"Jocelyn," Dina whispers. "Oh my God."

"She told me it was what she wanted, so I went along with it. Mostly because a few nights before, she asked me if I loved her or Julianna more and I told her it was Julianna—that it would *always* be Julianna. Anyway, the day after the hotel thing, she sent me emails, still pretending to be Jocelyn, and I went along with it for her sake. It seemed to be making her happy."

Dina shakes her head. "This can't be true."

"Dina, I'm sorry you have to find out like this, but I'm worried. Julianna has known there was someone sort of providing for us. I was honest with her from the start and she was okay with me . . . continuing to do things with Adira to make her happy if it meant our bills could get paid and we could have whatever we wanted."

"You mean you *used* her?" Dina snaps.

"No—it wasn't like that. I wanted it to stop, Dina."

"If you wanted it to stop, you would have ended it. But you didn't, you just kept stringing her along and capitalizing off her. And now you're set, huh? And you're pulling away? That's why you're worried. That's why I'm worried." Dina breathes evenly through her nostrils to calm herself.

"When's the last time you heard from Adira?" she asks.

"Two days ago. I've been trying to call her, but she isn't answering, and now Julianna isn't answering and she didn't come home last night after an event she had. Look, Julianna told me Adira ran into her at the store the other day—said it looked like she'd been watching her for a while. Adira has been stalking her for some time now and Julianna said she pretended to be someone else just to talk to her."

"How did your girlfriend react to seeing Adira at the store?" Dina asks as she marches to get her purse.

"She blew up. Got scared. Told her to leave her alone or she'd call the police next time."

"*Damn it.*"

"I'm worried, Dina. You told me to call you if things ever got strange with her and I always found it a random request from you, but now I get it. And that's why I'm calling. Julianna isn't answering me, and she always does. And I checked Adira's house—she wasn't there. I also called her job and no one has seen her. Both are missing right now, and I think Adira has done something."

"Oh, it's not Adira whose done something," Dina snips, snatching open the door. "It's the other one inside her."

CHAPTER SIXTY-SIX

"Here she is," Claudette said, smiling up at me.

"M—momma, what are you doing with her? Why is she in there?"

"There are lessons to be taught and learned, Adira." Claudette extended her arm to reach her hand out to me. "Come."

I couldn't move. I was stuck in place, my eyes moving from Claudette to Panda, whose body lay sideways in the boat. Her wrists and ankles were bound with rope and her eyes were closed. A white bandanna was tied around her mouth. She had to be unconscious.

"Momma, please. Let's just go back to the house and learn the lessons there."

"No. No. I've been praying on this and really thinking about it, and we have to do it this way."

My bottom lip trembled. "But I don't want to."

"We have to!" Claudette shouted. "And we won't disobey! Now get in the boat!"

In that moment I had two options. I could go back to the house, find a phone, and call the police, or I could get in the boat. If I went to the house, there was a chance Claudette would get away with Panda, and either way it would be too late. But if I got on the boat, *maybe I could do something. Maybe I could help somehow, talk her out of whatever she had planned.*

I couldn't leave Panda in the boat with her. I was her sister. I had to protect her, so I climbed down and sat on one of the wooden rows, right next to Panda. Claudette started the motor and took off. I don't know how she could see with so much fog, the wind whipping at our eyes, but she kept going for miles and miles until, finally, she stopped and killed the motor.

As she did, Panda woke up, her eyes nearly bulging out of her head. "Mmm!" she cried. "Help!" she said muffled around the bandanna.

I reached for the bandanna, but Claudette swatted my hand away. Then she diligently took off the bandanna and Panda cried, "Momma! Momma, please!"

"Don't beg me. I've been praying on this and my prayers have been telling me that Pastor Bower is right. For us all to heal, I have to cleanse you myself. This will absolve all my pain and your sins."

"I don't want to be cleansed!"

"Shh, shh, shh." Claudette pressed a finger to Panda's lips. Panda's eyes were lined with tears and so were mine, and mine became thicker when Panda turned to look at me.

"Adira," Panda cried.

How could I help? How could I protect her? Protect us? What could I do?

"Momma, please, let's go back to the house. I–I can make pancakes and eggs and we can watch that movie you love so much," I pleaded.

"No, no." Claudette pressed her finger to Panda's lips again, then used her other hand to stroke Panda's hair. " 'And this water symbolizes the baptism that now saves you also—not the removal of dirt from the body but the pledge of a clear conscience toward God. It saves you by the resurrection of Jesus Christ,' " Claudette murmured. I frowned at her scripture. "You will be cleansed and brought back again."

With that, Claudette stood up and yanked on Panda's arm. Panda screamed but was unable to do anything with bound wrists and ankles.

"No! Stop!" I screamed, shooting up to a stand, but Claudette knocked me back with her arm, causing me to collapse between the wooden benches of the boat. I struggled to get up while Panda thrashed as much as she could, and I continuously lost my balance while trying to stand upright.

Water splashed onto the boat and everything slowed as my grasp slipped on the wood and my feet slid beneath me. Panda thrashed and Claudette blasphemed scriptures and I cried for her to stop until my throat hurt.

I got up, finally, but it was too late. Claudette threw Panda into the water, wrists still bound, ankles still tied, and I screamed at the top of my lungs, despite how much it hurt, lunging across the boat to reach for her. I leaned over the edge of the boat, ready to fall in with her because if she was going, I was going too, but Claudette snatched me back by the hair and I hissed and then wailed as she continued shouting her scriptures.

In that moment I felt hopeless. I scrambled for Panda. I fought so hard, but all I could do was stare, one arm stuck in the water as she reached for me and reached for me, sucking in water, splashing and spluttering, until the splashing and spluttering became no more and she sank.

Sank.

Sank.

Eyes wide open.

My baby sister.

My Jessa.

"She will resurface and be reborn," said Claudette. "She will be cleansed of her sins and she will be ours again."

But she was never ours again. She never came back.

CHAPTER SIXTY-SEVEN

JOCELYN

I stare at Julianna with a grimace. It's all I can do to refrain from cutting her delicate face.

"It must be nice to be wanted by him," I say with my arms folded.

Julianna frowns up at me, her eyes lined with tears. I've bound and gagged her so she can't speak.

"You know, I find it strange that he'd choose you over us."

Julianna shakes her head, closing her eyes.

"Rejection doesn't suit women like us—especially Adira." I walk to the shelf, picking up the knife I took from Adira's mansion. "Do you know why she can't be here right now?"

I don't look to see if she shakes her head or attempts to respond.

"It's because she's weaker than I am. Whenever she catches herself in a bind, she needs guidance. She needs someone who will just do the damn thing without hesitating so that life can progress."

I carry the knife with me toward Julianna and she whimpers.

"Maybe we shouldn't," Adira whispers. And it's nothing but a whisper. One that can be ignored.

"She wants him to herself, and what Adira wants, Adira gets. She's had a shitty life, but I'm here and I exist to make her life easier."

"Jocelyn . . . he'll know I was behind it. He won't trust me. He won't stay with me."

"It's too late for that, Adira," I snap. "We've done all the work! We have her here now."

"Yes, but . . . it's not her fault," Adira counters. "I–I knew what Gabriel's answer was going to be when I asked him if it was her or me. I just . . . I didn't expect it to hurt so much and I didn't want to let him go, even though I knew I'd have to."

"No, you don't have to. If he doesn't have her, he will only have you. She's the only thing standing in your way." I wave the tip of the knife in Julianna's face, at which she flinches and leans back.

"He'll know. Even if something happens to her or we say she left, he'll be heartbroken," Adira goes on.

"But you'll have him."

"He doesn't want me! He rejected me!"

"You're the reason he is even worth a damn thing!" I shout. And then I see her again. Adira. Standing in the room with her fists clenched. "Oh, would you look at that? Seems someone finally decided to grow a backbone."

"Fuck you," she spits at me.

"Why did you even come out? Why didn't you stay in the dark where you're supposed to be? Why don't you hide like you always do?"

"Because this isn't right, Jocelyn. I can't always have it my way—this is . . . it's taking things too far."

"But if he stays with her—if we let her go—then you're heartbroken."

Adira's head moves sideways. *"I've been heartbroken for years, Jocelyn, and you know it. Panda—"*

"Don't." I move away from her, giving her my back. "Don't even start that shit."

"Panda would never do something like this. She was good."

"I said DON'T!" I roar, turning back to face her. "Just shut the hell up and go back to the dark! Go fucking hide like you always do when shit gets too hard for you!"

Adira trembles, her eyes wet.

Julianna makes a noise and I look down at her. She's staring at me, eyes full of confusion, her head shaking too.

"Let's just get this over with."

I march toward her and yank her by the hair. She screams, and even though it's muffled, it sounds loud to me, so I hit her in the face to shut her up, but she thrashes and bobs her head, trying to put up a fight.

Something bangs in the distance and I hear a voice—a familiar one that shouts my name and causes me to freeze.

"Jocelyn, stop!" the voice shouts again.

I breathe raggedly, slowly releasing Julianna's hair as I face the door. Dina stands several steps inside the basement, her hands in the air. And standing behind her is Gabriel.

Oh, God. Gabriel. Why did she bring him?

"Jocelyn," Dina says in a calm voice, both her hands in the air, as if she's taming a wild animal. She takes a step forward, and then another, and I know what she's doing.

"Stop! Don't come closer to me or I'll stab her!"

"Okay—okay." Dina stops immediately. "I won't come any closer, but I need you to let Adira go."

"I don't have her!"

"Yes, you do," Dina says. "Let her out. Let her speak."

My head shakes as I look from Dina to Gabriel, whose eyes are panicked.

"How did you find me?"

"You sent me your location."

"No, I didn't!"

"Yes, you did. You sent it to me several minutes ago, and I know why you did. It's because you're still you and you don't really want to go through with any of this."

"Yes, I do! This will help her!" I scream.

"Will it?"

"Yes, it will! Adira loves him! She's happy with him! She deserves happiness for once in her damn life!"

"Yes, she does, but this isn't the way to achieve it, and you know it, beloved."

Dina takes another step closer, and I bring the knife to Julianna's throat.

"I know the signs," Dina says, continuing to walk closer. "I've known for weeks, but you were smarter with it this time. You know me and you know what to do, and how to react. Adira was still in there, but . . . as I look at you right now, I don't see Adira. I only see you, Jocelyn, and I know you want to help, but I need you to let her out now. Set Adira free. End all of this once and for all before you completely ruin her life."

I scoff. "What? Ruin her life? Are you fucking kidding me?"

"Yes! She was doing well, Jocelyn! She was medicated, meditating—she was fine and you know it! Every time you come back in whatever form you are, she sinks into those dark places and you don't make it any better for her. You leave her there to swim alone in her own darkness."

"If she was so great, why am I here then? Sure, she may have blocked me out for a couple of years with all your Reiki bullshit and meditations and the medication, but she will *always* need me. She's needed me since she was ten years old!"

"That's where you're wrong. You know she doesn't need you. That's why you're sabotaging her life. You want her in this chaos so you can stay here permanently while she continues to hide."

"I'm sabotaging her life? Do you hear yourself? I'm the one who got her away from that demented woman who claimed to be a mother! I'm the one who saved her after she watched her sister sink to the bottom of a fucking lake and drown to death! I'm the one who told her to run away just to get to you! *Me!* Not anyone else but *me!* I'm the one who had that evil Bower fucker sent to jail to rot there! Adira would be *dead* if I hadn't intervened!"

"Bower is dead," Dina murmurs. "I know you know that because Kellan told me he sent you the article. That's what has really triggered you. Not Julianna and Gabriel's relationship. It's Bower's death."

"Shut up," I growl, gripping the handle of the knife tighter.

"I understand you're upset," Dina says soothingly. "But you can't take this out on other people. This couple—they're innocent and you know it. Yes, you may have fallen in love with him, but this is not you, Adira."

"I'm not Adira!"

"Yes, you are. You're Adira Bennett, and you're my smart, bright, cheerful girl. You're sweet and giving and you care about people! Jocelyn—she doesn't care. She will *never* care about you. She only wants to control you—she wants to use you!"

I release Julianna and stumble backward, pressing my palms to my forehead. "No, no. That's not true."

Don't listen to her. Get rid of Julianna. You said you wanted him to yourself. This is how you do it. Get rid of her!

"No!" I scream.

Don't fight me! I'm helping you! Don't I always help you?

"Adira! Release it!" Dina yells. "When I say your sister's name, you will tell Jocelyn to leave, just like we've practiced!"

Don't listen to that bitch! You need me, Adira! You need me! You will always need me and you fucking know it!

"Jessa!" Dina cries.

I drop to my knees, and Julianna manages to scramble away from me. Gabriel runs around Dina, snatches the knife out of my hands, and drops to his knees to cut Julianna out of the ropes and tape.

"Jessa!" Dina yells again.

I wrap my arms around myself, sobbing, rocking.

You need me! Jocelyn screams, but her voice sounds distant now.

"Jessa! You love her, right? Think about Jessa! Live for Jessa, Adira!"

I suck in a breath so deep my eyes prickle and my body shakes violently. I fall down, convulse, and immediately feel hands stripping me out of my shirt until I'm in nothing but a bra.

"What's happening?" Gabriel asks. "She looks like she's having a seizure!"

"She's fine. She's fine. Help me turn her over." Dina is above me as she directs her command to Gabriel.

"Is she really okay?" Julianna asks, staring down at me.

"She's fine. She's releasing. This is normal for her after an episode." The hands are on my face. My neck. "Thanks for helping, you two, but I need you to get the hell out of here and never speak of this."

"But I—"

"Now!" Dina shouts at Julianna.

Gabriel and Julianna hop to their feet, and I hear them scramble away. A creak of a door and a heavy slam and they're gone.

Warm hands press to the center of my chest and Dina inhales through her nostrils before exhaling through her lips. "You are healed, Adira. You are healed. You're here. You're safe. Can you hear me?"

I want to nod, but I can't. I feel like a passenger in my own body. Every limb is numb, everything tingles.

"Blink if you can hear me."

I blink once.

"Good. You are healed, my sweet girl." Her hands travel south, pressing on my belly. "You are healed. Let this go. Let

Jocelyn go. You're better than all of it. Remember who you really are. Remember your true self."

My eyes begin to close and darkness cloaks me, but before there is full darkness, I see Jocelyn standing above me. Her head shakes from side to side, and she's narrowing her eyes as she glares me down.

"Pathetic," she hisses in the hollows of my mind, then she turns away and walks in the same direction Gabriel and Julianna went to leave this place.

CHAPTER SIXTY-EIGHT

ADIRA

I'd never felt so alone—so afraid. But after Claudette drowned Jessa, I ran away from home. I ran so hard my lungs were hurting and I banged on Mrs. Stein's door.

As soon as the door swung open, I went into hysterics. "Panda!" I screamed. "Panda—please! Panda's gone!" I cried. "She—she killed her! She's gone!"

"What?" Mrs. Stein shrieked, and she quickly brought me into her house. What happened afterward was a blur. Mrs. Stein had the phone to her ear, and not too long after, the police arrived. They asked me questions, and I answered numbly, and from what I overheard, they were going to investigate at Claudette's house.

In the midst of it all, a woman showed up. She wore a burnt orange dress and her locs, which were baby locs back then, stopped at her neck. Her eyes were wide and she rushed to Mrs. Stein. "Momma, what's going on?" she demanded.

And Mrs. Stein told her everything. And I realized this was the woman Mrs. Stein always talked about—her daughter, Dina Holloway.

Dina found out what happened, and she took a good look at me. She didn't judge me. She simply sat right next to me and brought me into a warm embrace. I was left with no choice but to cry in her chest.

"We can't let them take her—they'll put her in foster care. She doesn't deserve that. She could stay here," Mrs. Stein said.

"No, Momma. With your health, no."

"I can do it. She's older. I'm sure it won't be too hard."

"No." Dina was firm this time, then she sighed, and I pressed my ear closer to her chest, listening to her steady heartbeat. "I'll look after her. I'll take care of her."

And Dina did look after me. She fought for me. Through all the court dates, check-ins with social services, my therapy—through everything, Dina was there. And no, she didn't have it all, but she made life worth living and she made it fun.

But oftentimes, I ruined it by letting the ugliness inside me come to the surface. I'll never forget when my therapist diagnosed me with DID—dissociative identity disorder.

It was after I'd destroyed a painting that was given to Dina by a friend of hers I didn't like. This friend was a man named Blair, and for some odd reason I didn't trust that man and didn't want him to be around. Perhaps it was my trauma that'd snuck up on me, but because of it, I destroyed the painting. A painting that had taken Blair four months to make. It hurt Dina, but what hurt her even more was when she called it off with Blair for my sanity.

After that, she relayed her worries to my therapist at the time, who concluded that I have alters. At first, the alters didn't make sense. And they often popped up out of nowhere. The alters were more assertive, more direct. Each of them was different, but none of them were like the real me, and I liked that . . . until they became hard to control. Harder to hide. And all these years, Jocelyn was cooking up a storm inside me, ready to be unleashed at the perfect time.

I realize now that I'm damaged, dangerous, and wicked because of my alters. Dina knows this. Everyone who enters my life will eventually know this.

And how can they blame me? How can *anyone* blame me? I watched my only sister drown to death. I live with eternal darkness and it swirls inside me, and if I don't let it out by being Jocelyn—by being the others—then I'll hurt myself. And I don't want to leave this world. At least, not yet. Because I know there's nothing left for me after this. I'll be nothing but dust in a vase, tossed into a sea—if I'm even that lucky.

Because of Claudette and Bower, I have no faith. I've lost all of it. Claudette drowned her own daughter. She betrayed our trust by putting a man before us. I will never forgive her for that, and because I allow my unforgiveness to fester, I've unleashed the darkness it creates through something else—or more like *someone* else.

CHAPTER SIXTY-NINE

JOCELYN

I took over that horribly tragic day Jessa drowned. But back then, my name wasn't Jocelyn. She has given me many names, the sweet Adira, and each time she resurrects me—brings me out to protect and guide her from self-destruction—I possess the same qualities for her.

I'm fearless. Powerful. Honest. And I do exactly what needs to be done so she can live a better life. Sure, my methods may be unorthodox, but I like to consider them bold and cutthroat.

I could've killed Claudette right on that boat, but I didn't. Because Adira was hurting. I felt her pain in every single fiber of me, felt her crying internally, hiding in the darkness of a tomb she'd built to protect herself. Anytime I tried to enter the tomb with a candle, she'd blow out the light and demand that I handle it.

She'd been itching for me to come out for a while now. She'd sneak into this tomb, talk to me, ask me for advice, but was never bold enough to let me surface. Maybe because she knew if she did, there would be no turning back.

But after losing Jessa, she was left with no choice. Adira can't do what I do. She cowers and hides. She weeps and whines and curls into the fetal position until it's over, but me? I get shit done. I take the initiative because I know she has potential. So long as she has me with her, sharing the tomb, I know what she's truly capable of, which is why when I surfaced from the darkness, I ran away from Claudette's. I ran half a mile until I came across the house that belonged to Dina Holloway's mother, Mrs. Stein. Dina's last name had never been Holloway. That was just the name she used to do her Reiki and healing—her practice name, so to speak.

I banged on Mrs. Stein's door and told her everything. I cried with snot and nearly vomited because Adira was crying, and her pain was my pain, and Mrs. Stein took me in and called the police first thing. Within the next twenty minutes the cops arrived, an investigation was ignited, and the cops hurried to Claudette's house. But by then, Claudette had bled out on her kitchen floor, a rusty kitchen knife jammed into her left rib cage.

I remember the police asking me who I thought had done it, and I told them I saw Bower do it, which is why I ran half a mile to Mrs. Stein's house. He was going to kill me next but couldn't catch me, so he fled.

I can imagine the look of pure shock on his face when the police showed up at his doorstep to arrest him without so much as a warning. And how much more shock he was in when they interrogated him about the girl who drowned in the lake.

That's a secret that only Dina knows. Why? Because I told Dina when she took me in. Mrs. Stein was too old to carry me on, so Dina stepped up to the plate. Little did she know what she was signing up for.

I formed a deep attachment to Dina, even more so when Mrs. Stein became sicker.

Dina knows that Claudette is the reason Jessa died. She knows it was me who stabbed Claudette and left her there to bleed out on the floor, and since then, she's been trying to heal Adira—bring her out of the trauma—but how the hell do you pull someone out of that? Adira has spent her entire life building this deep, dark tomb within herself—a place where she can hide so that all her worries might disappear. All that work over the years doesn't just go away.

Sure, she can medicate herself, allow the drugs to temporarily pull her to the surface again, but she will always be triggered. She will always have the tomb to run back to. She will always have *me*.

Rejection is a trigger for her.

Heartbreak as well.

So was seeing that article about Bower being stabbed to death in prison.

And when Gabriel rejected her, choosing Julianna over being with her, that's what officially brought me back. She quit the medication, hoping to find a way to keep him. She feared being alone again—the same way she felt when she lost Jessa—and knew that was where she was headed. She didn't know how to cope with the news about Bower. Should she have been relieved? Should she have been upset? Should she have been angry because, to her, that was the easy way out for him? The man deserved to rot inside and out.

Adira didn't know what to feel, and because she didn't know, she shut down. Two days later, she created me. Jocelyn Vann, a wealthy woman who owns a lounge. A lounge Adira has personally owned for three years called Jessa's, but suddenly it was mine, and I was the woman meant to save her. I was who she needed, who she craved to be—who she *wanted* to be. The one who didn't take Gabriel too seriously. The one who didn't fear rejection. The one who minded her own business and did her own damn thing and never put a man first. The one who would *never* experience heartbreak because, to Jocelyn Vann, heartbreak is bullshit. There are more important things and boss moves to make and a man can never take that away.

Gabriel was nothing when she met him. Just a man in the food court of a mall who was giving her the eye. He knew what he was doing and he knew what he was after. Their one-night stand was only supposed to be that—a one-night stand—and Adira had no plans to linger, but he kept calling, kept texting, kept making her blush, and she liked him. And to be fair, he was honest with her. After a couple of months, he told her he was seeing someone else, but being the push-over she is, Adira said she didn't mind—that she would take him however she could. *So fucking desperate.*

She provided for Gabriel, but then she found out that she wasn't just providing for Gabriel. She was providing for his girlfriend too. Julianna didn't care about sharing him because her bills were paid and she didn't have to work. He had the looks, he had the charm, so she let him use it to take care of her, and damn, did she get what she wanted.

She got everything. The ugly pink car. The barre classes and the money to invest in her makeup artistry. An apartment near the bay that costs more than she could ever make from doing makeup, and at the end of the day, she and Gabriel fucked and laughed about how foolish and desperate this random woman was to give them all that.

Adira always thought he'd come to his senses, realize she was better, that she could give him more. He never did. I remember the conversation very clearly.

"Would you leave her for me?"

"I can't," Gabriel replied.

"Why not?"

"Because I'm in love with her, Adira."

"So, what is it that we have, then?"

"You know what we have," he told Adira. *"You know what we are. I pretend to be yours and we take care of each other's needs."*

"And I take care of hers."

"She comes with the territory. You said you were okay with that."

"But I don't want you to be with her anymore. I want you to be with me. Let her take care of herself."

"Adira," Gabriel said, clasping her face in his hands as they stood in her kitchen. *"I can't."*

"Why not, Gabriel?" Adira pleaded.

"Because . . . I'm not in love with you. I wish I was, but I'm not. I love you so much, but I'm in love with her and always will be, and if you can't accept that, we have to stop this."

And that was enough to get Adira to spiral. Down the slippery slope she went, sliding right back into herself, right into her tomb, where she removed the stones to breathe life back into me.

Gabriel had constructed all he needed through Adira. He no longer needed her or her money and she knew it. He'd ride the chariot she built for him, but not with Adira at his side. Julianna would be there, taking all the praise, as if she built him into the successful man he was.

"I want her gone. I can't lose him. Please, you know I deserve happiness," she pleaded to me in the darkness. "Please. Make it happen. Make me happy. It's all I want. I don't care what you have to do, I just . . . I can't lose him. I can't lose any more people who matter to me."

It's what she wanted and, sure enough, I was going to make it happen for her, no matter the lengths.

We're in bit of a bind now, but that's the good thing about having someone like Dina to vouch for you. She knows me more than anyone else and she loves Adira. And to love Adira, she must accept me.

She knows I won't leave for good. I'll never leave. I'll come up with new names, new schemes, and new ways to resurface, because without me, Adira may as well not exist. Without me, Adira would be no one at all.

CHAPTER SEVENTY

ADIRA

When I open my eyes, there is a light above me so bright it's blinding. I close my eyes and breathe in, counting down from five.

Five.
Four.
Three.
Two.
One.

I exhale. My eyes pop open again and I wait for color to fill the room, some sort of vibrancy or detail of real life, but there is none. Only white. Blinding white. When I realize the color won't arrive, panic sets in.

I sit up, only to feel my wrist get snatched back down. I glare down at the leather cuff bound tightly around my right wrist, then look to the left hand, which is cuffed too. Both cuffs are attached to a chain on a hospital bed.

"Adira, relax," a voice murmurs. I turn my head to the right and sitting in a chair in front of the window is Dina. She's several feet away, and probably for good reason. Anytime I'm brought here, everyone keeps a distance. Even her. They don't know which side of me they'll get.

"How are you feeling?"

"I'm fine," I croak. I try to swallow, but my throat feels like sandpaper. "Can I have some water?"

"Sure." Dina stands and walks to a tray at the end of the bed. She picks up the Styrofoam pitcher and pours water into the matching Styrofoam cup. She walks toward me with careful, measured steps, assessing me, and when she safely presumes that it's actually me, Adira, she extends her arms and helps me drink the water. I gulp it all down and ask for more, and she goes back to pour it, then returns.

"How long have I been in here?" I ask after my next gulp.

"Three days."

"Three days? Oh my God, Dina! What about Lovely Silk? I had meetings—designs to look over and someone is trying to invest—"

Dina's laugh stops me from talking. "What's funny?" I ask. "This is serious. I'm going to lose so much money. I'm off track."

"This is how I know it's you." She chuckles. "My Adira. My little workaholic worry-bot." She rubs my cheek and smiles down at me and I return a smile, sighing. "You had me really worried about you this time, Adira."

"I know." I drop my gaze. "I'm sorry. I—I'm really, really sorry, Dina. I—I didn't mean for it to go that far. I just thought Gabriel would choose me and when he didn't, I just . . . I felt like I needed to make him choose me, but—"

"Shh. It's okay. You don't have to apologize to me." She sets the cup down on the tray at the end of the table. "But you do need to apologize to someone else."

"Julianna," I whisper, lowering my head.

"And Gabriel."

I frown, and Dina raises her hands in the air. "Look, I know he strung you along. He used you, but you gave him the right to do it, Adira. Gabriel isn't the only man out there for you. There are plenty out there who run their own show and are ready to take care of their women. Gabriel was just a leech and he sucked too hard, made you lose touch with yourself in the process.

"It's not all his fault."

"No, it's not. At the end of the day, you're responsible for your own actions, but Adira, my beloved. Why didn't you come to me?" Dina pleads, grabbing my hand and wrapping it in hers. "Why didn't you let me help you?"

"You always help me, Dina."

"So you went to the tombs and sought someone like Jocelyn. I've never even met Jocelyn."

"There are a lot of them."

"How many more do I need to worry about?"

"There are no more. There was Lonnie, but she was immature. Then there was Zee, who was sneaky and quiet—sort of like a sleuth, but Zee was also lazy. But Jocelyn . . . well, she was who I wanted to be. Confident. Smart. Bold. Doesn't take any shit from anyone."

"You *are* Jocelyn, Adira. You don't have to put on a face to be her."

"Try telling my brain that."

Dina sighs and peers around the room. "You won't be able to get out of here unless you medicate. And you told me if this ever happened again, I have the right to assign someone to watch you whenever I can't. When you're out of here, you'll be under watch for however long I need you to be so I can make sure you're doing what you need to do, and so Jocelyn never returns."

I nod. "I understand."

Dina sighs, then walks around the bed to drag a chair toward it. "You've been thinking about Jessa a lot too, haven't you?"

"Yes."

"It would've been her twenty-fifth birthday the day you took Julianna. You were deflecting."

"It's not just that."

"Then what is it?"

"I, um . . ." I contemplate telling Dina what I have to say next. Sure, I could tell her the truth, but that'll only cause more stress, and if I want to get out of here, I have to keep some things to myself.

"I just really wish I could've saved her," I say instead. And it's the truth. Had I been stronger and faster, I could've saved Jessa. But I wasn't. I just stretched out an arm and threw out a hand, but it wasn't enough. I watched my baby sister drown, then when they found her body, I saw it, bloated and pale and blue.

Such trauma. It's no wonder I have so many alters. I use them to save me from myself. Because if it were only me, I'd likely have killed myself by now.

Dina doesn't think I need them. She thinks that, in a way, all of the alters are me. They're the layers within myself that I keep hidden and only bring to light when I'm in survival mode, or when I want things to go my way. She believes I use my alters as excuses—a way not to take blame for the bad things I do.

Like the girl Shakayla who I hit in the face with a lunch tray in high school because she sat in my spot and wouldn't move. It was a spot I'd sat in the entire school year. I'd kindly asked her to move and she told me to *leave her the fuck alone.* And that's when Lonnie showed up and smacked her with a tray.

Then there was Zee, who saved me from this disgusting man at a club who was trying to follow me to the bathroom during my college days. I never could've done it, so Zee was the one who sprang out, grabbed him by his worthless balls, twisted them, and told him, *"If I see you following me around again, I'll rip your dirty fucking balls off."* I never would've had the courage to tell him that. But Zee did. And sure, Zee tended to be lazy and only came out when she wanted to, but when she did, she made sure I always remembered it, and she always had my back.

And I suppose Jocelyn is an embodiment of both of them. Jocelyn hasn't always had a name, but she's always been the one to save me during my hardest days. She's the perfect blend of them all, only she's much more patient and much more calculating, which, in the end, makes her the most terrifying.

CHAPTER SEVENTY-ONE

ADIRA

A doctor enters the room in a white lab coat as Dina mentions how she needs to text a client to reschedule with them. The doctor wears a black skirt with blocky heels. Her hair is silky black and comes down to her shoulders, her skin pale like Snow White's—but not in a porcelain manner. Her face doesn't have the sweet rosiness tinting her cheeks. It's rather plain, minus the dark red lipstick she's swiped her lips with, which reminds me of a vampire having just sucked blood.

I know and remember her all too well. Dr. Whitman. She was the only doctor in Tampa brave enough to take on my case.

"How are you feeling?" she asks, approaching the bed.

"I'm okay."

"Just okay?"

"I'm good."

Dr. Whitman smiles, then glances at Dina. "Do we suspect this is actually Adira?"

"Yes, I would say so. The first thing she panicked about was work."

Dr. Whitman laughs and then digs into her lab coat pocket

to retrieve a set of keys. She unlocks the cuffs around my wrists and I sigh with relief, bringing them up and rubbing them gently.

"You had a rough couple of months," Whitman says, and it's a firm statement. A knowing statement. Dina must've told her everything. "Do you want to tell me what triggered you?"

"I guess stress from work. And the rejection from Gabriel. I didn't want it to end. Plus . . . the news about Bower."

"You always get this way when you don't get what you want, Adira. You have to unlearn that."

"I know."

"You're lucky no charges were pressed against you."

"Well, it would've been rather stupid for them to press charges, considering she's the reason their bills have been paid for the past two years," Dina says with a roll of her eyes.

Whitman presses her lips together and doesn't bother getting on that subject. "As for the news about Bower, I can understand why it bothered you."

"When can I leave?" I ask her.

"Sixty days."

"What? Sixty days? I can't be here that long. I have to work!"

"I understand that, but the police will be coming soon with questions. Fortunately, there are no criminal charges against you, but you still committed a crime, which means you'll be spending more time in here than you'd like. Once we've done your therapy and we've gotten you properly medicated, everything should be better." Dr. Whitman reads something in her notebook. "There was no trace of any of your medication in your blood tests."

"I stopped taking them in March."

"Hmm. Three months ago. Very dangerous, Adira," she says while scribbling something in the notebook.

"Are you sure it has to be sixty days?" I ask.

"Well, like I said, we want to keep you here for a little while longer. We'll do everything we can to make sure you're comfortable, but in the meantime, no cell phones, no sharp objects, and *no lying*. Got it? I want complete and utter transparency if you plan on getting back to work anytime soon. And I'll need you to tell me more about Jocelyn."

"How do we know Jocelyn won't come back?" Dina asks, worried creases forming around her eyes.

Dr. Whitman looks from Dina to me, then back to Dina. "We won't know. We can only know if it happens again. But if Adira is done with Gabriel and Julianna and we can get her back into a routine, she should be okay. Anyway, the police should be here any minute for their report now that she's conscious. Be honest with them, Adira, and don't leave *anything* out. We've done what we can do, submitted a notice of your mental status and health. All we can do is hope this doesn't escalate further."

I grab Dina's hand and smile. "I'll be okay. I have to be."

Dina smiles back, but it doesn't reach her eyes. She has doubts, and I understand. She didn't know going into fostering me that it would come with this. A lunatic who has multiple personalities protecting her. I've never understood why Dina holds on or why she has so much faith in me. She could literally walk out of my life right now and never look back, but that's not Dina. She loves with all her heart, and I've been like a daughter to her.

She fights for me . . . so the best I can do is fight for her too. I can't drag her into my mess again. I have to let it all go.

The past with Claudette and Bower.

The complicated mess with Gabriel and Julianna.

And even Jessa. I don't have to let my love or good memories of her go, but for the sake of my future and Dina's, I must let go of the bad I remember happening to her.

I have to stop blaming myself for something I couldn't control. . . .

If only it were that simple.

CHAPTER SEVENTY-TWO

ADIRA

Four Months Later

Velvet's Café is just how I remember it. But my demeanor coming here has changed. I walk to the counter to order a caramel macchiato, then sit at a table that faces the door.

I sip my coffee, respond to a few emails, and when two people I was hoping would show up step inside, I sit up straighter. Julianna smiles and peers up at Gabriel as they walk toward the counter, and along the way, Gabriel's eyes wander and land on me.

I smile and give a small wave, and his eyes grow wide and rounded as he stops walking. Julianna notices him come to a halt and stops with him, and when her eyes follow his line of sight, her mouth gapes. Grabbing his hand, Julianna walks to the counter with him and I sigh, taking another sip of my coffee.

It's not what they think. I'm aware that they don't live in the same apartment anymore. They moved sometime after the whole Jessa's basement showdown, and I only know this because Dina took me to Julianna's place after I was released from the facility, so I could apologize. But they weren't there, and security said they'd moved months ago. After that, Dina figured they didn't want to be bothered and told me to leave it alone, but I couldn't do that.

That's why I'm here, at Velvet's. It's one of Julianna's favorite places and, according to her Instagram, she still takes
her barre class a block away. I knew she'd be here eventually.
I thought I would catch her alone, but with Gabriel here, it's
even better. I can kill two birds with one stone.

After they've gotten their drinks, Julianna and Gabriel turn
and walk for the exit. But before they can reach the door Julianna is so desperate to get out of, Gabriel stops, sighs, and
then turns to look at me. He grabs Julianna's hand and leads
the way toward me.

"Adira, what are you doing here?" Gabriel asks, standing
next to the table.

"I was hoping I'd run into Julianna," I tell him, and Julianna looks up at Gabriel, her eyes swimming with fear. "It's
not what you think," I tell her. "I just . . . I was hoping to
bump into you—again—ha ha." I make a joke of it, but Julianna doesn't laugh. "Anyway, I was hoping to run into you
so I could apologize in person. To both of you. And to thank
you for not pressing charges."

Gabriel clutches his coffee cup a little tighter and Juliana
shifts on her feet.

"I don't expect either of you to forgive me, but I just want
to put it out there." I draw in a deep breath, then raise my
hands. "So, that's it. I won't waste any more of your time."

"That's it?" Gabriel deadpans.

"You tried to kill me," Julianna hisses.

"That . . . wasn't me."

They both frown.

"Well, not entirely."

"Dina told me what was going on with you," Gabriel says,
studying my face. "I wish *you'd* told me instead. Maybe it
never would have come to what it did."

"You're right." I drop my gaze to the lid of my coffee
cup, the tint of shimmery brown lipstick on the rim. "I didn't
want to scare you."

"A little too late for that," Julianna grumbles. "Look, you're sorry, we get it. But it would be nice if we don't ever have to see you again. *Ever.*"

"Jules, come on," Gabriel mumbles, glancing at her. "She's apologizing."

"No, I mean it, Gabriel. All of this is really fucked up. I get it, she's fucked in the head, but I will probably never recover from what she did to me. I appreciate the apology, but fuck it, you know? Fuck all of it. If it weren't for that Dina lady asking us not to press any charges and getting us to sign those stupid NDAs, she would be in fucking jail, but we've got her money, right? That's gonna fix it all. We're rich now, so I guess nothing else matters." Julianna tears her hand out of Gabriel's. "I'll meet you outside."

She marches out of Velvet's, swiping her eyes with her hand along the way, and I draw in a deep breath.

"For what it's worth, I'm the one who's sorry," Gabriel says as I meet his eyes. "Dina was right. What I did was wrong, no matter what you did in the end. I think about my time with you, and all the things I did. How I took advantage of you . . ." His throat bobs as he swallows. "None of it was okay. I'm part of the reason you went off the deep end. Will you forgive me?"

I huff a laugh, dropping my gaze and then shaking my head. "You're asking *me* to forgive *you* after what I almost did?"

He smiles and nods. "Yeah. I am."

"Okay," I sigh. "Yes, I forgive you. Just so long as you forgive me."

"Deal." He sips his coffee and turns, then stops abruptly. "Oh, by the way, championships start next month. I know you don't give a damn about rugby, but I'll mail some tickets to your office anyway, just in case you ever wanna attend a game."

I smile as he walks away, and then he's gone, walking hand in hand with Julianna. I sip my coffee, satisfied with where me and Gabriel stand now.

CHAPTER SEVENTY-THREE

ADIRA

Two Years Later

When I look in the mirror—the one hanging on the wall of my brand-new bedroom, in my newly built house—I smile because I've never felt better.

"You are smart. You are beautiful. You are brave," I say to my reflection. I repeat the mantra while applying my makeup. "Smart. Beautiful. Brave."

Life is going great and work is perfect and has given me the home of my dreams. It's a simple ranch-style home with a contemporary design that melts my heart every time I step into it. It's smaller than the mansion was—four bedrooms— and doesn't have the water view, but it does have plenty of space for me to garden and a swimming pool I've been making use of quite often. It's peaceful here, and the neighbors are friendly. I'm happy. Of course, none of this would've happened had I not gotten my shit together.

After checking out of the psychiatric clinic and making amends with Gabriel and Julianna, I went on a vacation. Dina stuck with me for seven weeks afterward, and for two of those weeks we went to the Maldives to unwind. There, we did a lot of meditating, and she performed several Reiki techniques on me. It was nice, and it made me feel alive and whole and human.

We had no cell phones, no laptops, no devices. Just ourselves and the earth and clear minds. However, when I returned, I went straight back to work and ended up closing a deal for a collaboration with one of the most popular e-commerce stores in the world. They handle the distribution and shipping and all I have to do is continue launching and creating new products, upgrade merchandise, and much more. It feels undeserved after what I've gone through, but then again, I had to accept that I've worked hard for this. I started this company and allowed it to flourish, and no one can say that but me.

I finish applying my makeup and once I'm ready, I march out of the bedroom in my heels and enter the kitchen, where my purse and keys await.

My eyes swing to the stove, and I feel an ache in my chest as I remember there's no one to cook breakfast for me anymore. He used to do it and he was good at it. But he's gone now, and I can't think that way anymore.

Dr. Whitman says whenever I find myself thinking about Gabriel to think about Jessa. Jessa helps me not spiral. Jessa keeps me going. I live for her. I take my medication, downing the pills quickly, then pick up my purse and keys and leave the house. I lock it up and hop into my Maserati, driving straight to work.

Work is in a new building downtown with even more windows than the office I had before. I love my office, decorated in ivory and soft blues and small touches of black and white.

"You have three missed called and two emails from last night to respond to," Alaina says, marching into my office with a cup of coffee. "I forwarded the emails to you."

"Thanks, Alaina."

"Absolutely. I'm happy to see you looking so alive, Adira."

"I feel alive," I say, then pick up the coffee. "Hey, what do you say we catch dinner this weekend? Maybe some drinks?"

"Oh, I wish, but I'm going with Ricardo to a Kendrick Lamar concert. It's going to be so fun!"

"Oh—well, hey. Don't let me stop you." I laugh.

"Ricardo is so good to me, Adira." She sighs dreamily. "He's seriously the man of my dreams."

I smile at her as her eyes wander out of one of the windows.

"I think you're even more in love than the last time."

"You better not be referring to Deveon!" she snaps. "I told you—he is Voldemort around here! We only speak of Ricardo. And for your information, I *am* in love." I laugh as she twirls around in her pastel-blue dress and leaves my office.

I make my first call after having my coffee and realize this is where I need to be. With my mind running and my hands doing something, being surrounded by people who enjoy my company. So long as I have this, I won't need anyone or anything else.

My phone vibrates on the desk, and it's a text from Dina.

How are we feeling today?

I respond with a smile. **Better than ever. I planted petunias last week and they're flourishing.**

I'm so proud of you, beloved.

I shoot her back a whole chain of heart emojis.

I make my final work call and, after I feel satisfied, I open my web browser to check my Facebook account. It's been months, and I have thirty minutes until my next meeting. I scroll through, seeing images of partners and colleagues with new babies or grandbabies. I smile at a baby girl with curly, dark hair and rosy cheeks, and there's that familiar ache again. I ignore it, scrolling some more, skimming past the ads for robes and candles and lotions, but then I stop when I see a name I haven't seen in two years.

Gabriel Smith.

It's too late to scroll back up. The image is right there—right in my face, and the sight of it causes my stomach to clench. I minimize the browser instantly and shake my head.

"No. Not today."

I check some work emails instead, respond to those, and then get off the computer to go to the coffee station. I prepare myself another coffee and strike up a conversation with one of the interns, but I know eventually I'll have to go back to my office. I'll have to face that screen and log out of Facebook, but not without seeing his name and that picture.

I'm tempted to tell Alaina to come in and delete it for me without opening it, but a part of me *deep deep deep* inside is drawn to his name. This part of me wants to know the when, the where, and the how.

I return to my office, sit at my desk. I tap my finger on the mouse, then I sigh and click open the browser again. It pulls right open to Facebook, right where I'd left off.

This is okay, I tell myself. *I'll be fine. I'm medicated. I had my coffee. I'm in the right headspace. I'm happy. I'll be fine.*

Only when I click the image, I'm not fine. It's an image of Gabriel and Julianna kissing on the beach. She's dressed in a blush pink A-line dress and he has on a taupe button-down and white linen pants. Above the post are the words, *We're Getting Married!*

I read the caption about how she's the love of his life, and how he's gone through so much with her, how she's his soul mate, etcetera, etcetera. I read it, absorb it—study the image repeatedly, and when I feel like I can't breathe, I log off, exit the browser, and sit back in my chair.

Getting married? Wow. I should've seen that one coming.

CHAPTER SEVENTY-FOUR

ADIRA

The rest of the workday is somber compared to my mood from this morning. I leave work early and make my way home, where I march to the wine fridge and take out a bottle of my favorite sangria.

I pour half a glass and sip it slowly. Carefully. Then I carry it with me to my office, along with my phone, and open Instagram. I search for Julianna's page and her username is the same.

The first image is of her and Gabriel. The same images I saw earlier of them are presented as a slideshow on her profile. They're kissing. Laughing. The sun is setting behind them and the blue water sparkles like wet glitter. Based on the location tagged above, they're in Hawaii.

I sip my sangria again, but it tastes bitter going down.

"I should send them a wedding gift," I say to no one in particular. "That's the nice thing to do."

I close the app and walk to the kitchen, dumping the remainder of my wine down the drain. Then I go to my bedroom, take out my weed pen, and pull from it several times. Marijuana helps. Dina would agree.

I shower. Listen to music. Meditate. I do everything I'm supposed to do when I feel like my world is tilting on its axis.

But it isn't fully helping this time. I have all these thoughts and questions running through my mind, like why she decided to marry him after all he put her through and all he did. They're using the money I worked my ass off to make to fund their wedding. And, sure, giving them money to keep quiet was better than ending up in prison, but still. If it weren't for me, they wouldn't be in Hawaii taking pictures, and she wouldn't be able to buy a fancy wedding gown or pick an expensive cake to cut with him when the time comes.

Is he planning a romantic honeymoon escape in another country, where he can fuck her one way to the next in an overwater bungalow while calling her his *wife*?

No. None of what I do helps and I can't ignore them. The dark thoughts that nag at me. They're screaming, trying to claw their way out, but I have to fight them. I have to ignore them. What they're doing with that money is no business of mine. What they're doing with their life is no business of mine. Not anymore.

My life is fine. I'm fine. I'm happy.

You're not happy.

I lay my head on my pillow, feeling the urge to cry. I paved their way to happiness. He used me. *She* used me. Now they'll have it all.

They'll have it *all*. They'll have each other.

And I'll only have myself.

I'll have nothing. Just myself.

I curl up in bed, feeling myself drifting off to sleep. But before I do, the doorbell rings, causing me to gasp and sit upright in bed. I check the time on my phone and it's nearing midnight.

I rush for a robe, my slippers, and hurry downstairs. "Who

is it?" I call as I walk toward the front door. There's no response.

I check the peephole and there's a woman standing on the other side of it. She's looking down so I can't see her face.

"Who is it?" I ask again.

"It's me." I keep the chain lock attached to the door and open it partially, and the woman finally picks up her head so I can see her.

Her eyes are hazel beneath the porch lights, her curly-kinky hair dark brown and swimming with pink highlights that run down to her shoulders. She's dressed in jeans overalls, a black T-shirt beneath, and scuffed black and white Chucks.

She smiles at me. "Hi, Adira," Zee says with mischief swirling in her eyes. "I'm so glad you need me again. Can I come in?"

ACKNOWLEDGMENTS

This book drove me crazy! And as crazy as it made me, I wouldn't have been able to complete it without the people who dealt with all my whining and griping during the half a year it took me to write it.

The person who got it the worst was my husband, and I'm so thankful to have him in my life because without him, I'm pretty sure I would've given up on writing this one a long time ago. I'm beyond lucky to have a life partner like him, someone who understands and motivates me every single day.

Secondly, to Dani Fuselier and Hannah May, I'm surprised y'all are still my friends because how do I *not* annoy you with all my writing rants by now? I love y'all so much! Thank you for always pushing me in the right direction.

Traci Finlay, you know what you did and I'm so incredibly grateful for you! Thank you for being there to help me make my books the best they can be!

I'm grateful to MJ Fryer for being the most incredible alpha reader in the world! Thank you for always making time for me and my stories, no matter what the story is about or how insane the idea seems.

To my readers, I adore you all and you push me so much to be the very best writer I can be. I wouldn't have this career without you, so thank you for supporting and loving me, especially my Queendom! You're all so incredible!

And to you, the person reading this very sentence: Thank you for your support and for taking time to read my book. I'm so glad you enjoyed it enough to reach the point of the story where I can show you my gratitude.

Discussion Questions for *The Other Mistress*

1. What are you first thoughts about Adira when she's watching Julianna?

2. If you found out your life partner was sleeping with two people *other* than you, how would you react? What would you feel? Explain.

3. Why do you think Claudette was so angry and bitter toward her children?

4. What's your first impression of Bower when he's introduced?

5. Considering all that happened between Adira, Gabriel, and Julianna, do you think she will remain successful for long?

6. Should Gabriel and Julianna have gotten any money after Adira's downfall? Why or why not?

7. Adira had a very harsh upbringing and witnessed a lot of things in her younger years that she shouldn't have seen at her age. Do you think Adira's disorder makes sense considering all she's been through?

8. What do you think about Dina's role in Adira's life? Do you think Adira would be where she is now without Dina?

9. Do you think it's possible for someone like Adira to heal from the trauma she's endured?

10. After reading the last chapter, what do you think will happen now that Zee is back in the picture?